NEVER ENOUGH

A SAM POPE NOVEL

ROBERT ENRIGHT

For Jacob William Enright.
Welcome to the family, little man.

CHAPTER ONE

Four months was a long time to be hunting a ghost.

The word 'Veilmont' had become all-consuming for Sam Pope, ever since his former comrade, James Murray, had handed him the card with the name printed across it. Sitting on the steps of Trafalgar Square in the bitter cold of January, Sam had been shown his next target by a man who had been paid to kill him.

Sam could have just walked away.

Should have just walked away.

His body would have thanked him. It had been years now since Sam had taken the first step on his path that had led him to going face to face with some of the most dangerous criminals the world had known.

From sex traffickers to global terrorists.

From arms dealers to corruption within his own government.

Sam had been steadfast in his belief in justice, knowing that somebody had to fight back. That sometimes, the law wasn't enough and a man of his skillset and freedom from the systems put in place, allowed him to reach those outside the law.

But it had come at a price.

His reputation as one of the most highly decorated and respected snipers the British armed forces had ever known, had been tarnished. Despite a level of mutual respect with the current Commissioner of the Metropolitan Police, and her predecessor, Sam was painted as a dangerous vigilante and was the most wanted man in the country he had fought to protect.

His body was battered. A walking tapestry of scars that were constant reminders to the wars he had waged. The two bullet wounds that dominated his chest were the constant reminder that he had once been deemed disposable, when General Ervin Wallace had tried to have him executed. Now, they were accompanied by a such a multitude of stab wounds and bullet holes, that Sam often wondered how he managed to keep going.

Why he kept getting up and kept fighting?

But he knew.

When he had proudly served his country overseas, it had been the thought of his son, Jamie and his wife, Lucy, that had kept him sharp. Returning home to them both had kept Sam alive through multiple missions, and when Project Hailstorm had seen him almost return home in a body bag, Sam had stepped away from his military career to start a new life.

Then Jamie was taken from him.

Run down on one fateful night by a drunk driver, who, due to a technicality, didn't face the consequences of his crimes.

In one moment in time, Sam had lost everything.

His son.

His wife, who couldn't stand to watch him fall away.

Himself.

But now, as the train pulled into the modern station in the centre of Vienna, Sam peered out at the glorious capital of Austria, lit up against the night sky. The warmth of spring clung to the air, and as he stepped off the train with the sports bag over his shoulder, joining the hoard of commuters on their way to the barriers, he knew that losing his son all those years ago was what was powering his every step.

His need to hunt down and uncover what 'Veilmont' was.

His need to fight back.

But the name 'Veilmont' was nothing more than a whisper in the wind, and despite the intel he had collected, Sam knew he was still no closer to knocking on their front door. It was a door that Murray himself had walked away from, insinuating to Sam that even he, a man who controlled a network of mercenaries, was too disgusted to walk through. Their reacquaintance, years after Sam had saved Murray's life in the heat of battle, had set Murray on a new path of redemption, and as his parting gift to Sam, he had given him the name and the arsenal to do what he did best.

To rattle the cages.

To bang down the doors.

Whatever he could do to locate the myth of 'Veilmont' and shut down whatever it was that had scared his former comrade away.

Country by country.

City by city.

Lead by lead.

It had taken Sam from Spain, across to the Netherlands, and now, as he made his way out of the station and into the busy metropolis of Vienna, to Austria. In his latest stint in Amsterdam, Wesley Van Hecke, a trust fund playboy with a large, digital footprint, had given him the address of a high stakes poker game in the city, and the man who ran it. Dangled from the fifteenth-floor balcony of his luxury bachelor pad, Van Hecke's pomp and bravado had evaporated as quickly as his bodyguard's consciousness. Sam had laid siege to the building, battling his way through the hired help until he finally had Van Hecke to himself. A few swift right hooks to the stomach and the promise of a fifteen-floor swan dive to the concrete below was enough to reduce the arrogant young man to a quivering and compliant wreck.

Eventually, Van Hecke had given him something. He had heard of a connected man in Austria by the name of Roland Bauer. The man was a heavy hitter in the city and had several connections through to Amsterdam where he had amassed a sizeable fortune in the drug and sex trade.

Two ticks against him from the off.

As Van Hecke panted heavily with fear, his legs dangling above the city skyline, he explained how Bauer had once alluded to a special proposition that only a select few were privy to. That was as far as the conversation went, but Van Hecke had been invited to a high stakes poker game, where the buy-in was half a million euros, with the promise of more information. The money was already withdrawn from Van Hecke's safe and stacked neatly in a sports bag, which he offered to Sam.

There was no guarantee that this was anything more than a wealthy criminal luring a young, naïve rich kid to a blatant robbery.

But the slightest chance that it could be more, meant Van Hecke was more use to Sam alive, than dead.

That was what had saved his life, and once Sam had hauled him back over the railings, he had marched him to the safe and unburdened him of the large sum of money. The half a million was now strapped to Sam's broad shoulders, as he followed the map on his phone through the winding streets of the busy city. The Austrian nightlife was in full force, with a cocktail of tourists and locals lining the streets outside numerous bars and restaurants, their good times echoing over the seemingly endless cacophony of traffic. With powerful strides, he followed the blue line on his phone, navigating the large group of young women who were enjoying a drink and a cigarette outside one of the trendier bars, the doors open with a promise of loud, thumping music and minimal personal space.

One of them flashed him a smile.

He ignored it.

As he rounded the corner, his destination loomed between the buildings, the jet black building in stark contrast to the welcoming lights of the other businesses desperate for footfall. There was no sign above the door, just two lights that cast their glow down upon the two bulky doormen, who had already locked their eyes on Sam. Without missing a step, Sam strode confidently towards them and as one took a step forward, Sam kept his eyes on the other, who made the slightest movement to the inside of his black jacket.

The men were armed.

'Walk away,' the doorman said in a thick Austrian accent.

'Mr Bauer is expecting me,' Sam replied, maintaining eye contact. 'Van Hecke.'

The man's brow furrowed, and he took a small step back, and looked Sam up and down, from head to toe. The name had clearly resonated, but whatever description the man had clearly didn't fit the figure before him. Sam was over six feet tall, and his muscular torso was stretching the fabric of his black t-shirt and the dark green bomber jacket that clung to his bulky frame. For the first time in what felt like years, his face bore no cuts or bruises, but the unavoidable wrinkles of his mid-forties dominated his forehead and eyes. His strong jaw was set, coated in a thick stubble that was peppered with grey. His dark brown hair had grown out, pushed back over his skull, with a few strands swooping down to his eyebrow. The colour all but faded from the hair that was tucked behind his ears.

'Walk away.'

Then the man shook his head and then muttered something to his colleague in German.

'*Ich habe das Geld.*' Sam replied, catching the men off guard with their native tongue. He unzipped the bag and offered them a glimpse as proof. The doorman gave a grunt and then nodded to his colleague who stepped forward aggressively. Sam stood his ground, allowing the man to yank the bag from his shoulder, and then begin a vigorous pat down.

The man quickly found the Glock 17 tucked in the back of his jeans and held it up.

'Can't be too careful.' Sam smirked, but the two men scowled in return. The doorman handed the gun over to his colleague, who held it by his hip, the barrel pointed at Sam.

'Inside.' He barked, and Sam, keeping his hands up, obliged, falling in step behind the other doorman, who held the bag of money in an iron grip. The other stepped behind, prodding the gun into the base of Sam's spine to shift him forward through the door and into the building. The door closed behind them, and the guard ensured it was locked.

The stairwell was dimly lit, with white lights built into the skirting board that ran alongside each step. With each step, the low hum of conversation grew, and the doorman holding the money pushed open the door and Sam was almost blinded by the bright lights that greeted him. The decadent room was furnished with oak tables and plush, leather chairs, and a well-stocked bar ran along the back wall, lined with bottles of the most expensive drinks. An attractive woman stood behind it, her attention drawn to the new arrivals, and the concern on her face only added to the growing tension.

All of the tables were empty, except the one in the middle, which was cloaked in baize, and a croupier stood, his hands expertly shuffling the cards. Stacks of chips were laid out before him, and his head spun, his eyes locked onto Sam, as did the three other sets of the men seated before him. One of the men was familiar to Sam.

He had been the focus of his internet searches for almost the entire journey from Amsterdam.

Roland Bauer.

The man's gruff facial features were juxtaposed with his expensive, designer suit, and his cropped, grey hair sat atop a furrowed brow. He was stocky, and as he stood to greet the intrusion, he never broke his eye contact with Sam.

'*Herr Van Hecke*,' the first doorman said, handing the bag over to Bauer, who sneered at Sam before peering inside. The doorman leant in and whispered something to Bauer, who nodded before turning back to Sam, who could still feel the barrel of his own gun pressed against his spine.

'My associate says you are English,' Bauer spoke clearly, his gravelly voice suiting him.

'Don't hold it against me,' Sam said.

'The problem we have, is that Mr Van Hecke is not English.' Bauer forced a smile. 'And the fact I have met him. Now, you have his money, but the question I want to know before I kill you, is who the fuck are you?'

Sam cast a glance to the other two men who were still sitting, seemingly unconcerned at the situation unfolding before them. Swimming in the same circles meant they were used to blood being shed, and Sam was sure if he probed deeply enough, he'd discover they'd shed their fair share.

But he wasn't here for them.

He was here for the man who stood before him, hands on his hips, and two murderous henchmen waiting to snap into action.

'I don't want any trouble,' Sam offered with his hands raised. 'I just need some information.'

Bauer began to chuckle, his unsettling laugh echoing in the silent room.

'Information?' He slapped his hand on the table, shaking the poker chips.

'You can keep the money.' Sam nodded to the bag. 'Tell me what I need to know, and nobody gets hurt.'

'Hurt?' Bauer looked to his guests, then to the henchman beside him still holding the bag. 'I am bored of this.'

Bauer gave the nod, and Sam could feel the man behind him shift his weight onto one foot, increasing the pressure of the gun against Sam's spine. Instinctively, Sam snapped his right hand back, his fingers locking onto the man's wrist and expertly finding the pressure points. Before the man could squeeze the trigger, Sam dug in, sending a shockwave pulsing through the man's arm and relinquishing his grip. The man barked with pain, and Sam swung his left elbow, connecting flush with a weak jaw.

Blood and teeth splattered onto the floor, and Sam twisted the man's wrist and took hold of the weapon. Behind him, he could hear Bauer yelling instructions in German, but Sam drilled the doorman in the temple with the butt of the pistol and in one fluid motion, trained it on the other henchman who was scrambling to drop the bag and reach for his own firearm.

'Don't!' Sam warned.

The man pulled the gun.

Sam pulled the trigger.

The gunshot exploded through the room, sending the other guests ducking for cover as the bullet ripped through the man's shoulder and burst out the back in a spray of red mist. The man howled, spun, and hit the ground.

Bauer remained still, his eyes locked on Sam in a mixture of confusion and hatred. Behind him, the barwoman had ducked down behind the bar, her cries of panic the only other sound besides those of the man Sam had just shot.

'Impressive,' Bauer said with a wry smile. 'I could use a man like you.'

'I'm not for hire,' Sam replied, stepping round the cowering croupier and kicking away the gun from the feeble reach of the wounded henchman. He turned back to Bauer. 'Now…tell me about Veilmont.'

Bauer frowned.

'I don't know what you're talking about.'

Sam rolled his eyes, and then launched forward, grabbing Bauer by the collar of his shirt, and drilling him face down against the table. The chips toppled over, and Sam pressed the gun to the back of the man's skull.

'Veilmont!' Sam yelled. 'How do I find them?'

'You don't find them. They find you. And if you keep pushing, then they will do just that.'

Sam pressed the gun down with more force, pinning Bauer to the baize.

'I won't ask again.'

'And I will still have no answer for you.' Bauer sneered. 'A bullet from you is better than the alternative.'

Sam gritted his teeth. Another dead end.

He scanned the terrified faces of the other guests, and then took a step back, releasing Bauer but still keeping the gun trained on him. Bauer stood, straightening his jacket, and he turned to face Sam with a look of smug satisfaction.

'Will that be all?' He gestured to the table. 'As you can

see, I do have a game to run and a member of my staff is in need of medical attention.'

The faint sound of sirens had begun to filter in from the outside world, and Sam knew that a gunshot on a busy street would sound the alarms. He scooped up the bag of money and hoisted it over his shoulder, and Bauer stepped to the side, as if he was offering it as a sign of good will.

'Phone.' Sam barked and held out his hand. 'Now.'

Bauer shrugged, and pulled his phone from his pocket, unlocked it, and handed it over. Sam snatched it, typed in a number, and let it ring once. He hung up the call and tossed it back to Bauer, who just about caught it.

'Is there anything else?'

'Yeah. Apply pressure to the wound,' Sam said as he zipped up the bag of money. Bauer glanced down at his fallen henchman, who had gone a deathly pale as the blood pumped through his fingers.

'Oh, I'm sure he'll be fine,' Bauer said.

'I wasn't talking about him.'

Sam lifted the gun and pulled the trigger, and Bauer roared in agony as his leg snapped back, as the bullet shattered his left shinbone. Bauer crumpled to the floor, whimpering as he clutched at his destroyed leg with blood-soaked hands, and as Sam fixed the rest of the room with a cold stare, Bauer cursed him through sharp breaths.

He promised that Sam that he was a dead man.

That 'they' would come for him.

Sam pushed through the door and headed back down the shadow-laden stairwell and then out into the night, where the warm, spring night welcomed him, and the wailing of sirens filled the air. He tucked his weapon away, readjusted his sports bag, and headed off into the city, hoping that this time, he had taken just one step closer to Veilmont.

No matter how small it might be.

CHAPTER TWO

Sam woke the following morning, blinking through the brightness of the sun that cut through the gap in the curtain. With a grunt, he hoisted himself from the uncomfortable mattress and shuffled across the meagre hostel room that justified its low cost. A small, rickety desk was pushed against the wall beneath the window frame, and the carpet underfoot was coarse and well-worn.

But a bed was a bed.

He reached across the desk and opened the tatty curtains, squinting as the full blast of the spring sun burst through. Vienna was already alive and well, with the morning traffic blaring its worldwide symphony. Across the street, a luxurious hotel stood proudly, and Sam felt a twinge of envy at the hot shower it could afford him.

And he could afford it.

The funds that he had in the bank account to fund his war against organised crime was in the millions, left to him by a good friend and a former ally, Paul Etheridge, who had disappeared years ago. The two of them had served together in the military, and Sam had saved his life, and when Sam had called upon him when he was desperately searching to save a young girl from the clutches of a sex trafficking gang, Etheridge had come through for him. The man had transformed himself into a cyber security guru, amassing a fortune that could have allowed him to see out the remainder of his life on a tropical island with a continuous flow of cocktails and women.

But deep down, Etheridge was still a soldier.

Still born to protect.

And for a while, he had aided Sam's fight, working tirelessly behind the scenes to cipher information and hack security systems.

But the years had passed, and all Sam had to remember his friend by was the vast fortune now at his disposal, and the promise that Etheridge's reason for going dark wasn't in vain. Sam had been cuffed and sentenced to a life behind bars when Etheridge had intervened, and by doing so, had made himself a marked man.

A man who had everything had risked it all for what Sam was doing.

The last thing Sam could justify was using that money for comfort.

A bed.

A shower.

A locked door.

That was all he needed. And as he scanned the street below for a coffee shop, part of him wondered where Etheridge had ended up. He'd lost people over the past few years. His war against organised crime had come at a price.

At least Etheridge, to some extent, had been able to walk away of his own accord.

Buzz. Buzz.

Sam's head snapped to the desk, where his phone screen had lit up, and was shaking the furniture violently with every ring. The name filled the screen.

Ranjit Siddique.

Sam hoisted the phone to his ear and connected the call.

'Ranj. What have you got?'

'*Well, good morning to you, too.*'

Ranjit's voice was laden with sarcasm, as had become a frequent occurrence. Sam was still working his way to trusting the man, who up until a few months ago, had been on the payroll of 'Guardian', the security outfit run by James Murray. An elite level hacker, Ranjit had fashioned a cushy role within the organisation, using his skills to bring down security systems and pilfer intel for Murray and his crew. The man may not have got his hands dirty in the field, but they were plenty grimy, and Sam knew that a man like Ranjit would find it hard to return to the normality of the working world. Sam had extended the invitation to Ranjit, offering him the chance to not only make some money, but to do some good in the world.

Good work that would see him become a wanted man.

Ranjit accepted without a single question.

'Sorry,' Sam shrugged. 'You weren't the one who had a gun shoved to your spine last night.'

'*True. But I did have to watch Frozen for the hundredth time this week.*'

The response drew a wry smile from Sam, who enjoyed Ranjit's recounts of parenthood.

It helped him remember a calmer time in his life.

'So…' Sam continued, peering through the window and locking his eyes on a coffee shop. 'Tell me you have something. Roland Bauer wasn't as helpful as I'd have hoped.'

'*How did that go?*'

'I shot him,' Sam said. 'In the leg. He'll live.'

Sam could hear Ranjit take a deep breath. Despite being fully supportive of Sam's mission and having worked in an environment where violence was the main currency, Ranjit wasn't a man of war. His life had been keyboards and computer screens.

The reality that guns were fired and blood was shed was still something that didn't sit easily with him.

'Well…I'm glad you're okay.' Sam could hear the clicking of a keyboard. *'And to answer your first question…yes, I do have something for you.'*

Sam stood up straight.

'Go on.'

'That number you dialled me from. I assume that was Bauer's phone?'

'Yup,' Sam said. 'You're certain it can't be traced back to you, right?'

It was the one thing that Sam held against Ranjit. Unlike Etheridge before him, Ranjit had a happy home life.

A loving wife.

Two beautiful young daughters.

Sam would never forgive himself if he sent danger to their doorstep. Ranjit's cocky laugh set him at ease.

'Trust me, Sam. That number is being bounced off so many networks, they'd go through an entire fuckin' phone book before they traced it back to me.'

'Okay!'

'So, I've run through the call history on the phone, and the contacts. Mr Bauer certainly enjoys some of the more fucked up things in life. Fits the brief.'

Ranjit had been the one who had done the digging when Murray and his outfit were approached by a man representing the elusive Veilmont. He hadn't found much, but what the dark web had been able to provide had been enough for them to walk away. When Sam had pressed him for more, all Ranjit knew was it involved an awful lot of money, and that one 'survivor' had said they had experienced hell on earth.

'Survivor'.

That was the word that had confirmed to Sam that he needed to find them.

To rattle the cages until he got their address.

Until he was able to knock on their front door.

'I don't need the details,' Sam said. 'I need something useful.'

'Well, there are a few calls to a private number in Paris. Lots of barriers put up to protect it, you know? Rerouting to other countries. Other numbers. Anyways, I'll spare you the details of the hard work I've put in.'

'Please do,' Sam said with a smile.

'Anyway, like I said, I traced the number back to Paris. Its last call came this morning, and I've pinpointed it to a Mr Yohan Cheyrou. Ever heard of him?'

Sam's silence was an answer in itself.

'Big time diamond dealer. The man has a net worth of over two hundred million. When I say he's one of the richest men in France, I ain't lying. He's got a few swanky properties in the city, including the building where the ping came from this morning. I'll send you across the address.'

'Thanks, Ranj. I owe you one.'

'It's what you pay me for.' Ranjit replied merrily. *'So, what's the plan? I'm digging into the company records…well…what little exists of them…and Cheyrou is a hard man to get in a room with. Private security. I've got invoices for military grade lockdown systems in his buildings. What's the plan?'*

'I'm going to knock on his front door and ask to see him.'

Ranjit laughed.

'Always so subtle. But looking at these financial records, the man only takes a meeting with a potential customer for a fee.' Ranjit let

out a whistle. *'Fuckin' half a million Euros just to meet with him. Those better be some pretty nifty diamonds.'*

'Or his meetings are about something else.' Sam could feel his free hand balling into a fist.

He thought about that word again.

'Survivor'.

'You able to pull that kind of money together?'

Sam turned to the sports bag that he had zipped up and stored under the crooked old bed.

'Funnily enough, I can.' Sam smirked.

'I would say I'm surprised, Sam. But I'd be lying.'

'Send me that address and then get to work on finding me a base in Paris. Also, work your magic and ship some of that arsenal across. SA80. Two Glocks. Few grenades. Plenty of ammunition. Pay off whoever you need to, and I'll reimburse you.'

Ranjit let out another whistle of exasperation. As a parting gift when Murray had folded Guardian, he had handed Sam the keys to the company armoury. Although procuring a weapon in his world wasn't impossible, Sam wasn't going to turn down his own personal arsenal.

'That's quite the order, Sam. You're going to a meeting. Not to war.'

Sam turned and caught his reflection in the window pane.

His rippling physique was covered in battle scars.

He was willing to add more if he had to.

He was built to survive.

He felt his muscles tighten and his mouth twist into a snarl.

'Survivor'.

'We'll see,' Sam finally said before he disconnected the call. He tossed the phone down onto the unmade bed and felt a surge of purpose strike him like a lightning bolt. For months now, he had been traversing the continent, following the finest shavings of breadcrumbs to find answers. Now, he had a genuine lead and there wasn't a second to waste. As he marched into the murky, cramped private bathroom, he heard his phone buzz again. Ranjit had sent him Cheyrou's address, which meant he now had his destination.

He now had a target.

Another domino to topple. Van Hecke had led to Bauer. Bauer had led to Cheyrou.

And now there was a chance that Cheyrou would lead him to the spectre that had been just beyond his grasp. Over the years, Sam had faced off against a number of dangerous groups and seedy organisations.

The Kovalenkos.

The Death Riders.

The Foundation.

Poslednyaya Nadezhda.

But none of them had carried the same sense of dread that Veilmont did. Every syndicate or organisation, even government, that Sam had gone to war with, had been steadfast in their beliefs. Had been bold and brash with what they wanted to achieve and the blood they were willing to spill for it.

Power.

Money.

A change in the political landscape.

But Veilmont was nothing more than an echo. Something more sinister. Something hidden. And as Sam washed himself under the tepid, feeble dribble that fell from the shower, he couldn't shake the feeling that when someone finally answered the door he was knocking on, it would be the devil himself.

When Sam returned to the room, he quickly pulled on a fresh black t-shirt and his jeans and then gathered his minimal items. His phone, which now had the requested address, along with a second one for where he would set his base. His wallet, which contained the watertight forged identity of Ben Carter that had been provided by an off the books government agency.

In his rucksack, he had another change of clothes, his bomber jacket, and a loaded Glock 17.

In the sports bag, he had half a million Euros, generously donated by Van Hecke, which should get him a face to face with Cheyrou as long as Ranjit worked his magic.

And as he set out of the hostel and towards the busy streets of Vienna, Sam could feel his heart pounding like the drums of war. But before he made his way to Cheyrou and a potential step closer to Veilmont, or before he even figured out his route and booked his next trip across the continent, there was an urgent matter to attend to.

As the red lights burst into life and brought the oncoming traffic to a halt, Sam marched across the road to the coffee shop he had settled on and made his way in for a caffeine fix.

CHAPTER THREE

A year was a long time to be wearing a noose.

That was how it felt for Agent Renée Corbin, and every time she was summoned to a meeting by her superiors at the *Direction Générale de la Sécurité Extérieure*, she felt a slight hesitation that this time she'd be led to the hangman. As a leading light in the DGSE, Corbin had been responsible for some of the most vital investigations in the name of keeping France safe from international threats. For nearly two decades she had served with dignity and had cultivated a reputation that saw her respected in every room she had walked in to.

But that had changed nearly a year ago.

Pierre Ducard had served their great country for years as the *Chef d'État-Major des Armées* and had left the seat unfillable when he finally retired from the role. But his time as head of the French armed forces had built him an unbreakable credibility with the rich and powerful, and he soon began his campaign that would see him rise up the political ladder, scaling rungs at an alarming rate until he finally took the reins of the entire country.

The people were behind him.

Despite his right-wing leanings, Ducard carried himself with the authority that only three decades of war could build, and last year, as he embarked on the final overseas tour of his campaign, the man was readying himself for his seat in the Élysée Palace. But a man who wielded such power for so long wouldn't just know where the bodies were buried, there was a good chance that he'd buried them himself, and Corbin, under the orders of *Direction Générale de la Sécurité Extérieure*, Jean-Pierre Vivier, had opened an investigation into the potential war crimes of their soon-to-be president. Agent Martin Agard, a man Corbin had known for years, was tasked to aid the investigation, and soon, the two of them were heading down blood-stained avenues towards the point of no return.

A massacre in Cambodia.

A brutal execution in Croatia.

Assassination after assassination.

All of the blood seemingly on Ducard's hands, but not one fingerprint to prove he had touched any of it.

Despite Vivier's best efforts to shield the investigation, threats began to filter through, as if the duo's banging on the doors had echoed loudly enough to reach Ducard himself. Threats were made towards the agents, and Agard even had to put his wife and two children into protective custody to ensure their safety. All roads were careening towards dead ends, before a known conspiracy theorist online, came across Corbin's desk.

Olivier Chavet.

The surname immediately rang alarm bells, and through a painstaking process, Corbin was finally able to locate the files on the abduction and deaths of Didier Chavet and Simone Rabiot from a decade ago. The two French diplomats were abducted on a visit to Brazil and were held to ransom in the Amazon jungle.

They never made it back alive.

Ducard had done everything in his power to ensure their safe return, even aligning with the British military to bring them back alive. But the extraction mission had been a massacre, with nobody making it out alive, and when the bodies were finally recovered, Ducard ensured that the soldiers who had laid down their lives, and the diplomats who had been executed, were given their rightful sendoff.

But Olivier wasn't buying it.

In the young man's mind, Ducard was complicit, if not responsible for the death of his father, and through a relentless investigation, he had built a compelling case and a rabid following who wanted the world to listen to what he had to say. In the weeks before Ducard's expected coronation, Chavet went on a British news network to relay his investigation and put himself firmly in the crosshairs of the French military. Corbin and Agard had rushed to the UK to intercept, but somebody had beaten them to it.

Sam Pope.

The known vigilante eliminated the attack of Chavet and had revealed that he was the lone survivor from the failed attempt to rescue Chavet's father. He had also revealed that the two diplomats were already dead when the extraction team had arrived, confirming Olivier's and Corbin's own suspicions on Ducard. In doing so, it set off a chain of events that saw Pope lead a full-scale assault on Ducard's estate in Theuville, forty miles north of the nation's capital.

Ducard was captured and was already serving the first year of his life sentence in a military jail. Justice had been served, a man who had served his country with such ruthless distinction would now never take control of it's future.

But it had come at a cost.

Martin Agard had lost his life.

As had Olivier Chavet.

Corbin herself had had to fight a trained assassin and had only survived thanks to Sam's intervention.

But it had cost her so much more.

Despite the medal of bravery she was awarded, Corbin's career had been steered into the same dead ends she had been chasing previously. Despite Vivier's insistence that the promotion she would receive would open up new avenues of investigation into the French elite, bringing down Ducard had left a negative taste in a lot of powerful mouths. Corbin felt the shift instantly. Serious investigations were set up without her input, and despite pleading for involvement, the best she was offered was busy work that kept her within the walls of the government building, one of three glass panelled infra-structures that formed a looming crescent in the city of Paris.

Nearly a year on from the biggest result of her career, one that had come at a significant personal cost, Corbin blew out her lips and gazed out of the floor-to-ceiling window of her plush, private office. The sun cast a wonderful glow across the city of Paris, with the Eiffel Tower, as always, drawing her gaze from the rest of the magnificent skyline. Serving her country had always filled her with immense pride, and her father, a farmer, had shed tears when she had sworn-in all those years ago.

She wondered now if he, along with her mother, was looking down on her with the same pride or with the same scepticism almost every one of her colleagues had.

A knock against the glass door to her office drew her back into the room, and as Director Vivier stepped through the door, she stood to attention.

'Please.' Vivier held up a hand and gestured for her to take a seat. She obliged, as he took the one opposite her desk.

'How can I help you, Sir?' Corbin said. Her constant

requests had fallen on Vivier's deaf ears one too many times for her to offer any warmth.

'Agent Petit has brought to my attention that you have been accessing the files for the Project *Cheval Blanc*.' Vivier interlocked his hands and rested them on his lap. 'Care to explain?'

Corbin sighed.

She was expecting this to come up sooner or later, especially with the increase in surveillance ever since the Ducard incident. Information had been shared outside of the DGSE, and with the DGSI, their internal arm, now treating the DGSE like a potential threat to national security, every single agent with a badge and an access code was being tracked.

Corbin couldn't even book a dentist appointment on her work laptop without the DGSE knowing the state of her teeth.

The silence grew between them and began to gain weight.

'Well?' Vivier encouraged, not showing his disappointment.

'I was trying to cast my eye across what we have so far.' Corbin began. 'The trade patterns are similar to Project *Tomber* five years ago. Considering I brought down that cell, I thought maybe I…'

Vivier held up a hand, cutting off Corbin's hopeful trip down memory lane.

'The only response I should be getting, Agent Corbin, is 'I'm sorry, Sir. It won't happen again, Sir.'

The director kept his eyes locked on Corbin, who gritted her teeth and shook her head. The promises he had given her after Agard's funeral, of a brighter future and a key role in his hierarchy felt like a lifetime ago.

'But I am more help to this organisation if I am involved.' Corbin stated. 'Sidelining me is a mistake.'

Vivier sighed and leant forward.

'We've been over this, Renée.' Corbin shifted uncomfortably at the use of her first name. A lame attempt to build a bridge. 'There is still so much heat after what you did to Ducard, you're lucky this office hasn't burnt down.'

'You mean by bringing him in?' Corbin snapped.

'I mean aiding and abetting a known international terrorist in a full-scale attack, right here, on home soil. By turning this country's political landscape into a circus.' Vivier abandoned the niceties, his tone switching to menacing. 'You're lucky that I intervened in the investigation, otherwise you'd be in the cell next to him.'

'With all due respect, Sir. My job is to track down and eliminate threats to this nation. It's not my fault that the DGSI don't know their arse from their elbow and let everything that man did be swept under the rug.'

'Enough.' Vivier slammed his hand down on Corbin's desk, rattling the pens and the laptop. The impact echoed loud enough that a few heads from the open-plan office spun in their direction. 'This isn't a witch hunt, Renée. There are just certain people who are still not quite sure where your loyalties lie.'

The insinuation hurt Corbin, but she refused to let it show. Her progression through the DGSE ranks had been a testament to her own fortitude, and allowing any sort of weakness to shine through would be pounced on. The DGSE was still a male dominant organisation, and her success had been earnt by double the work of her peers.

'Sir. My loyalties should never be in question.' Corbin waved a lazy hand towards the window. 'Why not check the loyalties of those who were made promises by Ducard, or those who took a hit to their bank accounts when the truth came out?'

'Agent Cobin.' Vivier made no attempt to hide the threat in his voice.

'Or the bank accounts that began to grow the closer he got to the throne.' Corbin turned back to her boss. 'Just remember, Sir, it wasn't any of them who lost a good friend through it all. Or do you not remember the sacrifice Agent Agard made.'

Another hand slammed down on the desk; this time followed by Vivier hauling his large frame to his feet as he loomed over Corbin.

'How dare you?' He spat. 'You are on very thin ice as it is, Agent Corbin, and considering the heat you continue to attract, do not be surprised if you find it beginning to melt.'

'Is that a threat, Sir?' Corbin looked up at him, ignoring the voice in her head to stop. 'Should I add it to the pile?'

With a sullen shake of his head, Vivier stepped away from the desk and straightened his tie. He marched back towards her door, striding through the increasingly toxic atmosphere. Before he reached for the handle, he stopped and turned back to Corbin.

'I know this last year has been hard, Agent Corbin. I do. We have all lost a good friend.' Vivier glanced at the framed photo of Corbin and Agard on the bookshelf behind her. 'And I know it is hard for you to believe right now, but I am taking you out of the firing line for good reason.'

Corbin sat up straight in her seat, defiant.

'Not good enough for me, Sir.'

'Well, then. That's up to you.' Vivier pulled the door open. 'The best way to get back into the fold, Agent Corbin, is to do what you were trained to do.'

'Which is?' She asked dryly.

'Learn how to follow orders and stay out of fucking trouble.'

Vivier marched out of her office, and instantly, every

prying head dropped back to their desks as the director stormed through the office and out of sight. Corbin watched him until he disappeared, anxiously clicking the back of the pen her idle hands had landed on. Angered, she tossed the pen back onto the desk, collected her things and shut down her system. She yanked the laptop from its port, and then strode through the office, her head held high, knowing that the gossip machine would be in over-drive once she had left the building.

Had she been suspended?

Fired?

Corbin didn't care. The other agents could speculate all they wanted, as long as they continued the good work that she would be proud of. It just stuck in her craw that she wasn't allowed to be involved. But what sickened her the most, was that the corruption clearly didn't end with Ducard. The man held court with some of the most influential men in the country, including those who laid out the very foundations for which both the DGSE and DGSI operated.

Senior figures from all parts of the government.

CEOs of the biggest companies in the country.

All people with considerable sway when it came to deciding the top jobs in the organisations that were built to keep France a fair, and most importantly, free country.

Power didn't go to those who had earnt it.

It went to those who were chosen for it.

With that notion latching itself to her train of thought, Corbin didn't even appreciate the warmth of the sun as she pushed open the doors to the *Direction Générale de la Sécurité Extérieure offices*, codenamed CAT, and marched to her car. An agent walked past, offering her a pleasantry that she ignored as she made her way to her car. She dumped her bag and laptop in the back seat, along with the jacket of her pant suit, dropped into the driver's seat and accelerated away from what was beginning to feel like a prison.

And away from what felt the first of many steps that would see her eventually removed from her position.

Her anger soon dissipated as she drove through the city, and as she sat in the usual traffic, she began to do what she did best.

Find solutions to problems that everyone had given up on.

Despite making enemies of those in power, Corbin knew that her record was exemplary, and she had enough credit in the bank to at least make a case that she could still be an asset to the organisation. She'd given decades of her life to the safety of her nation, and she knew if she made the right pleas to the right people, there was still a way to divert the clear direction everything was heading in.

Still a way to take the noose from around her neck.

As she made her way to the small village on the outskirts of Paris where she lived, she was already making mental notes on how her apology to Vivier would go.

By the time she had returned to her car with a bottle of wine and a ready meal for one, she had her grovelling speech almost word for word.

And by the time she pulled into the gravel-laden courtyard in front of her quaint, secluded cottage, she had made a promise to herself to do what she needed to do.

What Vivier had demanded.

Follow orders and stay out of fucking trouble.

Corbin stepped out of the car, gazing across the vista of fields that were painted orange by the sun that was setting beyond them. Her beautiful country laid bare before her, once again re-emphasing why it was so important for her to protect it.

To get back to what she did best.

Why she had to stay out of trouble.

Her focus was swiftly stolen by the sound of feet crunching on the gravel behind her, and as she spun and instinctively went for the firearm that would usually be glued to her hip, her eyes widened with shock.

Her jaw dropped.

As did the bag of groceries, which spilled across the stones beneath her feet.

A smile formed across the world-weary face that was approaching her, one she never thought she would see again.

One that set her pulse racing.

And one that would make a mockery of her promise to herself.

'Hello, Renée,' Sam said as he stopped a few feet from her. 'Been a while.'

CHAPTER FOUR

Looking out across the fields that surrounded Agent Corbin's house sent a wave of memories washing over Sam's mind. The year before, as he'd stood in exactly the same spot, Amara Singh had walked back into his life after years of silence. Their relationship had been complex, forged in her determination to bring him in that soon blossomed into a deep affection due to their shared dedication to the greater good. She had been a fast-rising detective within the Met, but as their paths continued to cross, and their mutual attraction grew, they were always heading towards a crossroads that neither one of them wanted to reach.

There was never a future for them.

They had both known it, and although they got to spend one evening in each other's arms, when the time came for them to make their choice, it was always going to be to separate. Singh was recruited by a clandestine government operation known as 'Directive One', whilst Sam had a promise to keep that would take him to America.

But she'd walked back into his life the previous summer

and guilted him into the most terrifying mission of his life. One that would see him infiltrate an underground fighting tournament to stop an impending continental attack that would shake the entire world to its core.

They had succeeded.

Barely.

But now, as Sam gazed out over the eerily familiar fields, sipping a familiar coffee, he allowed his mind to wander to her once more.

Was she still with Directive One?

Was she still alive?

He didn't know. And with the levels of secrecy that Director Blake kept Directive One under, there would never be a way to know. All he knew was that Singh was more like him than she would care to admit.

She was a fighter.

A survivor.

And the wry smile that cracked across his jawline told Sam that in his gut, he knew she was all right.

'So?' Corbin's perfect English carried her heavy accent and cut through Sam's train of thought. He turned to her, smiled and lifted the mug.

'Nice coffee.'

'Thank you. If I knew you were coming, I would have brought some tea.'

A cheeky grin spread across the agent's face, and Sam chuckled. One of their first interactions, not long after Corbin and her partner had arrested Sam and Olivier Chavet had been over a cup of tea in a small cottage in Hertfordshire. At that point, Sam was expecting to be handed over to the authorities. Little did he know then that Corbin would help him bring down the next leader of her own country.

'It's good to see you, Renée,' Sam said. 'How have you been?'

Corbin sighed and dropped down into one of the wicker garden chairs that were positioned around the glass table. When Sam had stayed with her to recover from his injuries after the onslaught on Ducard's estate, the two of them had spent many an evening around it, sharing food and building a genuine friendship.

Those were few and far between in Sam's world, and he felt a rare surge of happiness as he took the seat opposite.

'I'm surviving.' She shrugged as she sipped her coffee.

'That promotion not all it was cracked up to be?' Sam probed, detecting the sadness in her voice.

'Surprisingly, taking down the most powerful man in the country doesn't make you the most popular person in the room.' Corbin shook her head. 'I don't know. Maybe it's time to move on.'

'And let them win?' Sam sat back in his chair, his muscular arms resting on the wooden arms. 'Trust me, this country is a better place because of what you did. And yeah, you'll piss people off – trust me, if anyone knows that it's me – but the only thing you can do is see it through to the end. Otherwise, all of it was for nothing. All of it.'

Corbin shuffled on her seat uncomfortably. They both knew he was alluding to the death of Agent Agard, and reluctantly, Corbin met Sam's stare.

'You're right.' She scoffed. 'God, you're annoying.'

'It's just one of my many gifts.'

'Well, considering your gifts seem to be destroying governments and causing political chaos, what brings you to Paris, Sam? Our government is still pretty broken from the last time. Or am I to take this as just a personal visit?'

Sam finished his coffee and stood, casting his eyes back out across the rolling green fields. In the distance, a tractor was motoring across a field, weaving fresh lines into the grass.

'Like I said, it's good to see you…'

'But?'

'But I need a favour.'

'Ah.' Corbin placed her mug down and sat up straight. 'If it's access you need, then I'm afraid it's a bad time. Apparently, I can't even cough in my office without someone checking in to see if I'm okay.'

'You're being watched?' Sam turned; an eyebrow raised.

'Monitored.' She corrected. 'They gave me the fancy new position, some extra cash, but with it, I've been shut out. Like I said…I've upset some pretty powerful people.'

Sam waved it off.

'You get used to it.' He took his seat again, his smile replaced with a cold gaze. 'Does the name Yohan Cheyrou mean anything to you?'

Corbin frowned, pursing her lips as she tried to place the name.

'Cheyrou?' She finally repeated. 'He's a dealer in jewellery I believe. Diamonds. From the little I know, a pretty rich man.'

'Not someone who's come across your desk before?'

'I deal with international threats to my country, Sam. A wealthy man selling diamonds to other wealthy people isn't considered a threat to national security.'

'But he's known.'

'Yes.' Corbin nodded. 'But as far as I'm aware, he's not considered a legitimate threat.'

'Not right now.'

'Sam. If you're thinking of doing what I think you're thinking of doing, I'd strongly advise you rethink it.' Corbin leant forward with a hint of concern. 'Just because Cheyrou isn't deemed a threat doesn't mean he's not dangerous. A man with that much wealth has connections.

Connections that run so deep they can't be traced back to him.'

'I just want to talk to him. Scout's honour.'

Sam held his hand up in the trademark signal, and Corbin rolled her eyes.

'Well, from what I understand, it's near on impossible to speak to him. The man doesn't take a meeting without a fee, and that includes with the authorities.' She shook her head. 'Apparently his time is money. So, unless you have a lot of money to hand…'

Corbin trailed off, as she noticed Sam's eyebrow raise.

'…which I don't want to know how you got, I would still strongly advise you don't do what you're going to do.'

Sam smiled and nodded, absorbing her warning but instantly discarding it.

'Like I said, I just want to talk to him.'

'Dare I ask what about?'

Sam met Corbin's gaze with a steely focus.

'I want to ask him about Veilmont.' He noticed the slight twitch at the corner of her lips. 'You heard of it?'

Corbin slapped her hands onto her thighs and stood.

'I think I'm going to need a real drink.'

———

They spent the entire evening in the secluded garden, the warm sun setting beyond the fields and making way for a pleasant evening breeze. Corbin had offered to cook, but the longer their conversation went on, the sooner the hunger seemed to dissipate. Sam had filled Corbin in on the past year.

His time spent in a Serbian prison and the horrors that followed.

His participation in *Boytsovskaya Yama*.

The murders of two police officers, orchestrated by Dominik Silva at the behest of the British government.

Admiral Wainwright.

Guardian.

Everything.

By the time he had finished, the shocked Corbin was already onto her second bottle of wine, admiring Sam's resolve that after all he'd been through, he still maintained his sobriety. As she topped up her glass once more with a slightly shaky hand, she looked across to Sam in amazement.

'How the hell are you still alive?'

'Dumb luck I guess.' He shrugged. 'But, like I said, a man that I trust put me on the hunt for Veilmont, and so far, I've had next to nothing. A few murmurs here and there. Some rich prick in Amsterdam was my strongest lead, and that took me to Bauer in Vienna. Now, my guy, he's managed to connect Bauer to Cheyrou and…'

Sam sat back, shrugging slightly, and Corbin sipped her wine as her brow furrowed.

'And you think Cheyrou can take you to Veilmont?'

'That's what I'm going to find out.'

Corbin ventured back into her cottage and emerged a few moments later with her laptop in hand. She placed it down on the glass, booted it up, and ran through the fingerprint protocol to access the database.

'What are you doing?' Sam asked.

'Last year, Sam, you saved my life.' She looked up at him fondly. Her mind lurched back to the drunken pass she had made at him not long after, and then it quickly vanished. 'I'm going to see if I can pay you in kind.'

Corbin hammered the keys with impressive dexterity, and a series of windows and databases popped up on her screen. Sam didn't even begin to try to make wind of the information before him but watching Corbin in action was impressive viewing.

She was an attractive woman. Sam would have been a blind man not to see that, and that combined with her alluring accent and her determination made her an enticing proposition.

But for eighteen months, Sam's heart had belonged elsewhere. To a wonderful woman in a small bar in Glasgow.

Mel.

Sam steered himself away from the pain and regret of leaving her and turned back to Corbin, who was shaking her head as she hammered away at the keyboard.

'Fuck.' She uttered, hitting another digital brickwall.

'What is it?'

'Everything is classified.' Her eyes scanned from tab to tab. 'I have one of the highest security clearances in the DGSE, but…'

'They don't want anyone to see it.'

'Veilmont. Cheyrou.' She slammed the laptop shut in frustration and took another long swig of wine. 'All of it off limits.'

'To you.' Sam felt the vindication of his trip coursing through him. 'But not to me.'

Sam turned on his heel and looked back out to the fields. The darkness had engulfed them all, shielding the stunning view and offering nothing but shadow. Behind him, he could practically hear the cogs in Corbin's mind turning, and she took a deep breath and pushed herself up from her chair.

'I guess I'd be foolish to say you should just stay here with me, huh?'

Sam turned and looked into her sad, yet hopeful eyes. He shook his head.

'You know I can't walk away from this.' He turned

back and gazed back out into the darkness. 'It's not who I am.'

Corbin wrapped her arms around her slight frame, shuddering slightly as the spring breeze began to carry its usual brisk chill. She stopped beside Sam and followed his gaze out into the vast nothingness.

'Then I guess all I can do is wish you luck.'

'There is something you can do for me. But it could get you into even more trouble.'

He turned to Corbin, who shook her head.

'Trust me, Sam. I don't think I'd even notice it. But it can't be as messy as last time. You know that, right? And let's be honest, finesse isn't exactly your strong suit.'

Sam scoffed, pretending to be offended.

'What makes you say that?'

'Well, last time you basically blew up the President's private estate and killed his entire security team.'

Sam shrugged.

'Fair.'

'But if I do help you, Sam, I need to do it as by the book as I can. Any information you get, you bring it to me, and I'll run it through the channels. If it gets cut off, then you'll know who and where. Deal?'

Corbin reluctantly extended her hand. Sam looked at it, back to her, and then shook it firmly.

'Best one I'm going to get.' He let go and then rested his hands on his hips. 'So…how quickly can you assemble an armed response unit?'

Corbin began to laugh and pointed to her laptop.

'I might have had a drink, Sam. But I'm pretty sure I just told you that I can't get you into Cheyrou's offices. It's like a maximum-security prison.'

Sam's eyes flickered with excitement.

'I don't need you to help get me in.' The smile matched his eyes. 'I need you to help get me out.'

CHAPTER FIVE

Yohan Cheyrou ensured he looked a person in the eye when he spoke to them.

Especially when he was about to have them killed.

Eye contact was one of the non-negotiables that he lived his life by, and the strong code of ethics that he abided by may not have been deemed 'ethical' by the weak minded sheep that comprised most of the world, but it ensured he had a blueprint from which he never veered.

He never veered from it.

Not once.

By adhering to the rules, he had set himself, he had been able to amass a fortune in the hundreds of millions, along with a reputation that was as bulletproof as the car that his chauffeur drove. People knew him, and those who were lucky enough to find themselves sitting across a table from him had the two qualities that he insisted upon.

Deep pockets and scant morals.

For over three decades, Cheyrou had been the biggest exporter of illegal diamonds from the far reaches of Africa into the French capital, building an empire that ensured that the blood was wiped from his product several stops before they arrived in his possession. Many people were brutally murdered or tortured throughout the process, but Cheyrou kept his conscience clean by maintaining that in any walk of life, there was a pecking order.

The haves and the have nots.

And he had built a chain of command that meant the money trickled down, so even those who were subjected to the horrors of digging for diamonds under the watchful eyes of brutal armed guards, still ended up with a little money in their pockets. It wasn't his responsibility to stop the bloodshed or the tyrannical rule of war lords in countries he would never visit, but his vast wealth and ruthless enterprise meant that no matter how many lives were lost, he was always able to cater to his wealthy clients.

The hierarchy was what it was, and as far as he knew it, there was only one person who sat above him.

And it was that person who had made it clear to Cheyrou what needed to be done, and it was why Cheyrou was now looking into the eyes of Jean Auclair, telling him he was about to die.

'You understand why this is happening, Mr Auclair?' Cheyrou asked, an air of nonchalance to his voice. Unlike Auclair, Cheyrou's eyes weren't filled with horrified tears.

'Please.' Auclair begged, gasping for breath. 'I won't say anything.'

'You need to speak up.' Cheyrou insisted, adjusted the custom-made cufflinks on his shirt cuff. 'It's hard to hear you over all this noise.'

They were standing on the metal walkway that ran across the upper floor of the printing factory, which despite the near total move to digital media, still held a number of clients. Magazines and newspapers may have been in decline, but the few printing press' that secured their slow demise still made enough to keep the lights on. To Cheyrou, the factory, as well as the entire printing industry, was a relic, holding on to the way things used to be.

The factory, whilst organised, was an eyesore, and the prime real estate on the outside of the city centre, meant he had bought it outright with the idea of allowing it to slowly die a death along with the rest of its industry. Then, he would construct a lavish high-rise to cater to the younger generation of wealth. Luxury apartments that would become just another arm of the vast business enterprise that he had built.

Jean Auclair was one such member of that generation, a man born into incredible wealth, like Cheyrou, but without the business nous to turn a few million into hundreds of millions. Auclair had inherited his money after his father had passed away, selling the family business and trying to live at a level where he just didn't belong.

Making decisions he shouldn't have made.

Making promises he couldn't keep.

And now, as Cheyrou's private security team dangled him over the edge of the steel balcony, the young man was weeping for his life. He'd already gone through the expected stages of bargaining. He'd offered Cheyrou all of his money. He'd begged and pleaded, offering to work off whatever debt he may have accrued.

But it was pointless.

All four of the men on the balcony knew it, as did the other member of Cheyrou's security detail who was waiting patiently beside the machine below.

'Please.' Auclair begged once more, tilting his head back to see what awaited him below. 'Please don't kill me.'

Cheyrou sighed.

There was nothing more pathetic than a man who couldn't take account for his actions. Despite having an almost limitless wealth and the option for a life of leisure, he was still a man of strict habits and unshakable routine.

His day always began promptly at five a.m., where he would begin his daily exercise routine and take his coffee and breakfast on the balcony of his top floor suite in one of the most prestigious apartment blocks in Paris.

He was in his office before eight, working through deal after deal with client after client, and arranging his day before it had even begun.

Everything was regimented and in place, and it meant there were no surprises.

Nothing to catch him off guard.

Every element of his life played nicely into the next, and it was why he had complete control over everyone who walked into a room with him. The *Préfecture de Police* were in his pocket. The DGSE.

The DGSI.

Interpol.

Direction nationale de la police aux frontières.

Cheyrou lived in a world without barriers, and as he stood in his custom-made suit, he ran his hand through his neatly parted, grey hair and gestured for his men to haul Auclair from his perilous position. As they did, Auclair collapsed to his knees, taking sharp breaths to try to control himself.

'Thank you.' He finally stammered.

'Stand.' Cheyrou commanded. 'No man ever felt pride on his knees. Stand.'

Auclair obliged, and as he stood, Cheyrou once again adjusted his cufflinks and took a step towards him, smirking as the man cowered.

'You knew the risk involved.' Cheyrou began, his eyes locked on Auclairs. 'In this world, it is good to understand one's place. You…you have been afforded a life of semi-luxury by the hard graft of your father, yet that has never been enough. You came to me on a pitiful notion that expensive diamonds would lead to an elite status. When you realised that beyond the approval of the materialistic have-nots, you had nothing, you begged me to open the door for you. Do you remember? Once again, on your knees, begging me for a life.'

Auclair was snivelling as Cheyrou's words cut through him. As he gave the order, Cheyrou's men hauled Auclair back to his feet, and he wiped the tears away before they trickled into his beard.

Cheyrou regarded him with disdain as he continued.

'Now, I took pity on you, Jean. I really did. I told you that the world you wanted to enter wasn't built for weak men such as yourself. Yet, you insisted, and as you know, Mr Glass has a very strict policy. Once you are in…once you have seen what exists beyond the reach of men of your ilk, there is no going back.' Cheyrou reached out and began to straighten the young man's shirt. Auclair flinched as he did so. 'Which brings us to where we are now, doesn't it? And surely, you must see the predicament I am in?'

'Please, tell Mr Glass that…'

A crisp backhand caught Auclair firmly across the jaw, rocking him backwards into the metal railing that protected him from the drop below. Cheyrou's sovereign ring ripped through the skin of his lip, and Auclair dabbed at the blood with his hand.

'You are not permitted to say his name.' Cheyrou said coldly, pulling a handkerchief from his jacket pocket and wiping the blood away. With his options dwindling, a desperate rage exploded within Auclair, who launched forward towards Cheyrou, his arms splayed as he lunged for the man's throat. A few inches away from the unflinching Cheyrou, Auclair felt the powerful grip of both security guards once more, who wrenched his shoulder tendons to breaking point. He let out a roar of anguish as they lowered him to a knee.

Cheyrou gave a slow and mocking clap.

'Finally. A little fight in you.' He wrenched Auclair's head back by his hair. 'But once again, you find yourself on your knees. Where is your sense of pride?'

Auclair spat in Cheyrou's face.

It was a brave act of defiance, one that Cheyrou would have genuinely applauded had he not been so disgusted.

'Fuck you.' Auclair barked through gritted teeth, feebly struggling against the grip of his captors as Cheyrou wiped the saliva from his face.

'As I said, no pride. Therefore…' Cheyrou took a step closer. 'No use.'

He peered over the railing to his henchman down below and gave the nod, and the man obligingly pulled the large lever attached to the side of the machine. With a monstrous roar, the enormous pulping machine shook into life, and the two metallic cylinders began to whirl against each other. The contraption was a necessity for the printing factory, used to drop old editions and other unwanted publications into, to render it down into pulp to be recycled elsewhere. Ten feet above the hungry mouth of the machine, Cheyrou turned back to Auclair, who's face had drained of its colour.

His eyes had lost all hope.

Calmly, Cheyrou adjusted the man's collar and smiled.

'There is no going back.'

Cheyrou gave the nod, and as Auclair's helpless screams echoed across the factory, the two men rolled him back over the railing and released him. As he plunged between the spinning cylinders, the screams of terror turned to blood curdling cries of pain, as the machine began to suck him through the small gap. His bones began to shatter, and blood sprayed across the cylinders as they began to render him to nothing. After a few moments, the anguish died down, and what was left of the man was ripped apart and pushed through the machine, filling the pulping container with the red, lumpy remains of Auclair's body.

Nobody said a thing.

One of the security guards looked visibly distraught, but when Cheyrou glanced in his direction, he knew well enough to straighten up.

Finally, Cheyrou gave the nod for the machine to be shut down, and as it went to sleep, an eerie silence fell across the murder scene.

'Clean that up.' Cheyrou ordered, unperturbed by what he had just witnessed. He then glanced at his watch. 'I have a dinner reservation.'

Turning on the heel of his expensive, leather shoes, Cheyrou marched down the balcony, taking the steps calmly as the three other men began the stomach-churning job of cleaning up the remains of Jean Auclair. As he strode confidently past the blood-stained container, Cheyrou pulled out his phone, used his thumb print to bypass the encryption and found the number.

It answered on the second ring.

There was no greeting.

Only expectation.

'It has been taken care of, Sir.' Cheyrou said, confident he had hidden the quiver of fear in his voice. After a few moments of uncomfortable silence, the man spoke up.

'I will not allow for that to happen again, Yôhan.'

The line went dead.

Cheyrou pocketed the device and stepped out of the factory, welcoming the pleasant evening breeze that was weaving through the city of Paris. The car was waiting for him, as was Jerome, his head of security, who stood by the open door of the car.

'Everything okay, Sir?' Jerome asked. He was a tall, broad man, a testament to his powerlifting days before he branched out into private security. He was as loyal as a dog, and ferocious as one, and Cheyrou enjoyed having such a man on a short leash.

'Perfect,' Cheyrou said as he approached. 'Make sure they do a thorough job.'

'Yes, Sir,' Jerome said, his deep voice laced with purpose. 'Enjoy your evening.'

Jerome turned and marched back towards the factory and Cheyrou dropped into the back seat and helped himself to a glass of champagne as the driver pulled away, knowing better than to engage his paymaster in idle chit chat.

As he threw back the glass in one mouthful, Cheyrou gazed out of the window, watching as his city whizzed by.

The driver kept his eyes on the road and his mouth shut.

Everybody had a place in this world.

And after that ominous warning, Cheyrou was well aware of his.

CHAPTER SIX

'It's going to be a busy one today, love. Lots of meetings.'

Ranjit was so used to telling white lies to his wife, it was practically a second language, and most days, it wasn't until nearly lunchtime that the guilt had finally surpassed. When he'd met Rita, they were both fresh out of university, both with their respective degrees and the world at their feet. Both of them had achieved first-class honours, the highest marks available, and with Rita's business management degree, and his data analytics background, the pair of them moved to London to make themselves rich.

They met soon after, fell in love, and were then hit with the harsh realities of the working world. Most businesses valued experience over education, and although their qualifications meant they *could* do the jobs they had intended, their experiences meant they weren't given the opportunity. Rita fell into a digital marketing company as an account manager, whilst Ranjit found himself moving from company to company, quickly finding disillusionment in working on an IT helpdesk.

They were both paid well enough, and as was the long,

corporate slog, the longer they worked in their respective fields, the more tiny rungs up the ladder they climbed. Pay bumps and benefits meant they could buy a house on the outskirts of the city, but their long hours and even longer commute meant they struggled to find time to enjoy it.

The years turned to a decade, and their comfortable life turned into a marriage with two beautiful daughters, which Ranjit often joked accelerated his hair loss.

But everything changed just after the birth of their second daughter.

The monotony of being the head of an IT department he didn't care about, for a company he cared even less for, saw him begin to stretch his digital legs, and soon, with the help of his data analytics degree, he began to manipulate the stock markets to his advantage. Forecasting potential drops enabled him to make a bundle, which paid off a significant portion of the mortgage. Rita was suspicious, but he was able to play it off as a bonus from work, until there was a knock at the door.

It wasn't HMRC.

It wasn't the police.

It was two men, James Murray and Fabien Jensen, who bundled him into the back of a van and drove him to what he would soon call his workspace. Guardian were an above-board team of mercenaries, put together by Murray after he had left the military. They took on wealthy clients, who either needed protection or problems to be solved.

And a CEO of a company whose stock Ranjit had decimated with a tactical sale, had hired them to set Ranjit straight.

Instead, they offered him a job, much to Jensen's chagrin, as Murray saw the benefit of a man with Ranjit's tech and data background. The fewer questions Ranjit asked, the more comfortable he'd be with their line of work, and they set him up in a kitted-out war room, with a wall of monitors and the most powerful equipment a tech nerd could dream of. It meant for the first time in his professional life, Ranjit was doing something he actually enjoyed, and as the contracts kept pouring in, he was tasked with a wider remit.

Creating specs for locations.

Monitoring calls and investigating targets.

Hacking into security systems and bank accounts to order.

All it cost him was his conscience, but the price, a six-figure salary, and more benefits than a nationwide charity, meant he was compensated well for it.

It was also when the white lies began.

Murray had helped him concoct enough of a paper trail to present to his wife that he had gone into contracting, and together, the two of them arranged the necessary invoices and calendar invites to at least make it look legitimate. When Ranjit was needed out in the field, usually in the high-tech van to provide on-the-job digital expertise, they were able to convincingly build a business case for it, and once the money rolled in, Rita's interest in the truth waned.

But when Guardian came to a premature end four months ago, Ranjit had resigned himself to a return to the nine to five slog. Murray had offered him a generous pay off, on the condition that he do one final job for him.

Remove all traces of Sam Pope's alias, Ben Carter, from any database they had run it through, and tighten up any gaps that could lead the authorities back to Pope.

Ranjit had been dumbstruck.

Not only had their contract to bring in Sam led to the dissolution of the company, but now Ranjit was being paid to give the man an easy way out. The thought even crossed his mind to hand Sam over to the authorities, but the money offered was enough to give him a buffer between needing to return to the working world.

As requested, Ranjit tightened up Sam's alias, and in doing so, auditioned for a job he didn't know existed.

Sam was a fighter, that much he had seen in person, but whilst there was no door the man wouldn't knock on, there were digital pathways he couldn't access.

Put a gun or a knife in his hand, and Sam Pope was the most lethal human on the planet.

Stick him in front of a laptop, and he was effectively a puppy dog.

The work Ranjit had done on his identity, coupled with a glowing reference from Murray, saw Sam offer Ranjit a six-figure salary to work with him and put his illegal expertise to good use. And despite knowingly breaking the law, Ranjit had never felt a more righteous purpose than when Sam had laid out what they were going to do.

They were going to track down 'Veilmont' and expose anyone who had profited from whatever it was.

Ranjit had spent months working through the dark web, collecting the scant breadcrumbs that Veilmont had left in their wake. Whoever or whatever they were, they didn't just cover their tracks.

They blew them clean off the digital landscape.

But from those crumbs, Ranjit had been able to follow a vague trail, which meant hacking into multiple databases across Europe. Most companies existed under the pretence that their cyber security was watertight, but Ranjit swiftly rendered them down to digital colanders with how quickly he punctured holes in them. His investigations soon helped him pinpoint Wesley Van Hecke, who had acquired his fortune from his father and who had some troubling correspondence on his phone. Ranjit didn't want to ask Sam how he got the name Bauer from Van Hecke, or how he'd managed to convince the young man to part with half a million euros, but that had then sent the rogue vigilante to Vienna, and it was Ranjit's job to facilitate that.

Then from Vienna to Paris, and all Ranjit needed to do was hack the CCTV companies that would have access to the videos that put Sam in the vicinity.

Trains. Train stations. Street cameras.

It was Ranjit's job to turn Sam into a ghost, as well as ensure he had the 'tools' he needed to get the job done. Manipulating shipping manifests, and paying off the odd baggage handler, meant it was relatively easy for Ranjit to send Sam's personal arsenal across the continent.

Everything Ranjit did now was completely illegal.

And he'd never felt like he'd done more good in his life.

But the white lies to his wife were an unfortunate byproduct of his job, as aiding and abetting the UK's most wanted fugitive would carry a severe sentence.

She would never approve.

It would put her and their children at risk, even though he was doing it for them.

That morning, the guilt was still sitting heavy in his gut when he arrived at 'The Hub', and even the taste of his takeaway coffee couldn't quell it. 'The Hub' was a fashionable office block in Kings Cross, set up by an Entrepreneur who wanted to 'change the working day'. Companies were able to rent out desks, meeting rooms, offices, even entire floors for as long as they needed.

A few hours.

A day.

A year.

It was an interesting concept, and in the four months that Ranjit had been stationed in the small, private office on the third floor, he'd seen many start-ups roll through the office block, but none with the same tenure as himself. His office was basic, with a wide, electronic desk, decked out with all the ergonomic hardware designed to maintain his 'well-being'.

The only personal artifacts he had contributed, were a picture of his family on one end of the desk, and a tall, looping plant that sat proudly in the corner.

Ranjit booted up his computer, and the four separate monitors flashed into life, and after running his usual checks across his own security network, he sat back and enjoyed the rest of his coffee. He commanded his voice activated speaker to play his 'chill-hop' playlist, and as the mellow beats thumped out of the small device, Ranjit began opening the software that would allow him to get to work. Sam had arrived in Paris the previous afternoon, explaining he had an old friend he wanted to lean on for support in his attempt to get to Cheyrou. Ranjit had already set up a new bank account in the heart of the French capital for him under his alias and could see that Sam had deposited the half a million that would at least get him on Cheyrou's radar.

Now, all he needed to do was work his way through the obstacles that the French millionaire would no doubt have in place to protect his business, until Ranjit had access to the man's personal calendar.

A man as careful and as potentially dangerous as Cheyrou wouldn't have skimped on security software, and Ranjit's suspicions were confirmed when he saw that Cheyrou had the best-in-class programs installed to keep hackers out of his business.

It took Ranjit seven minutes to bypass it.

Then, once he'd booked in an eleven o'clock meeting under the name 'Carter' – taking great care to mirror previous appointments – he set up an internal wire from the recently opened account to Cheyrou, which would offer him proof that his mystery guest had the necessary funds. Hopefully, Cheyrou would see it as an oversight on his part, but if not, Ranjit had confidence that Sam could handle himself.

That was Sam's area of expertise.

With all tasks complete, Ranjit sipped his coffee once more and spluttered as the ice-cold taste hit the back of his throat. He checked the time – it was just after nine – meaning he'd been working for over an hour without realising its passage, and so he stepped out, locked his office, and headed back through the building to the small, independent coffee shop across the road that now knew him by name.

By the time he'd stepped back out into the spring sunshine with a fresh flat white and neatly rolled cigarette, his smart watch buzzed to notify him of an incoming call. Swiftly, he lit the cigarette, located his phone in his jacket pocket, and took the call.

'Sam'. He answered chirpily, blowing smoke out of the side of his mouth. 'How's Paris?'

Just dandy. How are we looking?'

Ranjit chuckled. Always straight to the point.

But then again, Ranjit wasn't the one about to enter a fortified office with armed guards under false pretences. He could forgive Sam's haste.

'Good to go, mate.' Ranjit said, taking another puff. 'Dress smart. And good luck.'

Sam thanked him and hung up the call, and Ranjit took a few minutes to enjoy his cigarette in the warmth of the spring glow, along with the rich coffee, before heading back up to the safety of his office.

He may have been breaking the law.

But at least he wasn't in the line of fire.

CHAPTER SEVEN

Cheyrou's office was a nondescript building that blurred into the wall of architecture that lined the road opposite, and as Sam took a seat outside the coffee shop, he kept his eyes locked on the doorway. The entire street was composed of high-end jewellery stores, reminding Sam of Hatton Garden back in London, with hundreds of thousands of pounds on display behind fortified windows. An iron security gate sat behind every door, and Sam watched as paid security meandered up and down the street, trying, and failing, to blend in.

This street was money, both in the shops and in the pockets of those walking it, yet for all the celebration of wealth, Cheyrou's office remained discreet.

No sign above the door.

Nothing to indicate it was anything other than an administration office.

Yet the two armed guards who didn't budge from the doorway, and the outrageous half a million euro entrance fee, meant that Cheyrou's building was the heartbeat of the entire district. As Sam kept his eyes on the footfall ahead, Corbin emerged from the coffee shop with two fresh coffees and placed them on the table. Before she sat, she cast her eye over Sam and smiled.

'What?' He looked up at her, reaching for his coffee.

'Nothing. Just…' She looked a little embarrassed. 'You clean up well.'

Sam nodded his thanks, failing to disguise his discomfort. He'd grown up as a military child, and when his father, Major William Pope had passed away just as Sam approached adulthood, Sam had thrown himself fully into the armed forces in an attempt to feel closer to the man's legacy. A smart uniform wasn't something he was unfamiliar with.

A two thousand euro, three-piece suit with a designer label, however, felt like somebody else's skin.

'Thanks, I guess.' He forced a smile that broke across his clean-shaven jaw. 'My friend picked it out for me.'

'No offence, but I guessed that high-end fashion wasn't in your skill set.' Corbin smiled as she sipped her coffee. 'Has "your friend" done everything you needed?'

'He always does.' Sam said with a hint of pride in his voice. 'My meeting is in Cheyrou's calendar, the money is ready to go. Now I just have to do my bit.'

'You mean infiltrate one of the most protected buildings in this district, owned by one of the most powerful people in this city?' Corbin shook her head in disbelief. 'Tell me, do you ever doubt what it is you're doing?'

Sam took a thoughtful sip, letting the question hang in the air along with the distant bluster of traffic.

'Never.' He finally said, placing the mug back on the table. 'I did at first. For a while, actually. I used to think that I was just spiralling down a hole, and no matter how many people I put in the ground, I could never stack them high enough to claw my way back out.'

'That must have been hard.'

'It was. I mean, let's face it, what I do. It's not normal.

53

People go through trauma all the time, and they deal with it. They maybe never get back to who they were before it happened, but they get through it. And that's what I was doing, but the further I dug, and the harder I hit, I realised that what I do might not be normal…but it's necessary.' Sam took a deep breath. 'The people I've killed, Renée, they weren't good people. That didn't give me the right, but it sure as hell gave me a reason. And when the day comes that I have to face the consequences of my actions, I will face them with my back straight and my shoulders set. But right now…I have a feeling in my gut that tells me whatever Veilmont is…it needs someone like me to stop it. And if that means I have to walk into hell doused in petrol, then I don't have the luxury of doubt.'

Sam felt his muscles relax, the purpose of his mission causing them to flex against the expensive fibres of his suit. Calmly, he took his mug and finished his coffee, before checking his watch.

'You're a good man, Sam Pope.' Corbin finally said with a smile. 'Whatever pain you went through has helped a lot of people.'

Corbin hesitated slightly but continued.

'Maybe one day…it can help you, too.'

Her words cut through the designer suit and Sam's granite-like exterior, and he forced a smile to cover the pain. He knew she saw it, but to end the conversation, he stood and made a show of buttoning his blazer.

'Right…I have a meeting to get to.' He joked.

'Remember, you have ten minutes. Best I can give you.'

Sam nodded firmly and then cast his eyes to the end of the street where the black van was already in position.

'And you trust these guys?' Sam asked bluntly.

'As much as I trust anyone.' Corbin shrugged. 'But you stick a gun in their face, and they'll pull theirs.'

'Good.' Sam checked his watch again, then held out his hands. 'How do I look?'

'Uncomfortable.' Corbin joked. 'But you look the part.'

Sam nodded, adjusted his tie, and then fixed his eyes on the nondescript door to Cheyrou's office. Two potted plants stood proudly either side, partially hidden by the broad, militant looking men who made no effort to hide their responsibility.

'See you on the other side.' Sam finally said and then stepped out from the table. As he passed Corbin, he gently squeezed her shoulder, a potential goodbye if things went south.

And as he marched across the street, and the eyes of the security guards locked onto him, Sam was very aware that he was walking in unarmed.

Things could go south very quickly.

———

'Carter?' Cheyrou looked at the screen of his laptop with a furrowed brow, and then up at his assistant. Jasmine had been with him for the past thirteen years and was used to his volatile nature. 'Who is this man?'

'You accepted the meeting, Sir.' She stammered, looking around the expensively and carefully put together office.

Cheyrou's eyes narrowed. In his line of work, every detail mattered, especially when he knew a number of government agencies, both foreign and domestic, where looking for the thinnest of threads to dangle from his operation. One pull and they would hopefully unravel his entire organisation, yet Cheyrou prided himself on being nigh on untouchable.

Every account he owned was legitimate.

Every payment he made and every tax he filed.

Being on top of the details meant he was ahead of the curve, so seeing a name he didn't recognise had set an alarm bell ringing.

Being told he had accepted the meeting meant he was ready to go into lockdown.

'I did no such thing.' Cheyrou waved away his assistant dismissively and stood, looking up at the grand clock that adorned the fine panelling on the wall.

Two minutes until the scheduled meeting.

Anxiously, he adjusted his cufflinks, and as Jasmine disappeared through his office door, Jerome stepped through before it closed.

'Everything okay, sir?' The man's voice boomed even at a whisper.

'Ben Carter.' Cheyrou stated with a hint of disdain. 'I trust all checks have been carried out.'

'Of course, sir.' Jerome never showed any offence to being questioned. 'Works as a private contractor. Deals with more off the books problems for major corporations. He has quite the resume.'

'And you checked the legitimacy?' Cheyrou marched to the drinks cabinet that sat underneath the window that afforded him the view of the street below. The entire district was swimming in wealth and thus wasn't subjected to the same footfall or traffic as the inner-city. A few security guards paraded the street aimlessly.

An attractive, well-dressed couple sat outside the coffee shop opposite.

'Yes, sir.' Jerome nodded. 'We have also run checks on the proposed fee for the meeting. It is all accounted for.'

'Hmmm.' Cheyrou murmured, as he poured out a glass of expensive scotch whisky into the crystal tumbler. His evening meal had been accompanied by a few bottles of wine and an attractive woman, both of whom had provided him with a morning headache. He placed the stopper back into the decanter and then necked the drink in one, grimacing as it burnt the back of his throat.

'Is everything okay, sir?' Jerome asked again, his hands clasped behind his back. His Glock 17 protruded slightly from his jacket.

'Just a feeling.' Cheyrou said as his eyes glared through the window. 'Do we have a full team in place?'

'Yes, sir. Two on the door. Three throughout.'

'Armed?'

'Always, sir.'

At that moment, the shrill bell linked to the front door echoed from the corner of the room, indicating the door to the office had been opened. Cheyrou hurried to his desk and pulled up the CCTV platform, where he could see a well-dressed, muscular man obediently standing with his arms and legs spread in the foyer, whilst one of the guards patted him down.

Mr Ben Carter.

Without taking his eyes from his surprise guest, Cheyrou threw out his orders.

'Jerome, personally escort Mr Carter to my office, and then stay put.' His eyes flickered with mischief. 'We'll see who this man truly is.'

Jerome nodded and swiftly took his leave, whilst Cheyrou pulled out a few briefcases from the safe that was built into the wall. He took them over to the felt-covered display table on the far side of the office, where the sun cut through the curtain and cast its light on the stunning jewels he would display. It was all for show, and usually, seeing the sparkle pushed people to part with their cash.

But this was to keep up appearances, and as Carter was led through the door, Cheyrou startled slightly. There weren't many men who were comparable to Jerome, but Carter was certainly as tall and as stocky. His slick, brown hair was neatly parted at the side and looped down behind his ears.

The man was dressed to the nines, and as he approached Cheyrou with an extended hand, he certainly looked like a man who belonged in Cheyrou's office.

But something was off.

The handshake was powerful, the palm calloused and rough.

There were scars that littered the man's eyebrows.

The man carried himself like a soldier, and Cheyrou gave a small, undetectable nod to Jerome, who discreetly unclasped his holster.

'Mr Carter. It is a pleasure.' Cheyrou beamed his immaculate smile. 'Although, I must say, a little surprising, as neither myself nor my staff have a record of your booking.'

Cheyrou stared at Carter, who casually took a seat at the desk. Cheyrou glanced to Jerome, who slowly lifted a hand towards his jacket.

'Tell your guard he doesn't need to reach for his weapon.' Carter looked up at Cheyrou, the face vaguely familiar. 'I'm not here to cause trouble.'

'Then what are you here for?' Cheyrou asked, taking the seat opposite and turning to face his intruder, incorrectly assuming control of the situation. 'Need I waste time on presenting my latest collection to you?'

'I am also not interested in buying any diamonds from you, Mr Cheyrou.' Carter looked composed.

It was unnerving.

Cheyrou glanced to Jerome, who's hand was already clasping the grip of his handgun. Cheyrou shook his head slightly.

'Then, please. Explain.'

'Your money for this meeting is already in your account. You can check if you like.'

Cheyrou did and smirked at the recent deposit that made him half a million euros richer.

'So how can I help you, Mr Carter?' Cheyrou rested his hands on the desk. His eyes widened as Carter reached into the pocket of his jacket, and Jerome was already unholstering his weapon.

Carter held up his hand. Within the fingers, was a thin, black card.

Jerome eased up, slotting the gun back into the holster.

But Cheyrou understood the severity of the situation before Carter had placed the card down on the oak desk and slid it across to him with a finger.

It was step one on an irreversible process.

One that Cheyrou knew could have fatal consequences for the man before him.

Keeping his eyes locked on his mystery guest, Cheyrou lifted the card and inspected it, before tossing it back down onto the desk nonchalantly.

'I think you'd better be leaving now, Mr Carter.' He flicked his eyes to Jerome, who launched forward like a coiled snake. As he placed a meaty hand on Carter's shoulder, he was suddenly hauled forward, their guest expertly wrenching the man's wrist and then Jerome made a brutal, face-first introduction with the oak desk, that rattled everything on it.

Cheyrou leant back in his seat, his eyes wide with shock.

Sam pinned Jerome down, his elbow pressing into the man's neck, as he calmly looked back to Cheyrou who looked a mixture of fear and awe.

'Now…Mr Cheyrou. I want you to tell me about Veilmont.'

CHAPTER EIGHT

As Sam had stepped up from his seat and began his march across the sun-drenched road towards Cheyrou's office, Corbin had felt a sense of dread settle in her stomach. It wasn't the first time she had watched Sam walk headfirst into a dangerous situation, and just like last time, there didn't seem to be a favourable outcome. Taking down Cheyrou, if he was involved in something as bad as Sam feared, would rid the world of a potential evil, and could possibly save lives.

But there would be repercussions.

There were always repercussions.

When they took down Ducard together a year ago, they stopped a dangerous and violent man take control of Corbin's country and held him accountable for his war crimes. But it had come at the cost of a young man who had wanted justice for his father, and it had left two young girls without a father.

It had also sent her career to the doldrums.

Down the far end of the street, a tactical squadron, armed and ready to go at her notice, had been called in by her to deal with a potential terror threat. Corbin had slid the request in at the last second, ensuring any questions or rejections could be faced during the inevitable riot act that would be read to her.

Sometimes, it was better to ask for forgiveness rather than permission, even if forgiveness was at a premium.

Director Vivier was waiting under the thin ice she was skating on, and wrangling an armed unit to lay siege to the building of one of the richest men in the city would most likely cause him to reach up and drag her through it.

But she believed in Sam.

For a man whose path had been forged by trauma, he was a shining light of good in a continuously darkening world. Every step the man took was selfless, and through the few conversations they'd had, Sam had never once put himself first. When he had inserted himself in her pursuit of both Chavet and Ducard, it was because he wanted answers for the comrades who'd been sent with him to the slaughter.

When he'd left her last summer with the shady government agency, it had been to literally fight for his life to get to a terrorist cell.

He'd stopped a gold heist and exposed a politician, all because two young police officers had been senselessly murdered to provide a distraction.

And four months before, he'd allowed himself to become public enemy number one, just to bring down a well-connected admiral who had conspired against his country.

None of it was for Sam.

It was always for someone else.

And as she sipped the final remnants of her coffee, she watched Sam, resplendent in his expensive suit, get roughly pulled into the offices by the two security guards and the door slammed shut behind him. She knew he was unarmed and had walked willingly into a potentially fatal scenario.

All because he wanted the truth.

Because he *needed* to do the right thing.

The second the door closed; she started her timer and took a deep breath. Five minutes was the request, and as she watched the first few seconds tick away, Corbin knew it would be the longest five minutes of her life.

After a minute, one of the other guards reappeared, once again taking his post with stoic obedience.

Another minute, and his colleague appeared, and the two smartly dressed men resembled bouncers outside a trendy bar.

As the clock ticked down to another minute, Corbin lifted herself from her seat and stepped out onto the pavement. She gave a discreet hand signal towards the van, and she heard its engine roar to life almost instantly. Then she made a beeline across the street, and just before she reached the curb, she locked eyes with one of the guards, who shifted slightly towards her.

'Can I help you, madame?' It was more a threat than a question, and as she reached for her badge, she could see him make an intimation towards his concealed weapon.

'DGSE.' She yelled, drawing a few panicked cries from passersby, who saw her pull her Glock with her other hand, followed instantly by the two men pulling theirs. 'Put your guns down. Now. I have a warrant to search this building.'

The screeching of tyres drowned out the expletive tirade sent her way, and with expert proficiency, a four-strong team, strapped with vests and armed with handguns of their own, filtered out, their sights locked on the men before them. Corbin held up a hand to seize control of the stand off.

'Last time. Guns down and get on your knees.'

One of the guards looked anxiously to the other, and

relented, lifting his hands, and allowing the gun to swing harmlessly across his index finger.

The other pulled the trigger.

The bullet hit one of the agents in the neck, sending him sprawling backwards against the van, as blood splattered across the pavement. Terrified screams echoed out as the public raced for cover, and Corbin and the rest of the team returned fire.

Four bullets hit the man in quick succession, two of them thudding into the vest beneath his sharp suit, whilst Corbin's ripped through the man's right shoulder and sent him spinning. The other doorman, incensed, reclaimed his weapon, and opened fire, catching one of the agents in the knee, who went down in a heap, clutching his shattered shin.

Corbin and the other two agents lit him up with a contained burst, with his vest absorbing the first, before Corbin's bullet burrowed through the gap between his eyebrows.

He hit the ground, dead, and as the other agents tended to their wounded, Corbin raced to the other security guard and wrenched his shattered shoulder back and slapped him in cuffs. His anguished squeals were drowned out by the screeching alarm within the building before them, and the ominous sound of metal doors clamping shut.

Sam was locked inside, and Corbin knew there was nothing she could do for him.

Not when the next stage of the plan was to chase him.

As the terror grew throughout the street, and the wailing of sirens filled the air, Corbin went to work to control the scene, to give Sam the best chance of seeing his plan through.

Otherwise, there was no way back for him.

As a man who prided himself on being in control of every room and situation he placed himself in, Cheyrou made little effort to hide his displeasure at the man before him. When he'd finally agreed to discuss the matter at hand, Sam had let go of the man's head of security and allowed him to stumble backwards into his own embarrassment.

'Enough, Jerome.' Cheyrou had chastised, the glare in his eyes telling Sam that Jerome's next performance review might well be his last. Cheyrou turned back to Sam and in an attempt to wrestle control of the situation, calmly took his seat. 'Sit, Mr Carter.'

Sam obliged. If he'd given his real name, there was no doubt in his mind that the entire French military would have been ripping through the streets of Paris to claim him. As he sat, Sam straightened out his suit, still maintaining the role he'd walked in with, and he turned to Jerome who was holding a blood-soaked handkerchief to his nose.

'*Désolé.*' He offered by way of apology with an accompanying shrug.

Jerome just lifted a middle finger in response.

'You speak français, monsieur Carter?' Cheyrou asked. Sam tilted his hand slightly and shook his head. 'Then we shall speak in your native tongue.'

'I appreciate that.'

'What I do not appreciate is the interruption to my day.' The bass in Cheyrou's voice was returning. 'Now, I did have concerns at how a man of your means was able to make his way to this point. But my major concern is this right here.'

Cheyrou tapped the card on the table and continued.

'This right here, monsieur Carter, is not something that many men get to hold. Even less women. To have access to such a thing means that you have access to money and information that would put you in a very dangerous situation.'

Sam smiled and nodded.

'I'm used to dangerous situations, sir.'

'Ah.' Cheyrou sat back in his chair and pressed the tips of fingers together. 'Please, edify me. What is it you do, monsieur Carter? Private contracting does not provide access to the two, how do we say, characteristics that lead to this card.'

'So, you know what that is?' Sam said, leaning forward in his chair. Cheyrou kept a cold stare on him. 'I am a private contractor, Mr Cheyrou, only not for things most people are privy to. I…fix things for people.'

'Ah, so a hitman.'

'Not quite.' Sam sat back, matching Cheyrou's energy. 'Very powerful men in very powerful positions come across problems all the time. You should know that. Well, some-times those problems need to go away, and due to what I am then privy to, they pay me an extortionate amount of money. Not for my services you understand…'

'But for your silence.' Cheyrou nodded along and then lifted the card. The silence grew, and Sam arched his neck back to Jerome, who looked away with slight embarrass-ment. 'Perhaps you would like to work for me, monsieur Carter?'

'With all due respect, Mr Cheyrou, I don't think you could afford me.'

'Touché.' Cheyrou smirked and then tapped the card on the desk. 'You do understand that the moment you placed this card on my desk, you passed a point of no return. You understand this?'

'I understand that I have asked you to tell me about Veilmont, and you seem to be dancing around the conversation.'

Cheyrou's eyes glistened, and he then turned and nodded to Jerome, who pulled his weapon expertly and trained it on Sam. Hearing the unmistakable sound of a man arming himself, Sam arched an eyebrow, but didn't flinch.

'This card is not for you.' Cheyrou balled it up in his fist and dropped it on the shimmering oak desk between them. 'And I do not for one second believe you are who you say you are. Jerome.'

Cheyrou signalled for his guard to step in, but Sam raised up a hand.

'I wouldn't do that if I were you.' Sam threatened but kept his eyes on Cheyrou. 'The only way your boy will get me out of this chair is if he puts a bullet through my skull, and I'd wager you don't want the mess in your office. Like I said, I can solve problems for men like you, but I can also solve problems caused by men like you. So, one last time… tell me about Veilmont.'

Cheyrou stood Jerome down, and a cruel grin spread across his clean-shaven face.

'Have you ever heard of a man called Sebastian Glass?' Cheyrou asked. 'Suffice to say, you wouldn't have, but it is a name that will change your life. Now, I do not believe that you are who you say you are, but you are here now, so allow me to explain your final moments to you. You can either walk out of this room with Jerome, who will accompany you to a secluded place where he will kill you quickly and mercifully and I do not invest a small fortune in ensuring a lifetime of torture for all those you hold dear.'

'Tempting.' Sam shrugged.

'Or, I give you a glimpse of the true nature of this world, and then, monsieur Carter, when we find out who you really are, I will make it a personal mission of mine to ensure that the real world swallows you up in ways that will haunt you for however long they deem you worthy of living. The choice is yours.'

Cheyrou stood and adjusted his tie, and Sam followed suit. As he stood, he felt the floor beneath him rumble as Jerome shifted his body weight. He knew the gun was still trained on him, and didn't doubt that a sudden movement would set it off. He checked his watch.

Seconds.

'Well, it's a good offer on the table. But may I propose a third?'

'Monsieur Carter, you are in no place to make any offer.'

The tension in the room was sliced in half by the shrill, ear-piercing scream of the alarm system, and above the door, a red light began to flash. Instantly, Cheyrou threw open his laptop, and on the CCTV, he could see his security guards in a heated discussion with a woman in a suit who screamed 'government agency'. Behind her, armed men were pouring out of a van. His guards were reaching for their own.

Gunshots echoed beyond the window.

Screams of panic.

'Kill him.' Cheyrou spat at Jerome, who lifted the gun, only for Sam to shunt the chair into his legs. The impact caused Jerome to stumble slightly, and as he pulled the trigger, Sam had already clamped a hand onto his wrist and pushed the gun upwards. The gunshot bounced off the walls, as the bullet embedded in the roof, showering both men with white plaster. As the two men struggled, Cheyrou fumbled with his desk drawer, and Sam twisted Jerome's wrist until he felt the satisfying snap of tendons. Through gritted teeth, Jerome swung his left fist, but Sam leant into it and then drove a sickening headbutt into the guard's face. The already broken nose was rendered to dust, and blood gushed down the smart suit of both men. Sam let the man's body collapse to the floor, and then he scooped up the gun and aimed it the panicking Cheyrou, who had finally opened the drawer.

'Don't go for it.' Sam warned and then motioned for him to step back.

'You fucking rat.' Cheyrou spat. 'You brought them here.'

'They are not here for me, Mr Cheyrou.' Sam said calmly as he opened the drawer, took the loaded Glock, and tucked it into the back of his trousers. He then turned back to Cheyrou, his other gun still on him, and smiled. 'It seems you have a problem.'

The colour from Cheyrou's face was draining, and he gazed at the laptop, where the armed team had now breached his offices. The alarm system had initiated an instant lockdown protocol, but the loud buzz of an electric saw grinding through the metal security doors told both men that the agents would be in the room within minutes.

'Fuck.' Cheyrou sighed.

Sam slammed the laptop shut and then picked up the balled-up card and tossed it to the confused merchant.

'Like I said. May I propose a third offer?' He motioned to the card that Cheyrou had caught and unfurled. 'You take me to Veilmont…and I'll get us the fuck out of here.'

CHAPTER NINE

It didn't take long for Cheyrou to accept Sam's offer.

As the grinding of the metal blade echoed beyond the doorway, it was joined by the increasing wailing of sirens. Cheyrou had greased the right palms and padded the right pockets to ensure that law enforcement gave him a wide berth, but if the wrong agents searched his premises, he could lose everything.

His vast wealth would ensure he wouldn't see jail time, but his reputation would be tarnished and worse, Mr Glass would black-mark him.

And Cheyrou knew too much to be allowed to potentially bargain for his freedom.

'How do we get out of here?' Sam barked, snapping Cheyrou back into the room.

'Through here.' Cheyrou headed to the door at the far end of the office. 'There is a route through to the neighbouring building. I must warn you, my guards will…'

'Will not be a problem.' Sam said, ushering Cheyrou to the door with the gun. 'My aim is to get *you* out.'

Cheyrou nodded and scuttled in behind Sam as they dashed through the doorway, and out into the connecting corridor. As soon as they rounded a corner, one of the guards, on high alert, span and instantly drew his weapon.

'Claude, wait.' Cheyrou yelled, but Sam had already stepped in, driving his shoulder into the man's bicep and slamming the gun wielding hand against the corridor wall. Instantaneously, Sam drove his elbow back into the man's jaw, hooked him into a headlock, and shut his lights out with a vicious knee to the temple. As the limp body crashed to the floor, Cheyrou gasped in horror.

'Let's move.' Sam yelled, and without hesitation, Cheyrou scarpered through the door into the adjoining building and turned into the stairwell. As Sam followed, he heard the sound of the security door to Cheyrou's office burst open, and the thundering boots of the agents began to echo above them. As they approached the bottom, another guard stepped into view, clearly concerned by the commotion. His eyes landed on Cheyrou, then turned to Sam and instantly he drew his gun.

Sam drew faster.

The gunshot caused Cheyrou to startle loudly, and as soon as the bullet ripped through the guard's foot, he dropped to the ground, howling in agony.

'He's one of my men.' Cheyrou stammered, but Sam pushed him forward, shoving him into the metal handle of the fire exit door and sending him outside into the Parisian sunshine. As Sam stepped over the wounded man, he kicked away the outstretched hand and left him for the DGSE who were making their way through the adjoining corridor.

'Car. Now.' Sam ordered, and Cheyrou rushed to the metal shutter opposite the doorway. Fumbling for his keys, Cheyrou began to wrestle with the lock, and Sam ducked back into the stairwell and unloaded a couple of rounds, aiming beyond the agents who were now approached the top step. The bullets ripped through into the ceiling tiles, sending the agents back a few steps and buying Cheyrou some time. As the wealthy Frenchman finally pulled the shutter open, a burst of gunfire peppered the door frame, and Sam darted across to the garage, where the pristine Bugatti Veyron was waiting. Without a word said, Sam took the driver's seat, and Cheyrou dropped into the passenger seat beside him, and the engine roared to life with a powerful growl.

'Hold on.' Sam said as he pulled the car out and turned down the narrow alleyway, the sun glistening off the black paint of the supercar. In the rear-view mirror, he saw two agents explode through the doors, and Sam turned back to Cheyrou as they picked up speed. 'This car reinforced?'

'Excuse me?'

'Is it bullet proof?' Sam yelled.

'No.

'Head down.'

Right on cue, a bullet shattered the rear window, and Cheyrou squealed as he melted into his seat, as another bullet hammered into a brake light. Sam slammed his foot to the pedal, eating up the distance to the main road, and as the car burst through the buildings, he threw his weight behind the steering wheel. The tyres screeched as the rubber burnt across the tarmac, the car skidding out onto the main road, and between two police cars that were racing to the scene. In an attempt to cut him off, both drivers pulled their squad cars in, but Sam slammed his foot down and the car roared forward, zipping between both bumpers before they collided.

'Jesus.' Cheyrou cried out, panicked as the city began to race past him. Sam gripped the steering wheel with both hands, steadying the car is it raced beyond ninety miles an hour, his eyes scanning the disappearing road ahead. 'You'll kill us.'

Ignoring the terrified pleas beside him, Sam hit the brake and navigated the next corner, skidding inches away from a lorry that blasted its horn in frustration and hit the dual carriageway that cut through the city centre like a concrete vein.

'This is a nice car.' Sam said calmly as he brought the car back under his control. The wailing of sirens drew his attention to the rear-view mirror, where several flashing lights were weaving their way through the traffic behind them. 'Let's see what it can do.'

Sam threw his foot down and sank into his leather clad seat as the Bugatti opened up, hurtling up the dual carriageway like a bullet from a gun. As the cars ripped past as if they were stationary, Sam shot a few glances to the rear view, watching as the police tried their best to keep pace.

'Oh shit.' Cheyrou stammered, pointing up ahead, and drawing Sam's attention to the police blockade that was causing the traffic to slow down. Sam hit the brakes, his mind racing, as the cars ahead became a parade of brake lights, and instinctively, Sam wrenched the wheel to the left.'

'Hold on to something.'

The car jerked viciously to the side, hitting the kerb and after an initial bounce, burst forward across the grass verge, the back tyres swinging wildly to the side as Sam leant into the swerve and managed to pull the car straight. Pedestrians screamed and leapt out of the way, and a small walkway was obliterated by the speeding car.

Chairs.

Tables.

Welcome signs.

All of it rattled across the bonnet before disappearing over the windscreen, and Sam pulled the car down a sharp turn and into the backstreets. Slowing the car down, he carefully navigated through the narrow roads, turning as frequently as he could to disappear amongst the shadows. But there was only so long he could hide a Bugatti in the city centre and Sam pulled into a run-down car park behind a supermarket and killed the engine. Beside him, Cheyrou was seemingly breathing himself through a panic attack.

'We need to get off the road.' Sam said sternly, ignoring the man's plight.

'I have an apartment...' Cheyrou began.

'They'll have that covered.' Sam cut in. 'They were there for whatever reason, and logic would dictate they have eyes on any property you own. Take me to Veilmont and I'll get us out of here.'

Cheyrou shook his head and gasped for a few breaths. Outside, the sirens were beginning to grow again.

'I can't just take you there.' Cheyrou stammered. 'There are rules. Strict rules and...'

'Fuck your rules.' Sam slammed his hand on the steering wheel. 'In two minutes, these alleyways will be swarming with police and whatever agents were knocking down your door. You wanted me to fix this, right? Wanted me to get you out of here? Well, those are my terms.'

Cheyrou looked around panicked, as the impending sound of the police grew and behind them, some of the shadows were flashing a shade of blue.

'Fine. Fine.' Cheyrou snapped. 'Just, get me out of here.'

A police car slowly took the sharp bend ahead of them and entered the car park, and Sam threw open his door. In one swift movement, he drew one of the Glocks, and opened fire, ensuring the bullets riddled the front of the car. It stopped abruptly and began to reverse, and Sam ducked his head into the car.

'Get out. Now.'

Obediently, Cheyrou unfastened his belt and reluctantly left the vehicle, and Sam barged open the back door of the supermarket and ushered Cheyrou through, before firing one more warning shot at the police car. The two men then hurried through the stock room, and pushed out into the main shopping floor, ignoring the exasperated yells of the man behind the nearby meat counter. They hurried down the aisles, causing a mild panic amongst the shoppers who had already heard the gunshots, and as they approached the front door, two agents burst in, guns in hand.

'DGSE.' They called.

But Sam opened fire.

Two shots.

Two shattered shin bones.

The agents hit the ground amongst the terrified screams of the customers, and as they stepped out onto the pavement, Sam saw the sign for the Paris Metro. Beyond that, the black van that had been under Corbin's command roared around the corner, followed by two police cars.

'We've got to move. Now.' Sam yelled, and he darted forward, holding up an apologetic hand to the car that screeched to an emergency stop and honked its horn as the two men raced out into the busy street. Hastily, they weaved through the angry traffic, and took the stairs two at a time, just as two more agents leapt from the van that they had dangerously lifted up onto the kerb. Sam led the way, scaling the ticket barrier and then lifting the gun at the ticket attendant who made an attempt to stop him. The man held up his hands in fear, drawing an apologetic nod from Sam, who rolled his eyes as Cheyrou took a few extra seconds to clamber over the barricades.

Behind him, the agents leapt down the final few steps,

guns drawn, sending a wave of commuters ducking and screaming to the floor.

'*Arrêt!*' one of them yelled, drawing his weapon, but there were too many civilians. Using the public as a shield, Sam clasped Cheyrou by the wrist, kept low, and made a beeline for the escalator.

They raced down the side, barging a few errant stragglers out of the way, and Sam could hear the agents thundering down behind them. As they leapt off the botton, Sam led Cheyrou down a long, narrow walkway towards one of the platforms, but halfway down, he stopped and shoved Cheyrou into a station access door. It fell open, and Cheyrou stumbled into the wall, and Sam stepped in after him, as the agents raced a few meters behind them.

'Go.' Sam yelled, and Cheyrou began to run, as Sam took a step back, and the door flew open again, shielding him from view.

The first agent raced in, drawing his gun on Cheyrou, and as the second one crossed the threshold, Sam slammed the door shut and wrapped an arm around the agent's throat. As the man gasped for air, the other agent turned, and Sam stepped forward and drove his foot into his chest, sending him tumbling over and spilling his gun into the corridor. Sam tightened his hold on the other man, then spun him out of his grasp, drove his elbow into the back of his neck and slammed him face first into the brick wall.

A smear of blood accompanied the man as he slid motionless to the ground, and Sam approached the other agent, who had scrambled to his feet and raised his fists. He threw a few jabs that Sam blocked with his forearms and followed them with a brutal haymaker. Sam weaved to his right, and as the errant fist flew past his face, he stepped into the man's reach, hooked his arm, and swung a hard elbow that shattered the man's nose. The man stumbled back, dazed, but Sam caught his trailing arm, drew him back in, and drove a hard knee into the man's solid stomach.

As the air flew from his lungs, the agent dropped to one knee and was then sent sprawling across the tiles as Sam's elbow connected with the back of his skull.

Both agents were down, and Sam took a second to admire his handiwork, straightened his suit, and then turned to face the barrel of a gun.

Cheyrou was on the other end of it, his hand shaking with nerves.

'Who are you?' He asked, his words, like his grip on the weapon, lacking the courage of his convictions.

Sam took a step forward, and like a coiled snake, he snatched Cheyrou's wrist and disarmed him with ease.

'Let's move.' Sam said, ignoring the question, and a few moments later, Sam peered through the next door that opened out onto a train platform. The rumble echoed from the tunnel, and a piercing light flashed as the underground barrelled out of the darkness and came to a stop on the platform, which was heaving with impatient commuters. Through the crowd, Sam could see a few police officers scanning the throngs that were descending upon the carriages, and Sam pushed Cheyrou into the crowd and followed him onto the train.

The doors hissed shut, and moments later, the platform and the exasperated police officers, sped from view. The station vanished into the darkness of the underground tunnel, and Sam watched as Cheyrou battled with his disdain for the public and their idea of transport.

At the next station, they stepped off, hurried across to another platform and took a different line that would take them in a different direction, covering their tracks long enough for them to get away. As the doors closed on the emptier carriage, Sam guided Cheyrou into one of the vacant seats and took the one next him and blew out his cheeks. As they sat in silence for a few moments, Cheyrou tapped out a message on his heavily encrypted phone and then pocketed it.

'It is done.' He said curtly. 'You do understand, that when we get there, there is no going back.'

Sam looked at the haggared-looking millionaire and smiled.

'I'm pretty sure we crossed the point of no return a long time ago.'

The two carried on in silence, as the train disappeared beneath the city of Paris, and Sam silently hoped that the trail of carnage he'd left in his wake didn't get Corbin into too much trouble.

CHAPTER TEN

Agent Corbin was in too much in trouble, and she knew it.

It had been less than twenty-four hours since she'd had her chastening meeting with Director Vivier, who, in no uncertain terms, had told Corbin that her job was dangling by a thread. Her promotion had been a fast track to nowhere, and the rich and powerful people who lost a useful ally because of her had made sure to make her pay for it.

All she had to do was keep a low profile. Say 'yes' when she needed to, show up when she was asked and keep her head down.

The noise would soon die down and the fog would clear.

That was what Vivier had intimated, although in a sterner tone with harsher language.

But with Sam and Cheyrou now lost somewhere in the city, the ramifications of her assistance were becoming stark.

Six agents down.

Five wounded. One in critical care.

One dead body outside Cheyrou's offices. Four more injured.

Multiple traffic collisions.

Panic through the Paris Metro.

And as Vivier ran through the laundry list of fuckups that had brought Corbin to that moment, he sighed and dropped back into his chair in disbelief.

'I told you, Renée, to keep your head down.'

'But sir, I…'

Vivier held up a hand and shook his head with disappointment.

'Do you have any idea of how much trouble you are in?' Vivier slammed a hand on the desk and stood, gazing out of the floor to ceiling windows of his office within the *Direction Générale de la Sécurité Extérieure.* The man-made parks beneath, sandwiched between the other government buildings, were alive with springtime colour, and beyond the heavily crammed car parks, the city of Paris loomed large against the setting sun. 'There are people who want you removed, Agent Corbin. Do you understand me? Long before today happened…'

'Are you firing me, Sir?'

'No. Not yet anyway.' Vivier turned back to her. 'But you need to tell me, right now, why the hell you thought it was a good idea to lay siege to a man like Yohan Cheyrou. Do you have intel that links a man of his stature to international threats to this country? Or are you determined to piss off the most powerful people in this city on a seemingly regular basis?'

Corbin grimaced slightly. She was racking up powerful enemies like pool balls, and the truth seemed even more preposterous.

Vivier could clearly see the cogs in her head turning and stood, arms folded and gestured for her to answer.

'Well?' He snapped. 'What possible reason could you have had to lead that mission?'

'Sir, have you ever heard of the word 'Veilmont'?' Corbin asked, locking her eyes on his. It was her hail Mary, and she needed to make sure it landed.

A little quiver at the corner of Vivier's mouth said it might just have. He caught it quickly and then straightened his tie, before turning back to the window.

'I've heard of it.' Vivier nodded. 'But it's not something that falls under the interests of the *Direction Générale de la Sécurité Extérieure.*'

'Meaning?' Corbin pressed. Vivier turned to her, an eyebrow raised, and he marched back to the seat behind his desk and lowered himself.

'Meaning, it is not an avenue of investigation.' Vivier said sternly. 'It's a myth. A word. Somehow, people have attached stories to it, like they have done with the Catacombs. That there is more to it, but in reality…there had never been any evidence to prove that Veilmont even exists.'

'But what if we had proof?' Corbin sat forward. 'What if we had a lead and a possible way to get to them?'

Vivier sat back in his chair and squinted suspiciously.

'Then I'd question why this evidence, and this lead were not brought to me at the earliest opportunity, and I'd also question why an armed unit was sourced at the last possible second.' Vivier leant forward menacingly. 'Renée, you do understand that if you're hiding anything from me, then I can't help you.'

Vivier kept his eyes on Corbin, clearly trying to goad the information from her. But she met his gaze with resolve and shrugged her shoulders.

'I'm not hiding anything, sir. I'm just being cautious.'

'Cautious?' Vivier seemed offended.

'No offence, sir. I know you're probably the reason I

wasn't thrown out the door when Ducard was brought down, but you've not exactly gone to bat for me either.' Corbin straightened up. 'And it already feels like my days are numbered, so if I can do some good on the way out, then I'm going to do what I can.'

Agitated by her stubbornness, Vivier hauled up his laptop, slapped a few keys with angry fingers and spun the screen to face her.

'Who is that?'

His voice carried an accusing tone, and Corbin locked her eyes on the grainy image on the screen. It was footage, lifted from a security camera from the supermarket where two agents were shot that lunchtime. The image had been enhanced, which unfortunately pixelated the facial features to an extent. But the two men in the image were moving swiftly, and one of them seemed firmly in control of the situation. The man had brown, floppy hair, swept back in a messy parting.

A smart suit.

The look of a soldier.

Corbin controlled the grin threatening to crack across her face and then shrugged her shoulders.

'Is that Cheyrou and his bodyguard?'

'We've questioned his head of security, Jerome Baptiste, and he has identified that man as a British businessman called 'Ben Carter'.' Vivier spun the laptop back and accessed a few files before presenting them to Corbin. 'Apparently, Mr Carter had an appointment with Cheyrou today that neither Cheyrou nor security were aware of.'

'Okay?' Corbin shrugged. 'So, what…was it a set-up?'

'Mr Baptiste said the man physically assaulted him during the meeting and was making wild threats to Cheyrou. Basically, he was there under false pretences.' Vivier tapped the screen. 'Carter's record is almost too unbelievably clean for a man to be in such a position, and based on the intel from Baptiste, I'd say that this wasn't a raid. It was an abduction.'

Corbin looked to Vivier, who glowered at her accusingly before continuing.

'And if it is, Corbin, then questions will be asked as to why, on today of all days, was an armed raid of that office signed off?' Vivier slammed the laptop shut. 'And why, when an unknown British kidnapper has taken one of the city's most powerful men, was it signed off by the one agent who helped bring down Ducard?'

Vivier paused, offering an opening for Corbin to respond.

She took it.

'If anyone has any questions, sir, I'd happily answer them.' She stood, straightening her jacket. 'But just so you know, I'd be asking them the same thing I asked you. What is Veilmont? And I'd wager I'd get the same response.'

Angered, Vivier stood, trying to clasp onto his authority.

'What we have here, Corbin, is hard evidence. All you have is a name of a myth.'

'That's not strictly true, sir.' Her eyes flickered. She could hear the ice beneath her feet beginning to crack.

'Agent Corbin, unless you hand over any information that can explain your involvement in this incident, then I will have no choice to suspend you with immediate effect, pending a full investigation.' Vivier sighed. 'And believe me, those who will be doing the investigation have wanted you for a long time.'

Corbin pulled out her security pass and dropped it on the desk, and Vivier shook his head with frustration.

'If you need me, sir, you'll know what I'll be doing.'

She turned and yanked open the door as Vivier called after her.

'And what might that be, Renée?'

She turned and glared back at him.

'My fucking job.'

Later that evening, Corbin sat back on her patio, gazing out over the fields that surrounded her cottage. Absorbing the beauty of the vista, her mind wandered to Sam, and how he'd admired the same view the night before.

Now he was somewhere out in the city, on the run with one of the most powerful men in Paris, with every law enforcement agency tearing through building after building to find him. Once they caught up with Sam, and there was every chance they would, they would pull apart his fake identity and connect him to the 'terror attack' from last year. Although Ducard had been found guilty of his war crimes, there was still a baying mob demanding justice for the fact that a foreign operative attacked a high-ranking official within the French government.

It had not only caused a ripple effect throughout the French political landscape, but it had also strained the already tenuous relationship with the United Kingdom, a government already reeling from the aftereffects of Sam Pope's mission.

Corbin took a sip of her wine and smirked.

She had to hand it to Sam.

So many people went through life with the outrageous notion that they would change the world.

Never had she met someone who was the walking embodiment of it.

Yet he'd never ask for a thank you. That was what struck her, and it was why she had agreed to his outrageous idea. She had no way of verifying his 'lead' on Veilmont, no way of knowing if attacking Cheyrou would lead to anywhere other than the unemployment line.

Yet she trusted Sam.

All he had asked was that she cause a distraction, one big enough to instigate a panic that would not only allow Sam to get Cheyrou out onto neutral ground, but hopefully, along the way, gain his trust. Enough to back up his cover story of being a 'corporate fixer'. It meant putting herself and others in the firing line, and the guilt of her injured comrades was nibbling the back of her mind like a woodworm.

Corbin could square off enough of that guilt with the fact that Cheyrou had a heavily fortified office with trigger-happy guards on patrol, which set off enough red flags to justify her interest. It would give her a reasonable argument at her impending disciplinary hearing, but whether or not it would save her under the undoubted pressure Cheyrou would apply, was a fight for another day.

She wondered how hard Vivier would fight for her position.

Despite his constant political juggling, Vivier was a good man and ultimately, her actions had put him in a difficult position.

She owed him an apology.

That was enough to make her take another swig of wine.

But as the sun set across the expanse of green fields before her, Corbin's mind was back in the inner-city.

Back where her job and her reputation were hanging by a thread.

And back where, somewhere, Sam Pope had one of the city's most powerful men in his possession.

What she didn't know was that by the time that night was over, things would have escalated beyond her wildest imagination.

CHAPTER ELEVEN

It's easy to keep off the grid when you're not on it to begin with, and Sam knew that by the time anyone was able to link his alias of Ben Carter to the crime scene, he'd be long gone. But that afternoon, once he and Cheyrou had made their escape on the Metro, soon became a test of patience. Once they had put enough distance between themselves and the chaos they'd left in their wake, Sam had shoved Cheyrou into a coffee shop, brought them both a drink and then taken a seat in the far booth.

They were in the clear for a while.

Ranjit had already emphasised to Sam how untraceable Cheyrou's phone was. The phone had more layers of encryption than an onion, which meant even the best agencies in the world would struggle to pinpoint its location. And as for Sam's own, Ranjit had already put in the necessary precautions to avoid detection.

It was just the two of them.

No backup.

No sirens wailing and screeching towards their location.

Just Yohan Cheyrou, a multi-millionaire, illegal diamond trafficker with ties to Veilmont, and Sam Pope.

A relentless vigilante with a gun.

As the two men had settled into their booth, Sam had caught their reflection in the opposite window. Now that they'd caught their breath and collected themselves, they looked like a couple of well-dressed executives discussing business over an afternoon coffee.

The truth was far more sinister.

'So…' Cheyrou broke the silence. 'What is your plan here?'

'My plan?' Sam arched an eyebrow.

'Are you meaning to keep me hostage? Because I must say, I don't think I could do that again.'

Sam shook his head and smiled.

'No, what the plan is, is that you are going to uphold your end of our bargain. I got you out of there, I got you away from those agents, and you take me to Veilmont.' Sam shrugged. 'So, I'm going to let you finish your coffee, and then I'm going to let you start making those arrangements.'

'Or?' Cheyrou's arrogance was seemingly permanent.

'Or I'll hand your arse over to the DGSE.' Sam said coldly. 'I don't know what the hell they want with you, Mr Cheyrou, and frankly, I don't care. But I'm pretty sure this Mr Glass you mentioned probably won't want to be associated with someone who is in the firing line of the feds.'

The mere mention of his name brought a cold look to Cheyrou's eyes, and Sam felt a little unease in his gut.

'It will take some time. There are checks that need to be done. Things that need to be approved.' Cheyrou sipped his coffee and turned his nose up with arrogant disdain. 'Mr Glass is a very careful man.'

'How long?'

'Excuse me?' Cheyrou looked up from his phone.

'How long until I can meet him?'

'Who?'

'This Mr Glass.' Sam held out a hand to emphasise his point but drew nothing but a chuckle from his hostage.

'Oh, Mr Carter. You will not be meeting Mr Glass. Oh no.' He waved Sam away. 'Even if you threatened my life, he would tell you to pull the trigger. No, Mr Glass only attends the special events that he puts on for our more cherished members.'

'So, take me to one of them.' Sam felt his fist ball in anger.

'Again, he's a careful man. However, I can see that you are keen, and I do also value my life, so I will take you to Veilmont.' Cheyrou lifted his phone to show Sam. 'We have a 'spa' location known as 'The Haven', one of six across the country, about eighty miles from here.'

'Fine. Take me to it.' Sam relaxed his hand and blew out his cheeks. 'We'll see about Glass when we get there.'

'No, we shall not.' Cheyrou had stated firmly, undermining Sam's control of the situation. But there was no other way to play it. He needed to get to Veilmont, to see what it was before he made his next move.

He had the name of the head.

Mr Glass.

Whether it was real or fake, it was a name, and something for Sam to cling to.

But now, he was being taken to the front door, and once he got across the threshold, he'd see what he was stepping into.

Members?

Spas?

Points of no return?

It felt like a cult, and ninety minutes later, when a black car arrived in the car park of the coffee shop, a patched up and furious Jerome stepped out of the passenger door and ushered the two men in. Sam offered a half-hearted apology to the man, but even through the sickening bruising and the thick, blood-stained bandage across his nose, Jerome replied with a stare of complete hatred.

'He's a sensitive one, isn't he?' Sam nodded in Jerome's direction as he stepped into the car.

'Well, you did assault him, Mr Carter.'

Sam nodded his acceptance and then sat quietly as the car pulled away. The long journey was undertaken in complete silence, as Sam kept his Glock on show and trained on Cheyrou as a trade-off with Jerome. Sam had made it clear he didn't intend to hurt Cheyrou, but any attempt to halt their journey would result in a few point-blank shots to vital organs.

It was enough for Cheyrou to stand his men down.

The driver kept his eyes on the road, shifting expertly through the gears when the traffic changed. Jerome shot the odd look of thunderous vengeance towards Sam, who replied with a stoic look of disinterest. Soon, the city disappeared behind them.

The sun not too long after that.

The sprawling metropolis of Paris was replaced by winding, country roads that took them further from civilisation and the packed motorways that connected the major cities of the country. The clear sky was soon peppered with bright stars, and the final shreds of sunlight filtered out beyond the sprawling fields that soon merged with the darkness. Despite the unease, Sam just kept his eyes on the men in the car.

'Almost there, Mr Carter.' Cheyrou said casually. The sense of control had shifted once more. 'You won't be needing your weapon.'

'No offence, but I'd feel a lot safer if…'

'The door men will empty their assault rifles if you refuse to relinquish your weapon on the first request.'

Cheyrou turned and stared Sam right in the eye. 'No offence.'

Sam turned away, but clocked Jerome chuckling in the front seat. Not long after, the roughness of the country roads was soon replaced by the crunching of gravel, as the 4x4 began its struggle through the unlit, offroad pathways. As the driver carefully navigated through the unmapped road, Sam peered through the trees into the void.

Nothing but darkness.

All Sam needed now was a signpost that said, *'Point of no return'*.

Lights cut through the trees up ahead.

'Here we are.' Cheyrou said calmly, pointing to the windscreen.

A large, concrete block loomed large in the darkness, underlit by a few lamps that were bolted to the concrete wall. There were no discernible features of the building at all, and Sam could have mistaken it for an old war bunker. But as they approached, the details began to emerge.

Rows of fake plants lining the entrance.

The entire entrance was a series of large, tinted glass panes.

An industrial metal door, guarded by two men who made no attempt to hide the assault rifles in their hands.

As the car pulled up, Jerome asked Sam for his gun, and under Cheyrou's promise that nothing would happen, Sam handed it over.

Jerome turned the gun on him instantly, and Sam's eyes widened slightly.

'Bang.' Jerome joked, laughing with enough force that Sam knew he wasn't truly joking.

Cheyrou stepped out of the car, and as Sam followed, he saw Cheyrou greet the two doormen with a sense of formality. One of them trained the gun on Cheyrou, who stood with his arms spread, allowing the other to pat him down.

Sam followed suit.

'Good evening, Mr Cheyrou.' One of them finally spoke and pulled open the door.

Cheyrou nodded his thanks, and marched in, and Sam stepped through behind him. A vast, plain white reception welcomed them, with nothing but thick, white tiles that ran across the floor and then up the wall. There was no furniture anywhere, and fifty yards away, was a white reception desk where a woman, clad in a white dress, stood to attention. Their footsteps echoed as they approached, and Cheyrou greeted the emotionless woman with a grin.

'Denise. This is a guest of ours. Mr Carter,'

'Good evening, Mr Carter,' She spoke on cue. 'How may we serve you?'

'Serve me?' Sam's eyebrow arched as he turned to Cheyrou. 'Is this a brothel?'

Cheyrou started laughing, and when he turned and looked to Denise, she joined in too.

'Oh, Mr Carter. Allow me to show you what Veilmont offers its members. Your membership will cost five million euros a year and will offer you access to all Havens within the continent. Access to the Sanctuary is by invitation only, sent personally by Mr Glass himself.'

'Right. Like a golden ticket?'

Sam's joke didn't register as Cheyrou marched towards the grand door that split the back wall in two.

'As you have not yet paid your membership, consider this evening a taster for what is to come.' Cheyrou's smile faded. 'However, failure to pay the membership on your exit will result in your removal from the premises in a way that you would not welcome.'

Before Sam could reply, Cheyrou pushed open the door which led to the landing of a stairwell. Heading in both directions, luxuriously carpeted staircases spiralled out of view. At both instances of where the staircase bent out of sight, a scantily clad woman and man stood, their faces covered with a mask, and silken cloth covering their genitals.

'This way.' Cheyrou headed up the staircase, ignoring the masked people who didn't even flinch as the two men walked by. As they approached the upper floor, they passed two more masked servants, both of whom stood willingly to the side as Cheyrou offered them to Sam.

Sam declined.

As they ventured down the expensively decorated corridor, Cheyrou explained how the Haven was separated into four function rooms, and four private quarters. Each room had been pre-booked by a member with a designated theme for them to enjoy.

Drugs.

Sex.

Violence.

Whatever the member wanted, Veilmont provided it. As an ambassador and membership scout for Glass, Cheyrou effectively had the keys to a number of Havens across the country. As a show of his power and the luxury they could afford, Cheyrou used his watch to open the electric lock on the nearest door and threw it open.

A man was lying on a circular cushion, stripped nude, whilst three ladies tended to him. As their heads bobbed around his crotch, another woman held a cigar to his lips, and he took a long, smug puff. He turned to the two intruders, smirked, and went back to his cigar as Cheyrou closed the door.

'So...a brothel?' Sam didn't even try to hide his disgust.

'Oh, you think too small.' Cheyrou replied, and the next door opened upon a trashed room, where broken pieces of the furniture were sprawled through the shattered glass of the coffee table. On the sofa, a woman was lying, beaten half to death with her dress ripped and her eyes begging for help. Behind her, a man wearing a gimp mask, was strangling another woman over a wooden cabinet.

Sam went to step in. Cheyrou held his hand across and stopped him.

'Members do not judge other members.' He said firmly and pulled the door closed. Sam stared at the man in disbelief.

'Will he kill them?' He demanded.

'What? Those women?' Cheyrou shrugged dismissively. 'If he wants to.'

'That's insane.' Sam spat, knowing his cover was falling.

'No, that is power.' Cheyrou smirked. Behind Sam, one of the armed guards began to approach, and Cheyrou held up a hand to stop him. 'Mr Carter, this is what we offer. Whatever the customer wants, we can provide. This goes beyond your wildest dreams. Whatever you think you want to experience, we can provide. Once, Mr Glass arranged for four elk to be transported to the Sanctuary hunting grounds, so the customer could shoot and skin the animal.'

'Why?' Sam asked. Cheyrou rolled his eyes.

'Because that's what he wanted.' Cheyrou shook his head. 'Every room here, is a personal Nirvana for our customer. You want three women to blow you? Three men? You want to beat someone to a pulp? You want to fuck an animal? We don't judge. We just provide.'

Sam looked beyond Cheyrou to the soundproof door, where behind it, a woman was likely being strangled to death.

'This is wrong.'

'No, Mr Carter. Like I said. This is power. And this is what you demanded.' Cheyrou motioned to the armed guard, who took a menacing step towards them. 'Now, if you would like to sample something before you make your decision, we do have a room available. We can provide most things from our storage, so you just say the word. Men. Women. Children. Drugs. Weapons…'

'Children?' Sam cut in, wrestling control of his anger to keep himself calm. A cruel smile spread across Cheyrou's face.

'Why, yes. Not many of our guests are that open to the idea when they first arrive, Mr Carter. But we can provide one for you. You just need to select.'

Sam felt the rage boil up within him, but he countered its inevitable explosion with a long, controlled breath. He cleared his throat, straightened his tie, and then offered Cheyrou a smile.

'I just, didn't want to be judged.' Sam lied.

'Understandable.' Cheyrou patted him on the back. 'And we don't judge here, Mr Carter.'

Sam looked at the armed guard beside him.

Assault rifle in his grip.

Glock strapped to his waist.

Eyes that told Sam he'd killed before.

'Do you have children here now?' Sam asked, feeling his knuckles tighten.

'We do indeed.' Cheyrou said smugly.

'Take me to them.'

As Sam fell in-step with Cheyrou, who turned and headed back towards the stairwell, he could feel the looming presence of the armed guard behind him. And all he could think about was the best way to disarm him.

Because in a few minutes, Sam was planning on burning the entire Haven to the ground.

CHAPTER TWELVE

It wasn't fear.

It was resignation.

That was the heartbreaking look in the eyes of the children, who were dotted around the spacious, well-furnished room that acted as their prison. Vast white walls, all of them decorated with tasteful artwork, wrapped around the impressive underground dungeon, doing their best to disguise its true purpose. Bright, halogen bulbs bore down on the entire space, basking it all in a bright glow to try and distract from the lack of natural light.

A fully stocked fridge with as much fizzy drinks and sugary snacks a kid could dream of.

Enormous flat screens pinned to the walls, all of them hooked up to the latest consoles.

In any other circumstance, the room would have been a child's dream.

Yet, when the door was opened, half of the children huddled together on the plump corner sofa, squeezing each other's hands in the hope that they wouldn't be selected.

Girls.

Boys.

Aged between nine to fifteen.

The dream room was actually their nightmarish reality.

It turned Sam's stomach, and as he stepped in behind Cheyrou, it bored a hole through his heart as they looked at him with such terror. Cheyrou threw his hands out, and smiled, as the armed guard slammed the security door shut behind them.

'*Les enfants, nous avons un invité.*' He clasped his hands together as he addressed them. Two of the teenage boys ignored him completely, their soulless eyes locked on the wall-mounted screen as their fingers clicked across control pads. Cheyrou approached the younger kids huddled on the sofa and squatted down to their level. As he glared at them, he spoke out of the corner of his mouth to Sam. 'Your choice, Mr Carter.'

Sam shuffled uncomfortably. The dungeon was kitted out to be a children's dream, although it was just a waiting cell for a nightmare. Each child was dressed in floaty, white clothing, and Sam could see from the watering eyes, that they all prayed for freedom.

Or worse.

Anything other than what their life was.

'Are these children French?' Sam asked, swallowing the hatred in his voice. Behind him, he could sense the armed guard.

Three feet away.

Rifle pointed down.

Barrel in his left hand.

Cheyrou turned as he stood.

'Not all.' He shrugged. 'We collect them where we can. Orphans, usually. Taken from those who did something that caused Mr Glass to take their life.'

Sam nodded, as he scanned across the innocent, mortified faces of children who had grown up too fast. Had been violated by a cruel world, which had stripped them of their dignity, their innocence, and their childhood.

Sam felt his knuckles whiten.

He felt his muscles shake.

Behind him, he felt the weight of the guard shift ever so slightly.

'So...Mr Carter,' Cheyrou said. 'Which do you choose?'

Sam closed his eyes and took a deep breath.

He saw Cassie.

And then he saw Jamie.

His son, snatched away from him by a world that Sam refused to let grow colder. His eyes flicked open, and they met Cheyrou's, who frowned at the sudden change in his guest.

'I choose war.'

Before Cheyrou's expression could change, Sam swung an arm out, driving his knuckles into the millionaire's throat, and crushing his windpipe. Cheyrou's eyes bulged as he gasped for air, stumbling backwards towards the sofa where the children screamed at the sudden eruption of violence. As Cheyrou tumbled away, Sam swung on his heel, driving a brutal fist down onto the swiftly rising forearm of the armed guard, shattering the man's wrist, and sending the rifle scattering across the wooden floor. The man yelped as his left hand swung useless, but with his right, he pulled the Glock from his waist, but Sam stepped inside, hooked the arm, and wrenched until he heard the man's shoulder pop violently from its socket. The man struggled feebly, as Sam yanked the gun from his hand and raised it to his forehead.

Behind them, Cheyrou coughed and spluttered, struggling to his feet.

'W-what...w-what are you...' Cheyrou began over sharp, stilted breaths.

Sam drilled him in the throat again, this time with the hard steel of the gun. Despite his injuries, the guard burst forward, trying to knock Sam off his feet with a shoulder charge. Side-stepping at the last second, Sam gripped the back of the guard's collar, and using the man's momentum, diverted him headfirst into the wide screen television that clung to the wall bracket. An explosion of sparks accompanied the falling shards of screen, as the entire television rocked on its fixture, before collapsing onto the motionless guard, who was slowly being surrounded by the blood pooling from his skull.

Sam turned to the children, as he tucked the Glock into the back of his trousers.

'I'm going to get you all out of here. Okay?' He said to their vacant expressions. 'But you need to stay here.'

It was either the fear or the language barrier that caused them to huddle, but one of the elder boys stepped forward and nodded to Sam. He then turned and ushered the children away from the security guards twitching body, as Sam stepped across the dungeon and lifted the custom built HK416F Assault Rifle. The military issue weapon was in good condition, and Sam cast a keen eye over it, then hit the mag release and clawed out the magazine to check the ammunition. As he snapped it back and hit the bolt release.

'You have made a big mistake.' Cheyrou coughed, as he once again stumbled to his feet, his phone swinging loosely in his hand.

'How many guards?' Sam demanded, ignoring the threat.

'Mr Glass will come for you.' Cheyrou wheezed, trying to catch his breath. 'He will kill you and everyone you care abo…'

The butt of the AK416F shattered Cheyrou's nose on impact and send him rolling backwards over the sofa and hitting the hard floor. A few of the kids smiled as the blood soaked Cheyrou hit the ground, and Sam headed to the door.

'Back in a sec.'

He stepped out, swinging the weapon in both directions, clearing both avenues and then stepped back in. Cheyrou was on his knees, dabbing at the blood that pumped down his lips, and wiping away the tears that had tumbled from his eyes. Sam hauled him to his feet, and before Cheyrou could utter a word, he drilled him in the stomach with a brutal right and then swung him round and pushed him towards the door.

'You're coming with me,' Sam said. 'Every time you either question or don't do as I say, I will break one of your fingers. If we run out of fingers, we'll go to limbs. You understand?'

Cheyrou nodded feebly, taking deep breaths that gurgled as they tried to pass through his obliterated nose and his crushed airwaves. Sam nodded to the elder teenager, who had naturally assumed leadership and then marched to the door, his rifle drawn and he stepped through, once again checking each way. As he ushered Cheyrou out, a burst of gunfire ripped across the wall, sending Cheyrou scurrying back through the doorway, and Sam spinning to one knee.

He drew the sight to his eye.

He locked onto the guard on the stairwell.

He sent three bullets.

One burst through the side of the man's neck, ripping through the tendon and sending a spray of blood spinning out like a scarlet firework. The second bullet obliterated the man's skull, snapping it back and rendering him a motionless corpse on the stairwell. Sam stood, barked for Cheyrou, and then hurried to the stairwell. As he took the first step, he swung the rifle up, and he squeezed the trigger.

A burst of fire roared upwards, hitting the oncoming security guard in the legs and sending him tumbling down the stairs. As he crashed a few steps up, the security guard gritted his teeth and tried to wrench his Glock from his waistband.

Sam put a bullet between his eyes and carried on, followed by Cheyrou who was a deathly pale. As they ascended the staircase, the scantily clad staff ran in panic, and Sam ignored them, rounding the final corner to the hauntingly white reception area.

Gunfire echoed throughout, and Sam spun back, as a tirade of bullets embedded into and chipped away at the stone wall of the stairwell.

'There is no way out for you, Carter.' Cheyrou spat, his voice strained and gravelly.

Sam cracked him with an elbow, connecting with the squishy, swollen, blood-soaked mess that was once his nose. Cheyrou squealed and rocked back against the wall.

'Stop talking.' Sam ordered, and straightened against the wall, the rifle held tight.

The bullets relented for a split second, and Sam heard the expertise of a swift reload echoing through the lobby.

He swung out, the rifle drawn to his line of sight, the stock lodged expertly into the meat of his shoulder. Two short bursts, and both security guards hit the ground. As Sam stepped over the ejected bullet casings, one of the guards pushed himself up, growling with anger as he held a hand to the bullet that had decimated his stomach, and tried to feebly lift his Glock with the other.

The next bullet hit him between the eyes, and sent him, and his brain, sprawling backwards over the stunning white floor. The blood spatter looked like an ode to modern art, but the patterns were beginning to merge into the heavily pooling blood. The smell of gunpowder burnt in the air, and combined with the murderous scene before them, had reduced the Haven from a beacon of tranquillity to a war zone. Sam turned back to Cheyrou and motioned for him to head up the stairs.

'But the exit is that way" Cheyrou insisted.

Sam responded with a hard crack of his elbow, sending the millionaire sprawling onto the stairwell. Swiftly, he clambered to his feet, and Sam stayed a step behind him as they made their return to the first floor. The semi-naked staff had long since fled, but Sam did put down another security guard, who had made too much of a show of spinning out from one of the doorway alcoves.

Two bullets to the top of the chest put him down, and as Sam hurried past, he knew the man would bleed out within the next few minutes. Cheyrou stopped a few feet behind Sam as he approached the door.

'These members are innocent.' Cheyrou pleaded. 'They are not armed.'

Sam spun back, his eyes glaring with hatred, and Cheyrou cowered as Sam stepped back.

'Innocent? These people are all connected to this.' Sam shook his head. 'They are not going to die. But they sure as hell are not innocent.'

Then Sam planted his boot against the first door, taking it clean off its hinges. The naked man, scrambled in terror, pushing away the women tending to him, but stopped dead when Sam ordered him to. The man stood hunched, his hands covering his modesty, but any remnants of self-respect had left him.

Sam warned him he'd be back, and Sam ordered the women to collect their clothes and head outside. Once they had obliged, Sam booted down the next door, where unsurprisingly, he found the body of the woman slumped against the cabinet, her eyes vacant and her neck heavily bruised.

Beyond her, in the next room, the masked man was

violently thrusting into a woman he'd pinned down to the bed, whose face was covered with blood as she cried out for help.

Sam pulled the Glock from his waist, and stepped in, sending the man scurrying to the wall in fear. Before he could even say anything, Sam put a bullet through his right eye, painting the wall with his blood, before telling the other woman to get dressed. Once she had pulled some clothes on, Sam accompanied her out to the hallway, and he handed her the weapon. Without the need for words, he handed her the Glock, pointed it at Cheyrou, and tapped his watch and held up two fingers.

And for the next two minutes, a beaten and bloodied Cheyrou looked down the barrel of a gun, being held by a woman he had fed to a rapist.

Held by a person whose life had been irrevocably destroyed by his actions.

Sam cleared the other rooms, finding nothing but relieved workers who realised that the bullets weren't for them. With the woman still holding Cheyrou at gunpoint, Sam led the group back down the stairwell, and through the now blood-soaked reception towards the front door. The receptionist appeared from the desk, her face stained with streaks of mascara, and she joined the group as they headed for their freedom. As they approached the heavy, security door, a bullet ripped through one of the tinted windows, whipping past Sam and hitting one of the escaping women in the head. As a burst of red mist coated the screaming woman behind her, the woman's head snapped back, and she collapsed to the ground.

Sam dropped to one knee, pulled up the rifle and trained it on Jerome, who was standing behind the shattered glass.

Sam unloaded the entire clip towards the window, the bullets pounding into the frame and the surrounding brick, as Jerome swung back out of sight for cover. As Sam pulled down the trigger, he burst forward at speed, knowing his final few bullets were about to rattle the wall, and the second his gun clicked, Jerome would appear with an easy target ahead of him.

A few steps from the window, and his shoe crunched on the glass.

The final bullet thumped into the brick wall, sending a mist of cement into the air.

The gun clicked.

As expected, Jerome spun back round, his meaty arm extending with Sam's own Glock locked in his murderous grip.

Sam launched through the window just as Jerome pulled the trigger.

The bullet hit the wall, as Sam pushed the man's wrist to the side, before locking his arm over Jerome's wrist, and flipping him over his shoulder. Jerome flew through the air and landing painfully on his hip, his bone crunching against the gravel. Sam twisted the wrist back further, and Jerome's grip loosened, but before Sam could pull the gun from his grip, Jerome spun free from his grip.

The gun clattered into the gravel.

The two men stared each other down, and then Jerome pulled out a knife. With his face still swollen from their earlier confrontation, Jerome roared an insult in his native tongue then drove forward, slashing wildly at Sam, who managed to weave his way around the blade. As the metal sliced through the air, Jerome swung a violent shin kick that clattered into Sam's thigh, knocking him slightly off balance. As Sam stumbled, Jerome dived forward with the knife, but Sam stepped to the side, deflected the blow with his forearm, and connected with a rising knee into Jerome's gut. Two left jabs connected, and as Jerome tried to shake the cobwebs, he lazily swung the blade in Sam's direction.

But Sam ducked under, caught the knife-wielding arm by the elbow, snapped it back, and then drove the blade down into Jerome's thigh. The man roared with agony as the serrated edge ripped through his quad muscle, but before he could reach a higher octave, Sam slapped a hand on the man's shaven scalp, locked one hand on his jaw, and snapped Jerome's neck in one brutal twist.

The man flopped to the ground; his eyes open but the light shut down.

Sam stepped back through the glass, and summoned the remaining women to follow, and the woman with the gun shoved a defeated and bloodied Cheyrou towards the exit. Once outside, Sam threw Cheyrou into the other glass pane and told him to sit, before he asked around for any English speakers.

The woman with the Glock, and the receptionist spoke up, and Sam tasked them with protecting the children until the police arrived. He then told the other workers they were free to either stay and help the authorities, who could help them home, or to take their chances.

A few bolted for the darkness of the woods, concluding that even the dark unknown was a more appealing place to be. As the receptionist followed the armed worker back into the building, Sam asked her to use his phone to call the contact 'Corbin', and to use his phone signal as a tracer to bring them there.

He watched as she carried out the task before she soon disappeared down the staircase. With a deep sigh, Sam turned to Cheyrou, who was leaning uncomfortably against the glass, breathing heavily.

'Phone.' Sam held out his hand. 'Now.'

Cheyrou fumbled in his blood-soaked jacket and handed it to him. Sam frowned.

'Fingerprint.' He demanded.

But Cheyrou laughed. Despite the agony and the

promise of more, the millionaire hacked up blood as he laughed at Sam's request.

'You think this is a victory?' Cheyrou said, collecting himself. 'You have rung a bell that cannot be unrung.'

'Last chance,' Sam said through gritted teeth. 'Fingerprint.'

Cheyrou collapsed back against the glass, and chuckled again, gurgling blood as he did so.

'It cannot be unrung.' He repeated.

Sam stepped over Jerome's motionless body and retrieved the fallen Glock from the gravel. He lifted the gun to Cheyrou's head and pulled the trigger.

The bullet whizzed inches past Cheyrou's skull and shattered the glass behind him, sending him sprawling back amongst a shower of broken shards. As he rolled back, he howled in pain as the shards scratched at his body, but Sam stepped in and pressed his foot down on Cheyrou's right wrist, pinning the hand to the ground and embedding it with glass.

Cheyrou screamed in agony.

'You're right-handed,' Sam said.

Then he reached down, lifted one of the bigger shards of glass, and through the blood curdling screams of the millionaire who'd been beaten to a pulp, Sam hacked off Cheyrou's index finger. As he stepped back, he pressed the severed digit to the sensor on Cheyrou's phone and brought it to life.

With a smile, Sam handed the Glock to one of the terrified women and pointed to Cheyrou.

'If he moves, shoot him in the leg.' Sam patted his leg for emphasis. Then he turned and marched back towards the 4x4 that was still parked on the gravel, surrounded by darkness. The driver had long since gone, and Sam hopped into the driver's seat and brought the car to life.

Corbin would be there soon. She'd be there to pick up

the pieces he had left, and once again, he hoped that the chaos he'd left in his wake didn't bury her. The police would be there as well, no doubt panicked by what they'd find.

He'd left them the Haven, a pile of bodies, a group of beaten but brave workers, and the man with the keys to the front door.

It was enough to put Cheyrou away for a long time, but a man of his resource and standing would have low friends in high places, and Sam knew it wouldn't make any real difference. Cheyrou was never the target, he was just another name on the list that was leading to one destination.

Leading to a meeting with one man, who by any measure, was the man in charge of the entire operation.

Mr Glass.

And as Sam pulled away from the Haven and thundered down the gravel path into the middle of nowhere, he now had a way of contacting the head of the snake. All it had taken, was for him to go to war.

CHAPTER THIRTEEN

Wealth didn't equal power.

That was the harshest life lesson that Sebastian Glass learnt, and it was presented to him on his eighteenth birthday. Back then, he was known by his birth name.

Sebastian Winthorpe.

The third son of Duke Allister Winthorpe, Sebastian had grown up with a vast wealth that catered to his every whim. Whilst he never cared to learn or understand the true nature of his father's position, he'd appreciated the finer things that it brought.

The stately home.

The wave of staff who tended to it.

Multiple trips aboard a private jet.

A private education that placed him within the throngs of the next generation of the elite, all of whom were being groomed to hold valuable positions throughout the country.

But then, when he turned eighteen, Glass found out the true pecking order of the world. Despite the vast wealth that his father had attained, which had kept their lifestyle flash, and their status soaring, it came at the cost of his father's dignity.

Glass witnessed it firsthand, peering through the gap to his father's office when 'Mr Boyd' stopped by.

Boyd was always accompanied by the police, and at first, Glass had assumed he was a lawman. But in truth, Boyd was a drug dealer, who had ties to men like Harry Chapman and Frank Jackson, who had turned London into one of the prominent drug havens in the world. Boyd leaned on the police as his own private security, and as Glass peered through the door, he heard the truth of their standing.

Over eighty percent of the land belonged to Boyd and his multiple enterprises.

Drug storage and farming were standard practice.

Bodies had been buried on the grounds.

All of it, under Winthorpe's name, to ensure that when the axe fell, and it certainly would one day, it fell upon the neck of the family patriarch.

They paid Glass' father a fortune for the privilege, but from that moment on, the money felt insignificant. Boyd had demanded his father drop to his knees and forced the man that Glass had seen as hero, to watch as he assaulted his wife.

Glass' mother.

Nobody did anything.

His mother laid back on the oak desk and accepted it as part of the transaction.

His father stayed silent and looked away, refusing to acknowledge what he'd allowed to happen.

But Glass knew, from that, as his inheritance legally transferred to his bank account, that the money wouldn't make him a powerful man.

Leverage.

Danger.

Combined with the fortune he had acquired, it would make him one of the most powerful men in the country. But his sheltered upbringing and his well-known name would always be held against him, so a route to power through fear wasn't an option. At least not to begin with.

But a reputation as a problem solver, that could escalate his rise.

And the name needed to go.

Shedding the noose of the family name, along with their pathetic standing amongst the genuine elite was the first step, and due to the transparency of his actions, Sebastian chose Glass.

Sebastian Glass.

The man who could provide *anything*.

At first, that was just a clever line on the expensive, gold-tinted business cards he handed out at parties he either snuck or bribed his way into. After a few dangles, he got a bite and was able to secure a large amount of cocaine for a wealthy banker who was hosting an after party. Glass got the invitation too, and from there, his reach widened.

Suddenly, every major financial player with a drug habit was in contact, which meant within a year, Glass soon became the major mover within the financial sector. But he stayed the right side of the dealers, acting as a middleman to ensure the safe delivery of the product, but also establishing his reputation as a man of his word.

Within two years, he committed his first murder, when he slit the throat of a rival who was trying to undercut his service.

The news spread faster than the man's larynx, and before he had turned twenty-three, Glass had been able to orchestrate a hostile takeover of one of his drug suppliers. He'd accumulated millions by that point, more than enough to turn even the most loyal of foot soldiers, and after that acquisition, things began to fall into place.

Harry Chapman.

Frank Jackson.

Slaven Kovac.

The Kovalenkos.

All of them were on his books, all of them as providers and paying customers at some point. Jackson had even inspired Glass with his 'High Rises', to branch out across major European cities. By creating the Havens, Glass was able to establish central points of his business, where he could charge extortionate membership fees from his clients. He was no longer at the beck and call of the elite.

Instead, he was the one they were paying for access.

They wanted a seat at *his* table, and soon, the multi-million-pound empire grew to a billion.

Memberships were offered at discount or on the house to senior figures of power.

Heads of agencies.

Judges.

Politicians.

Anyone who could have pulled at the thread, were given access to their wildest fantasies. Glass underpinned it all under the name of Veilmont, which became a whisper that was only uttered in the most prestigious circles. All sides of the one percent flocked to him, with famous sports personalities and Hollywood actors all indulging their most depraved fantasies under his watchful gaze.

Everyone paid the price.

Five million a year.

For the pleasure and for his discretion.

There was no exit. Any attempt to break the member-ship or expose Veilmont to the uninitiated would result in death. And even then, Glass' reach was far enough to ensure those who did try to break free, were killed in a way staged to fool the public.

A car crash.

An overdose.

'Natural' causes.

Whilst Glass offered the rich and powerful *anything* they desired; it was he who had access to the world. He could have any door opened. Any room cleared. Haven after Haven opened across the continent, and Glass had spent the past few months dealing with a few Hollywood agents to build a Haven in the centre of Los Angeles. There were gaps in the market, and Glass was powerful enough to plug them permanently.

His wealth didn't equal power.

It was now his power that equalled wealth.

And as he sat in the study of his luxury suite at the top of the block of flats that looked over the Algarve, and the Atlantic Ocean crashed peacefully against the cliff face below, Glass reached out and lifted the curved wine glass and sipped the eighteen thousand pound red wine within it. Clasped between the fingers of his other hand was a cigarette, the smoke trailing off over the edge of the balcony and disappearing into the warm night.

His blonde hair was slicked back, still wet from the shower after his fifty lengths of the private pool he had demanded be built into the roof of the complex. His lean, muscular body was wrapped in his expensive, silk, designer gown and his piercing blue eyes were locked on the screen of his MacBook.

It wasn't often someone challenged his status.

It was rarer still, for someone to try to take down his business. A few had tried in the past. Disgruntled men who were not as rich as they wished had thrown stones, thinking his fortress was a glass house.

He had had them dissected alive.

But as he gazed upon the screen, the challenge he was witnessing didn't fill him with anger.

Nor worry.

A smile spread across his clean-shaven face, making him look almost a decade younger than his thirty-three years of age.

He took a sip.

Took a puff.

It filled him with intrigue.

His eyes flickered with excitement, as the smartly dressed man on the CCTV footage snapped Jerome's neck and then threw Cheyrou through one of the glass panes that surrounded the Paris Haven. The moment an unsanctioned guest had been granted access to the building, Glass had been informed, but had hoped that Cheyrou would have the sense to either strip the man of his cash or his life.

He'd failed, and for that, Cheyrou would go the same way as the many people Glass had sent to Cheyrou to dispose of.

The mystery guest had been checked in as Ben Carter, and on another tab, Glass had access to every shred of information pertaining to man, and every clear lie it told.

The bank accounts.

The long and well-travelled career as a contractor, working at numerous companies that either didn't exist, or were too big to delve into.

Everything about the man was a fabrication, and that only added to the excitement. As he tapped the ash of his cigarette over the perilous drop of the balcony edge, Glass pulled his phone from the pocket of his gown and patiently waited. The attacker had smartly taken both Cheyrou's phone and the finger required to access it, and as he closed down the video feed, the last thing he saw was the pathetic Cheyrou squirming in pain, clutching his bloodied hand as the women that Glass had once owned were holding him at gun point.

But he didn't care.

All of them, from the women to Cheyrou, were replaceable.

What Glass was waiting for, was contact.

Another hour passed.

Sixty blissful minutes, under the careful watch of the two-armed guards who stood at either end of the building-width balcony, as Glass enjoyed another expensive glass of wine and a few more of his thin, luxurious cigarettes. Wondering how quickly Cheyrou had panicked once arrested, Glass' head snapped to the phone on the table as it began to ring.

Yohan Cheyrou.

Glass smiled, puffed his cigarette, and put the call on speaker.

'You are very impressive, Mr Carter.' Glass spoke eloquently, his voice deceptively high. 'Tell me, did you need to make so much mess?'

'I'm just getting started. Mr Glass, wasn't it?'

Glass smirked.

'Please. Call me Sebastian. I would call you Ben, but I think we should get on real name terms, don't you?' Glass leant forward, tapping out another cigarette from the pack which he lit with the dying embers of the last. 'Tell me. Who are you really?'

'Who I am isn't important.'

'Oh, don't sell yourself short,' Glass said. 'It is important to me. It makes life easier for me when I brutally kill anyone you have ever held dear.'

The threat lingered in the air, and Glass felt his lip curl with anger. There was no response, but what irked Glass the most, was that it wasn't due to fear.

It was ambivalence.

'Haven by Haven. Name by name. I will find you.'

'And then what? You're going to kill me?'

'No, Mr Glass. I'm going to do worse than that.' The voice

paused for a moment, and Glass slammed a fist on the table, rattling the phone and angering himself for losing his cool.

'You have opened a can of worms, Mr Carter, that you cannot close.' He took a pull on the cigarette and let the smoke filter from the corner of his mouth. 'I will be seeing you soon.'

Before the voice could respond, Glass hung up the call and tossed the phone across the glass table. It clattered and slid to a stop next to the empty bottle of wine.

There was no fear.

That was what had burrowed beneath Glass' skin and irritated him. There was no hint of trepidation or worry. The mystery man had been clear and concise.

Which made him a threat.

Which made him a target.

As he collected himself and finished his cigarette, Glass reached for his phone and sent a message to his assistant. Instantly, the door to the balcony slid open, and the weasely man stepped in, as always wearing a tight-fitting suit that did nothing for his spindly frame.

'Yes, sir?' Glover asked, anxiously poking his glasses up his nose.

'Get the jet ready. We're heading to Paris.' Glass didn't even look at the man. He reserved his eye contact for people he respected, not those he paid handsomely. 'Pack for a week. Reach out to whatever triggers are in the area and have them meet us at the hanger.'

'Of course, sir. Right away, sir,' Glover said as he shuffled back towards the door.

'Oh, and have them prepare the Sanctuary for an event.'

Glover stopped and turned; his thin eyebrows raised above his sunken eyes.

'But sir, that's short notice?'

'I didn't fucking ask for permission, did I?' Glass snapped. 'Send the word out. Ten million to enter the ballot. A further ten if selected.'

'But…without any information to offer, they will be unlikely to bid?' Glover whimpered. Glass smirked, and looked back across the ocean, his view only hindered by the white smoke that filtered up from his cigarette.

'Oh, they'll bid.' Glass' eyes narrowed as he thought back to the conversation. 'Because if we're dealing with who I think we are…then everybody on the fucking planet will want a seat at that table.'

Glover scarpered away, leaving Glass to the warm Spring breeze, the darkened view of the Algarve and the tingle of excitement slithering through his body.

It had been a long time since he had been challenged.

A long time since he felt he needed to fight.

And as he flicked his cigarette over the railing and into the abyss, he felt that surge once more, and two hours later, he was boarding his private jet, ready to hunt the most wanted man in the continent.

Sam Pope.

CHAPTER FOURTEEN

The chaos of the previous two days had seen Corbin finally relent and crumble under the weight of her cravings. The entire DGSE office had been in overdrive for the past twelve hours, ever since she had taken the call from a woman, summoning her and the authorities to what they now knew to be the Haven.

Yet it was only Corbin who knew what to expect when they arrived.

A war zone.

A once 'off-limits' location rendered to rubble.

Corbin arrived with a few members of the DGSE, along with members of the armed police, who swept the building expertly, their rifles drawn and their trigger fingers ready. But Corbin knew it was a pointless task.

All they found were countless bodies of men in sharp suits and expertly placed bullet holes. Sam had clearly run through the security detail tasked with protecting the site, although they did find a naked man slumped against a wall upstairs, his brain smeared across the paintwork. A young woman was found, strangled, in the same room, and

Corbin didn't need to be the high-ranking agent she was to decipher why Sam had pulled the trigger.

A group of women and a few scantily clad men were gathered outside the building, all of them in varying stages of shock, and the police swiftly began checking them over and taking their statements as Corbin and the DGSE tried to establish control over the crime scene. That was when they discovered the children.

The group of them, of varying ages, huddled in fear in an open dungeon in the underground lair.

That was when the excitement turned to disgust, and that was when everyone's attitude towards the man responsible changed.

Leaning against one of the panes of glass was Yohan Cheyrou, the man who had been the subject of a city-wide manhunt the moment he'd been taken into the Metro by Sam, disappearing into the network of underground tunnels and relentless waves of commuters. A man of impenetrable standing among the city's elite, bloodied and beaten and looking every bit the criminal that Sam had labelled him. The expensive suit was tattered from the broken glass, and Cheyrou's pale face was twisted in agony as he clutched his blood-soaked hand.

Ambulances soon embarked upon the location, turning the once private and secluded Haven into a chaotic scene of flashing lights and broken bodies.

Chaos.

That's what it was.

From the moment Sam had caught her off guard at her cottage just over a day ago, to the moment she read Cheyrou his rights as he was tended to by the paramedics.

Whatever Sam was hunting, it was leaving a trail of carnage in his wake, and Corbin was well aware that the finger would be pointed in her direction.

In the early hours of the morning, she headed back to

the CAT, leaving her subordinates and the clean-up crews to work through the Haven with a fine-tooth comb and start piecing together the broken entity Sam had shattered. The bodies were taken to the morgue for analysis, although Corbin wouldn't need the pathologist's report to tell her that a well-placed bullet between the eyes would kill a man. But there was a trail of destruction running from the city centre to the outskirts of Paris, which meant there was already an avalanche of paperwork falling across her desk.

And judging by the look on Vivier's face when he had burst through the open plan office towards her private glass box, there was a riot act that accompanied it.

'My office.' Vivier snarled through the half open door. 'Ten minutes.'

There was nothing further, and as she watched Vivier storm back through the empty banks of desks, Corbin finally felt her cravings and her stress levels combine, and her hand yanked open her desk drawer and retrieved the emergency cigarettes that were tucked at the back. A few moments later, she stepped out into the twilight that was washed across the Parisian sky. The surrounding area of the offices, much like the buildings themselves, were empty, and the entire world felt like it was asleep.

But no matter the time of day, there was always chaos.

Always someone, somewhere, working to make the world a better place.

For a long time, Corbin had thought it was herself. Along with Vivier, and her late partner, Martin Agard, she had always known that the work they did at the DGSE ensured that the French people were safe. That they neutralised the international threats to the country, and no matter the cost, which Agard's widow and kids knew all too well, they saw it through.

It was why, as Corbin lit her cigarette, she didn't feel a shred of guilt or remorse for helping Sam.

She'd been to the remnants of the Haven and seen what Sam was unearthing. The scantily clad people were not there by choice, and undoubtedly, were subjected to months or even years of abuse at the hands of Cheyrou and whoever frequented the site. From the few women she'd spoken to who could muster a few responses in broken French, she'd quickly got the gist that the majority of them were sex workers.

Snatched from another country.

Sold into debauched slavery.

Corbin flicked the ash off her cigarette. Still no guilt.

There were dead bodies, men who were paid to keep the customers safe and the workers terrified.

There were dead customers. One of whom, when the required tests were done, would no doubt be proven to have raped and murdered the woman found in the room with him.

No remorse.

And of course there were the children.

Vacant eyes and broken wills, facing a freedom that they'd struggle to navigate.

No remorse. Not a shred.

Corbin stubbed out the cigarette on the wall she had perched upon and dropped the butt into the flower bed behind her. The bright lights of the building and the surrounding grounds cast the magnificent structures in a blend of light and darkness, and the early morning breeze carried a bitter chill on its shoulders.

With no desire to face the mountain of paperwork, red tape and potential disciplinary action awaiting her, Corbin pulled another cigarette from her box, lit it, and blew out a plume of white smoke with a grateful sigh.

'I thought you had quit.'

Vivier's stern voice cut through her moment of tranquillity, and she turned to face her boss, who was walking casually towards her, hands stuffed in his pockets.

'I did.' She blew out another plume of smoke. She tapped the box beside her. 'Have you?'

Vivier chuckled as he eased his overweight frame down onto the wall beside her. He gave a slight, involuntary grunt to hammer home his advancing years and then took a cigarette from the box and lit it.

'Marie will not like this.' Vivier grumbled through the smoke.

'I'm sure she's used to that, sir.'

Vivier turned and returned Corbin's smirk with one of his own.

'Touché, Renée.' He chuckled. For a few moments, the two of them sat in silence, looking up at their office and putting off the inevitable. As he finished the cigarette, Vivier coughed uncomfortably before leaning forward.

'How long have you worked for me, Renée?' He kept his eyes looking forward.

'Years, sir.'

'And you trust me, right?' He sat back and turned to her, the breeze whistling through the flowers and plants behind them. 'I know your promotion hasn't been what you would have wanted, but you do know I am just trying to protect you, right?'

'If you say so, sir,' Corbin said. 'Sometimes, it's hard to tell.'

Vivier nodded.

'I appreciate that. Well, the truth is, whilst trying to protect you, I also want to be transparent with you. So, when I tell you that you are in such deep trouble that I couldn't dig you out with an excavator, you know I'm being honest with you.'

Corbin finished her cigarette and condemned it to the flower bed.

'Is this about Cheyrou?'

Vivier leapt to his feet like he'd just sat on a pin.

'Of course it's about Cheyrou.' He looked around and lowered his voice, despite their isolation. 'Do you have any idea what keep your head down means?'

'Does it mean look the other way?' Corbin looked up at him blankly. 'Or does it mean just sit tight until someone gives you the go-ahead to fire me?'

Vivier stopped pacing and looked down at Corbin, who casually lifted a third cigarette from the box. Years of loyalty was filtering away faster than the burning end of her newly lit cigarette.

He sighed.

'You don't help yourself, Renée. You know that? I told you to keep a low profile, low enough so that when enough time passes, people forget the mess you made.'

'You mean exposing our next President as a war criminal?' Corbin shrugged and took a puff. 'Struggle to see how that is *my* mess.'

'Well, be that as that may, keeping a low profile doesn't mean leading a tactical unit into a fucking gun fight with the paid protection of one of the most influential men in the city.' Vivier scowled. 'In the middle of the streets, Renée. We've got an agent in critical condition; we've got dead bodies and chaos in the Metro. Not to mention, some secluded spa in the middle of nowhere filled to the brim with more corpses and sex workers.'

'And children, sir. Don't forget he had children on site.'

Corbin regretted the remark when Vivier glared at her, and he sighed once more.

'You need to give me something, Renée. Something that I can use to keep the vultures from circling around you. Because this right here…it's a mess. And they will bury you for it.'

Corbin rolled her eyes and finished the final few puffs

of the cigarette, regretting her relapse. With a sigh, she rocked back on the wall and looked up at her boss.

'You ever heard the word 'Veilmont'?'

Vivier frowned, but the slight flicker of his pupils gave him away.

'Veilmont?' Vivier continued the charade.

'Don't lie to me, sir. If ever there was a time not to lie to me, it's right now.'

Vivier placed both hands on his hips and looked down at his agent, clearly batting an idea around his mind like a game of squash. Finally, he spoke.

'It's a myth. It's something that Interpol and the DGSI have looked into at some expense and came away with nothing.'

'Nothing?' Corbin stood with renewed purpose.

'Look, I wasn't involved in the investigations, and they only share information pertinent to our own cases.' Vivier reasserted his authoritative tone. 'But it's not a name on the DGSE radar, which means it *shouldn't* be on yours.'

'What if I told you I had someone on the inside?' Corbin locked eyes with Vivier, who stopped still. 'Someone who is working his way through to find out what it is?'

Vivier gave a courtesy look over both shoulders before he took a slightly menacing step towards Corbin.

She didn't budge.

She would never budge.

In a low, almost deep whisper, Vivier leant forward and spoke.

'Renée, if you are working with an agency without the DGSE's knowledge, then I can't...'

'It's not an agency.' Corbin shook her short, brown hair. 'Just a man.'

'A vigilante?' Vivier scowled. 'Jesus, Renée. If it's the

same as last time, you *will* be arrested for treason. You know that.'

'Sir, whatever is coming my way, I can take it. But you've seen the photos. And I told you what I saw. Whatever my guy is doing, he's exposing some cruel people for what they are. Like you said, Cheyrou is a powerful man that our agencies would never even dream of touching. In one day, my guy has taken down his whole operation and linked him to a sex trafficking ring.'

'That's not been proved yet.'

Corbin chuckled.

'And it probably won't. I assume Cheyrou's already lawyered up?'

'More than we'll ever be able to afford.'

'Then you have to give this some space, sir.' Corbin pleaded. 'Whatever my guy is uncovering, he'll go right to the source. And if what we found at the Haven is the tip of the iceberg, then we're about to open the biggest fucking can of worms this country has ever seen.'

Vivier anxiously looked around once more and then stepped past Corbin and helped himself to another cigarette. One long drag was enough before he stomped it out under his Italian made shoe.

One long sigh let the smoke filter up and dance off into the night sky.

'Fine. I'll do what I can,' Vivier said with a clear reluctance. 'But you need to keep me posted, Renée. If you hear from your guy, I need to know about it. I can't have gunfights in the street. It's too messy.'

'Understood,' Corbin said, feeling her face contort into a genuine smile. As she went to step back towards the office, Vivier held out a hand and clutched her arm, stopping her in her tracks. She looked up at her boss, whose usual stern expression had morphed into one of concern.

'Be careful, Renée.' He uttered quietly. 'I've already lost

a good agent because of an off the books mission. I don't want to lose another.'

'Thank you, sir. But I'm always careful.'

Vivier relinquished his grip and Corbin headed back towards the derelict office, ready to push on with the paperwork that would give Sam the leeway he needed to do what was necessary.

That would make her complicit if things went wrong.

That would make her a target if things went right.

CHAPTER FIFTEEN

Glass peered through the window of his private jet as it began its descent, the clouds lifting from his view to reveal the tremendous city of Paris. The French capital was one of his busiest and most prosperous locations, and although he made the trip almost monthly, the stunning view always took his breath away. The flight from Faro to Paris had only been two and a half hours, but with the negotiations to clear a pathway, it had been almost seven hours since Glass had slammed the phone down on the man he believed to be Sam Pope.

The man who had promised he'd bring Glass' business down around him.

The Dassault Falcon 8X jet had cost fifty million euros off the shelf, and a further two to customise it to Glass' tastes. The upholstery was the finest Italian leather, blended with the wooden finish that gave the entire jet a touch of elegance. The bar was always stocked with the finest champagne and the warmest scotch, whilst a back area had been kitted out for a private chef, usually of Michelin star standard, who would prepare in-flight meals.

At the back end of the aircraft, the two ex-members of

the Sayeret Matkal, a premier arm of the Israeli Special Forces, were seated, their glasses only filled with water and their wits constantly about them. Every member of Glass' security detail was subject to rigorous drug screening.

Even a hint of alcohol in their system would see them removed from their position.

And considering what they were privy to, that removal would constitute a bullet to the back of the skull courtesy of their successor.

For this, Glass paid the men handsomely, ensuring that the most skilled fighters he could find came from some of the poorest countries. Highly trained and efficient killers, who had grown up on scraps, which meant their loyalty was easier to secure and their dedication to his strict set of rules would never be questioned. As the plane hit a sudden surge of turbulence, Glass reached for the scotch on the table before him, the ice cubes rattling as the plane shook. As he knocked it back, he peered over the rim of the glass at Glover, who meekly sat in the opposite chair, his puny frame hunched over a laptop as usual.

The turbulence sent a shiver of fear through the man, and as Glover gripped the leather arm rest in panic, Glass chuckled.

'It's fine.' Glass reassured him. 'Just a bump.'

'You know how much I hate to fly.' Glover's nasally voice carried a hint of resentment. 'I would have been happy taking the train.'

Glass planted the glass back down on the table and then motioned to the beautiful air hostess for another. She sauntered towards him in her black, lowcut, silk gown, offering him a wide smile and a generous view of her chest as she poured out the drink. As she walked away, Glass admired her for a few seconds before turning back to his useless assistant.

'How long have I known you, Charles?'

'Umm…' Glover mused.

'Ten years.' Glass answered for him. 'Ten years ago, you were being abused by those pathetic men in Canary Wharf, who thought they were the hottest shit on the planet. Low six-figure incomes, cheap, ill-fitting suits, and an arrogance that they "ran" the London financial market. And when that moment came, where I switched from being a drug hook-up to their go-to guy, you saw it coming.'

'Because I could see the desperation in their eyes,' Glover said proudly. Glass clicked his fingers and then slapped the table.

'Exactly. You, like me, could see the desperation that people have. For anything, really. For a good time. For money. For love. For anything. People are willing to sell their souls to cut out the hard work or the long road to what they really want, and I could see that you knew that. You were playing the long game with those guys, but it wasn't going to put you ahead of them.' Glass shook his head and took a sip of his scotch. 'No, you see the people who control those systems, are just an identikit version from a previous generation. Nothing really changes. A new name might be given to things. A few new buzz words will hit the zeitgeist that will get everyone riled up. People high up in the media will decide what the new mission is and who and what we get offended by, and that will drive the businesses to act in the way the elite want them to act. It never changes.'

Glass looked out at the Parisian skyline, as the sun began to threaten its early rise. Glover shrugged.

'What does that have to do with me?'

'Nothing. But it has a lot to do with me.' Glass smirked. 'I help those people make those decisions, and I can change them on a dime. I have every person with even a whiff of power in every country in this continent by the balls. That is power that you cannot buy, and that is control that you cannot relinquish. And that is under threat. Which is why, when this plane lands and I see who you have assembled to fix this issue for me, I don't want to be waiting for your fucking train to arrive.'

Glover turned away, looking back at his screen with a sense of self-loathing.

Not speaking up for himself made him weak in the eyes of Glass. Simultaneously, speaking back to his paymaster was a fast track to a bullet. As the Charles de Gaulle airport shone brightly below, the pilot expertly guided the Dassault Falcon 8X towards Paris Le Bourget. Usually, one of the busiest private jet airports in the entire continent, there was little to no activity as their wheels touched down in the Parisian dawn, the private jet bathed in the sudden glow of the rising sun.

It had been a long night.

It was threatening to be an even longer day, and as the pilot reduced the jet down to a crawl, Glass' security team began to rise from their seats, ensuring all safety measures were in place and their weapons were locked and loaded. Through the circular window, Glass squinted against the brightness, his eyes locked on his own private hanger. The front gates were open, but the inside was bathed in shadow, but he could make out numerous figures moving within.

'Who was available?' Glass asked, not peeling his gaze from the outside world.

'Tristan Duvall,' Glover said confidently. 'He was the only one within the perimeter. He's been able to make some calls. Says he has a nine strong team.'

'Fantastic,' Glass said, turning back with a smile. 'Good work, Charles.'

Glass knew that the compliment would be enough to restore Glover's sense of self-worth, and as the plane came to a stop outside the private hanger, the security team made the first move. As Glass stood from his seat, Glover's phone buzzed, and he took the call, and Glass heard him mention the name Cheyrou before his security detail escorted him down the steps that had unfurled from the aircraft like a tail. At the bottom, one of his paid guards had a Glock trained on the group of intimidating men who were standing, their muscular arms either folded across their meaty chests, or cradling FAMAS assault rifles in varying stages of construction. Glass stepped past the guard and patted him on the shoulder.

'Guns down.' He commanded and stepped towards the bulky figure before him with a hand extended. 'Tristan. It's been a while.'

'Mr Glass.' Tristan smiled; his pearly white teeth starkly contrasted to his thick, dark beard. A compensation for the lack of hair on his head. 'Your assistant didn't give too much information, just to…'

'Meet me here. I know. I gave the order.' Glass waved Tristan off and looked at the army of mercenaries he had assembled. A few of them returned the stare dismissively. Glass noticed it and smirked. 'Have you informed these men who I am?'

'No, sir,' Tristan said as he turned to face them. 'Some of them don't speak English. Some of them don't like taking orders, even from me.'

'Well, tough shit.' Glass looked to them all. He snapped his fingers, and one of the security guards placed a black carry-on suitcase on the table of the hanger, and Glass unzipped it.

Inside was five million euros.

He could feel the eyes widen around the room.

'Five million euros.' He announced, looking at them all. 'Split ten ways. If you accept the contract, then you are in until I have this man in captivity. Is this understood?'

'You don't want him dead?' One of the men spoke up.

Despite his hulking size, he seemed to shrink when Glass snapped his focus onto him.

'Oh, I do.' Glass' mouth twisted into a sinister grin. 'I just don't want you to kill him.'

'So, it's an extraction?' One of the English mercenaries questioned. 'A hell of a lot of money to snatch someone.'

'Well, that depends.' Glass noticed as Glover's head poked through the door of the jet, like a weasel emerging from the shrubbery. 'I don't expect this money to be split ten ways, put it that way. You see, the man I want captured, he single handedly took down one of my operations and the entire security detail. He seems to have a hard on for bringing me down, so I'd imagine any attempts to stop him will be met by considerable force.'

'So, what?' The merc spoke again. 'We can't hurt him?'

'Hurt him. Yes. Kill him, no.'

'Still seems excessive.' The merc shook his head. 'Who is this guy?'

'Sam Pope.'

The mention of the name sent the hanger spiralling into a silence that felt deafening. Anxious looks were exchanged between highly skilled men, and Glass could practically see the testosterone leaving the room. Clearly sensing the same wave of dread crashing over them, Tristan stepped forward, his muscular arms stretching the sleeves of his black t-shirt.

'You heard the man.' Tristan barked like a drill sergeant. 'We're going up against one of the most dangerous men in the country. We shoot to wound, we try to do things as quietly and as quickly as possible. Now, maths isn't my strongest suit, but five million divided by ten sure as hell makes things easier. So, let's all try to get back together.'

A few murmurs of agreement from the other mercs

echoed from the group, before some of them turned back to their weapons or their concerns.

Tristan turned to Glass, who nodded approvingly.

'Fine speech.'

'Just give us the information, and we'll get it done.' Tristan extended his hand. Glass took it.

'I want him alive.'

'Have I ever let you down?' Tristan added extra pressure to his grip, a needless display of defiance in the face of Glass' wealth. Whilst he may have been a powerful man, there was a reason why Glass wasn't the one leading the team into battle with a highly skilled vigilante.

Glass retracted his hand and sneered.

'My assistant will give you the location once we have tracked the phone in his possession.' Glass pulled a cloth from his pocket and made a show of wiping his hand. 'Once we've overridden the firewalls, we should have him. Be ready to go this afternoon.'

'Copy that,' Tristan said, as he patted Glass heavily on the shoulder blade, adding just enough to send him forward a step. As Tristan joined the rest of the meatheads who were now strapping up their armoury, Glass felt a sudden need to belittle someone. Tristan's display of physical dominance had left a throbbing pain in his back, and a sour taste in his mouth.

Right on cue, Glover arrived, open laptop in hand and his mobile phone in the other.

'Cheyrou should be released within the next few hours.' Glover stammered. 'Shall I send a car to pick him up?'

'Obviously.' Glass snapped. 'And have him taken to that printing press he was so fond of. His men will know where and how to clean up after.'

Glover nodded, swallowing his disgust at effectively sanctioning the murder of Cheyrou. Before he could scarper off, Glass rested a hand on his shoulder, just as the

Hyundai Santa Fe pulled up to the hanger. The reinforced vehicle, with the tinted, bulletproof windows, came to a stop before them both, and the guard in the passenger seat swiftly stepped out to open the back passenger door for Glass.

'Oh, and make reservations at *Le Ciel* for tonight,' Glass said as he approached the back seat. 'Tell them I want the room full.'

'Sir, that's quite short notice.' Glass shot Glover a firm glare and he sighed. 'Leave it to me.'

Glass smiled and patted Glover on the shoulder.

'See. That's the spirit.' As Glass shuffled into the seat, Glover tried to follow. The armed guard stopped him and closed the door.

'Sir?' Glover called out, his voice shaking. The window slid down, and Glass peered out at him.

'I need you to stay here. Ensure these men have everything they need for the task at hand.' Glass looked beyond Glover, where the dangerous men were tending to their weapons. 'Don't worry, Charles. They're harmless.'

'Sir, they are trained killers.'

Glass smirked as the window began to rise.

'Then don't upset them.'

The window cut Glover from Glass' line of sight, and the engine roared as they sped across the private runway towards the city. Glass let out a sigh, loosened the tie that pressed his shirt collar to his throat and finally felt his body relax.

Things were moving.

Plans were in motion.

And all going well, after a day spent resting, he'll be joined at one of the prestigious restaurants in the capital. By the most dangerous man walking its streets.

He'd sit opposite Sam Pope.

And tell him how he was going to die.

CHAPTER SIXTEEN

It was almost midday when Sam blinked himself awake, and with a groan that befitted a man in his mid-forties, pushed himself to a seated position. The mattress in the hostel was thin and lumpy, with coiled springs prodding through the fabric at seemingly frequent intervals.

It was in keeping with the rest of the room, and the rickety bedframe shook as Sam swung his legs over the edge and placed his feet on the rough, worn carpet. The thin curtain, punctuated with moth bites, did little to keep out the bright spring sunshine, and the pounding noise of the capital city hammered through the windowpane, shaking it in its frame.

It was the cheapest hostel Sam could find, and it did its job.

It gave him a bed, and it gave him a place to lie low.

It would also, undoubtedly, be a point of discussion when Ranjit called, especially as he'd booked Sam into a hotel when he'd arranged his travel to the famous French city. It was only three stars, but compared to the digs Sam had plumped for, he'd effectively turned down the Ritz.

But the money wasn't important.

The turn-down service or the name on the door held little value to Sam. He wasn't in Paris on vacation, nor was he going to flagrantly spend the millions that Paul Etheridge had left for him to fund his war on crime.

That money was to be put to good use, and paying for the cheapest bed in the most remote backstreet in Paris was a necessary cost.

Splashing out on a hotel with a pool, or even one that provided its own towels, didn't quite meet Sam's criteria for necessity.

Sam pulled his meagre toiletries from his sports bag and headed to the door, scooping up the cheap towel he'd bought from the nearby supermarket. He stepped out onto the landing and marched down the corridor, the floor-boards creaking underfoot. Sam had spoken to the owner of the hostel, a seedy, chubby man with a greasy, receding hairline and yellow teeth, who had confirmed to Sam in broken English that he was the only guest that night.

It meant he could amble down to the communal shower room in just his underwear without any concerns about prying eyes.

It also meant that there was nobody in the line of fire for what he knew was coming.

After a vigorous scrub under the lukewarm but surprisingly powerful shower, Sam took a few moments to inspect his body for any new injuries. Thankfully, the armed guards that had watched over the Haven were exactly what he had expected.

Intimidating men who were good enough to scare a rich person straight if they stepped out of line.

But not trained killers.

Those were to come next.

There were no new scars to add to his ever-growing collection, but Sam could feel the fingerprints of Father Time on his body. Every joint clicked when it bent, and the muscles that he worked so hard to maintain were constantly aching.

Recovering from battle was always a mission in itself.

It was just becoming harder with each passing day.

After returning to his room, Sam threw on his usual attire of a black t-shirt and grey jeans and then sat to pull on his boots. His spine creaked as he tightened the laces, but he ignored the clear signs that he needed to slow down.

But he couldn't.

Not yet.

As he slid his arms into his bomber jacket, his phone vibrated loudly on the rickety bedside table, and he glanced at the screen before answering.

Ranjit.

Sam took the call as he stepped out of his room and made his way through the narrow, dimly lit hallways towards the outside world. As he connected the call, Ranjit was already in full flow.

'It's as if the owner doesn't give two shits about cleaning his hostel. I swear, even a cockroach would turn his nose up at it.'

Sam chuckled, barely able to hear Ranjit over the grumbling of his empty stomach. His friend continued.

'Atrocious to look at. Horribly unclean. Disgusting smell. And that's just the vile bloke who calls himself the owner. Another one here says...'I've travelled most of my adult life and this is by far the worst hostel I have ever visited. Truly appalling.' Should I go on?'

Sam stepped out into the cool breeze and was hit by the explosive volume of the traffic like a slap in the face. He headed across the street to the coffee shop that had caught his eye, and as he navigated the busy roar, he responded.

'What have you got for me, Ranj?'

He could hear his friend take a pull on his cigarette, which meant he too was enjoying the spring sun.

'Apart from another six hundred one-star reviews of the place you are staying?'

'I told you; it doesn't matter.' Sam stepped into the queue, drawing a scowl from a surly looking businessman who was also on a phone call, and a flirtatious smile from the stunning brunette behind the counter. 'It's all I need.'

'I know, but come on? The place I booked you was hardly the Four Seasons, but at least it had fucking carpet on the floor.' Another pull on the cigarette. *'I mean, it ain't like you're shy a few bob, Sam. Fuck…I could even charge double, and you wouldn't notice.'*

'I would if I got the same level of bullshit from you.' Sam chuckled again, knowing his barb hit. 'But that money isn't for my comfort, Ranj. I told you that. A good man left me that money to keep fighting the good fight.'

'Yeah, yeah. Fuck me, Sam, you're such a boy scout. I'm sure your buddy wouldn't mind if you treated yourself once in a while.'

Sam gave his order to the beautiful barista and responded.

'I am treating myself.'

'Ordering a fuckin' croissant with your coffee isn't treating yourself, bud.'

'It is when you're in Paris. You should see the price of these things.' Sam gave the woman a polite nod as he collected his latte and croissant and headed back out through the door, ambling into the fenced off seating area that comprised a few metal tables and wicker-backed chairs. The businessman was in the throws of an argument on his call, and Sam took the table beside him and sat down. 'So, what have you got for me?'

'Well, you're right. Your guy is in Paris. Headed straight over the second you got off the phone with him. Either you are very persuasive or were a complete arsehole to him.

'I'd say a little bit of both,' Sam said with a grin and sipped his coffee.

'I tracked his private plane which landed in Paris Le Bourget

earlier this morning.' Sam heard the click of a lighter through the phone and Ranj's appreciative exhale. '*Managed to locate his private hanger in their database and ran a backdoor program into their security system.*'

'English,' Sam said as Ranj sighed.

'*I hacked the security feed for the hanger. No audio, but I got a clear visual of our guy. I'll send it across to you. For a guy worth that much money, he is almost completely off the grid.*'

'Yeah, when you see what he was offering at the Haven, you'll understand why.'

Sam felt his fist clench uncontrollably, as his mind raced back to the vacant eyes of the children he had rescued. Whatever he'd saved them from that night, he was certain they'd have been subjected to countless times. He needed to speak to Corbin, to ensure they were okay and then he'd see about putting that money to good use for them.

'*Well, I've got a visual anyway. It should be with you now. Also, just a heads up, there was a lot of firepower in that hanger.*'

'Military?' Sam's brow furrowed and he took a bite from his pastry.

'*Ex I'd wager. But a lot of scary looking dudes, with a lot of scary looking guns. And I'd bet all the money in your bank account that they're heading your way.*'

As Ranjit's words filtered into Sam's ears, his eyes locked onto the black van that slowed to a stop in front of the hostel he has slept in. Sam turned to the side, lifting his hand to his face to lower his profile, and through his fingers he watched as a large man with a bald head and a thick, dark beard stepped out of the passenger seat. He was clad in black, with his leather jacket straining against his solid build, and Sam could see the military training in the simplest of his movements.

'I think they already have.' Sam muttered into the phone.

'*Shit. Get out of there.*'

Sam sipped his coffee.

'Don't panic, Ranj. You're in a different country remember.'

'*Then what the hell are you planning to do?*'

Sam felt an alarming level of calm filter through his body, as if the following decisions were as easy as deciding what croissant he'd wanted a few moments ago.

'There's a reason I picked that hostel, Ranj. It's empty. Which means what comes next has as little collateral damage as possible.' Sam finished his coffee and slammed the cup down. 'I could have met Glass at the airport, but I'd have been walking into a massacre. But now, I know that he has at least six guys on my location but also has six less at his. Now, I'd imagine these guys don't want to shoot up a building in the middle of Paris in broad daylight, so once they confirm I'm staying there, they'll sit on the place, wait for me to return and then make sure I stay there until the streets quieten down. I'd say about four or five hours or so.'

'*And what…you'll be long gone by then?*'

Sam chuckled.

'I'll invite them in myself. In the meantime…'

'*Sam, you're a fucking mad man.*'

Sam ignored Ranj's outburst and continued.

'In the meantime, I need you to get into Glass' network. We know these phones have encryption out the wazoo, and I won't even pretend I understand how you get round that. But whatever you did to backtrace those numbers to Cheyrou, I need you to do that with Glass' phone.'

'*I'll try but I can't guarantee it.*'

'Just try,' Sam said. 'We want to bring this guy down; it isn't about putting a bullet between his eyes. It's about taking down his entire network, name by name. We expose

137

those who are involved, they'll turn on him and put him down themselves.'

At that moment, Sam watched as the door to the hostel flew open, and the intimidating hitman emerged, striding powerfully back to the van. Sam saw the man nod encouragingly, meaning the owner had confirmed their target's whereabouts. The van rumbled to life, and Sam watched as it slowly cruised down the street, before pulling a huge U-turn and parking up behind a taxi rank. It came to a dead stop.

All eyes would be on the hostel.

All eyes waiting for Sam to emerge.

'You could just walk away, Sam.' Ranj offered solemnly. *'Leave all of this to your friend in the DGSE. They must surely have enough to at least pull at the thread a little. You've done enough.'*

Sam took a deep breath, and his mind flashed to the broken stares of the captive children.

Their silence did little to quieten the sheer volume of horrors they'd been through.

Sam felt his fist clench again, and a surge of purpose struck him like a bolt of lightning.

'It's never enough.'

Sam hung up the phone, and then stood, lifting his empty cup and crust-covered plate and returned to the café. The brunette once again flashed her gorgeous smile, and through a mixture of her broken English and Sam's broken French, Sam ordered another coffee and hunkered down at the table beside the window of the quaint coffee shop. The cramped room was decorated tastefully, with distressed wooden tables positioned in various points in front of the long wooden bench that clung to the exposed brick wall. Plants hung from the ceiling, the walls were covered in tasteful art pieces, and on the long, wooden windowsill beside Sam, there were a stack of tatty, donated books. He thumbed through them, thinking about his long-abandoned promise to his son to keep reading and made a new one that if he walked away from his war with 'Veilmont', he'd pick it back up again.

In the meantime, he chose a book, plonked it open on the table and then locked his eyes on the front door of the hostel.

The hours past.

After the first hour, the intimidating bald man had returned to the hostel, flanked by two other men who screamed military. Minutes later, he and one other emerged, and the clear leader ordered the other to the back of the building. As the man disappeared down the alleyway, Sam understood what was happening.

They'd positioned a man in the hostel, most likely in his room, whilst another had taken up a position covering the back of the building. If he returned and somehow got the drop on his violent welcome party, then they'd hopefully flank him from both sides.

There was no element of surprise.

The only advantage Sam had; was he knew where the pieces were on the board. The only downside, he was the only piece left to face them.

After a hearty lunch, another coffee, which Sam insisted on being decaf, he watched as the Parisian day folded into a warm early evening, and the commuters began to flood to the streets, doubling the footfall and gridlocking the traffic.

As it reached six o'clock, the accommodating woman began to shut up shop, and Sam handed her a generous tip and then told her it would be safer if she forgot he was ever there. The look of disappointment in her eyes was clear, and in another life, one where his heart wasn't still yearning to return to Scotland, Sam could have been tempted.

But there were bigger things at play.

A vile, unreachable organisation that was closing in on him.

A death squad staking out his place of residence.

Those children.

And with a deep breath, and a double check that his Glock 17 was still pressed firmly against the base of his spine, Sam marched across the road to the front door of the hostel, very much in the mood for a fight.

CHAPTER SEVENTEEN

Tristan Duvall sat in the passenger seat of the blacked-out van, and his dark brown eyes were locked onto the front door of the hostel. His eyes matched the darkness of his thick beard, with the odd white hair flicking through. It suited his dark complexion, and Tristan had never been sure where he would call home. His ancestry was a mystery to him, and as he grew up in the care system in Madrid, he was told that he had an Argentinian father and a Spanish mother.

He didn't care.

He didn't have a memory of either of them.

Had never seen a photograph.

For all intents and purposes, they were young lovers who found a moment of happiness in a consistently shit world, and he had been the outcome. And from them, he had inherited their Mediterranean genes, and seemingly, from his father, impressive physical genetics. His hulking six-foot five frame was lined with thick, rounded muscles, and had been that way ever since the *Infantería de Marina* had moulded him into a walking weapon. He walked into a crummy town hall down a side street in Madrid, without a penny to his name, and had signed up with a shaking hand.

They steadied it and slapped a Heckler & Kock G38 in his grip and from then on, Tristan viewed most of the world through the sights of his gun, and with the view that it was either kill or be killed. For over two decades, he had served what he called his country with pride, never once questioning an order, nor hesitating to pull the trigger. As his celebrated and widely respected career threatened to take him towards a more strategic position, he made the decision to step away from the military and went into private contracting.

A moral compass wasn't something Tristan had ever been guided by, and putting a bullet in a man, woman or child for the right price was as easy as breathing. It made him a very wealthy and a very in-demand man, and with Dominik Silva now spending the rest of his life behind bars in a British prison, Tristan had taken up the mantle as one of the most lethal guns for hire in Europe.

He was a close associate of many rich and many powerful men.

And they didn't come richer or more powerful than Sebastian Glass.

It was a rare occurrence to see a man of such poise so riled up, but the remit was clear.

Bring the man he believed to be Sam Pope to him.

Alive.

Sitting beside him in the van was a man he knew as Johan, a trusted wheelman who was also capable with a weapon in his hands. Tristan had used him a few times, but the man spoke little French and even less Spanish, but he knew his role. In the back, three other men were playing cards, shuffling uncomfortably in the minimal space, all of them strapped up courtesy of the buffet of weapons that had been laid out for them in Glass' hanger. One of the men, Ronan, was loitering in the alleyways behind the hostel, an insurance policy against Sam trying to give them the slip.

Inside the hostel, a man named Kylian was waiting and had radioed in to inform Tristan that he had been allocated the room opposite Pope's and would walk him out at gun point.

Tristan wasn't so sure, but as the evening traffic threatened to block his perfect view of the hostel entrance from the comfort of his seat, his eyes flickered with excitement.

His pulse raced slightly, as the adrenaline began to kick in.

He lifted the radio and informed Kylian to get ready.

And less than five minutes later, as Ronan's panicked voice boomed through the radio, Tristan slammed his fist against the dividing panel in the van, the thunderous echo sparking his team into life. As they filtered out of the van, locked and loaded and sending the terrified civilians into a panic, Tristan joined them, his hand already clasping the Glock 17 and holding it low, as he barked out the reminder that they were to take Sam Pope alive.

Ronan's voice cackled through again.

'He's thrown Kylian out of the fucking window.'

———

Sam had thrown open the door to the hostel and instantly locked eyes onto the grotesque owner, who looked up from his desk with a sneer. Unlike before, when the man's greasy, sweat soaked skin was a result of his lack of personal hygiene, this time it was different. There was a nervousness to the man, who ran a hand through his thin, wispy hair, and his eyes looked everywhere but at Sam. The stench of cigarettes clung to every square inch of the room, turning the wallpapers a horrible shade of yellow as it threatened to peel from the wall.

'Is he in my room?' Sam demanded. The man stared back at him blankly. 'The man waiting for me. Is he in my room?'

The owner shrugged and reached for a cigarette.

'Je ne parle pas anglais.'

As the owner cockily chuckled, his eyes bulged in horror as Sam launched across the desk, gripping the scruff of his unwashed shirt with both hands, and then in an impressive show of strength, he hauled the rotund owner forward across the desk. A lamp tumbled to the floor, and papers and pens clattered after it, drowning out the owner's cries of panic as Sam drew him towards him.

'You spoke it this morning.' Sam spat angrily. 'Now, I would rather sort this issue out without you getting hurt. The only way I can do that is if you tell me the fucking truth. Understand?'

The man had gone limp through fear, and Sam could smell the stale stench of his breath.

'Yes.' He uttered meekly.

'Now is he in my room?' Sam repeated. The man shook his head. 'Opposite?'

The man nodded.

'They had guns…' The man began but trailed off. Sam pulled his own as the owner gasped.

'So do I.' He motioned to the stairs with the weapon. 'With me.'

The owner hesitantly walked across the room to the stairs, as Sam marched behind him. As they climbed the stairs, Sam tucked the weapon back into his jeans and then nodded for the owner to head to his room. The old floor-boards groaned underfoot, and Sam made no attempt to quiet them. Approaching his door, Sam stepped back and pressed his back against the wall beside the door opposite and then nodded to the owner. With a gulp, the owner did as he was ordered, and no sooner had he turned the key in the lock, the door behind him flew open.

Out stepped the man Sam had seen disappear into the building hours ago. Broad, decked in black, with a gun aimed at the owner, the man stepped forward with a furrowed brow, and his confusion dropped his guard. Lowering the gun, the man went to speak, but then swiftly tried to react to what was flying through his periphery.

It was too late.

Sam's knuckles collided with the man's jaw, the impact causing a sickening crack as the bone dislodged from his skull. The man stumbled back into the door frame, groaning with agony through his broken jaw, and as Sam stepped through, he lamely tried to lift the weapon. Behind him, Sam heard the owner scream in terror before his footsteps thundered down the hallway and disappeared down the rickety staircase. Sam swung his fist down, driving it into the man's forearm, causing him to drop the gun. Stumbling off balance, the man grabbed out at the cheap, wooden chair beside the tatty dressing table and swung it up, and it shattered as Sam lifted an elbow to absorb the blow.

Seeing red, the man launched forward, growling through his wrecked jaw, and he slammed his shoulder into Sam's stomach and sent them both hurtling back into the wall. The plasterboard indented, and dust burst out, and Sam drove elbows down into the man's spine to relinquish his grip. It worked, and Sam caught him with a knee to the face that sent him stumbling backwards, the blood gushing from his nose. Off balance, the man staggered towards the window, and Sam ran, grabbed the back of the man's shirt collar with one hand, and the back of his jeans with the other, and then hurled him towards the thin pane of glass that led to the outside world. The man's skull obliterated the glass, and as they showered down to the street below in a thousand twinkling pieces, the man hurtled down between them, before slamming to the concrete below with a sickening, life-ending thud.

Panic erupted, and Sam could hear a voice screaming in French, before a gunshot echoed and a bullet cracked into the wooden frame of the now obliterated window. As another bullet clattered the wood, setting off the inevitable timer for the arrival of the police, Sam pressed against the side of the frame, his gun drawn.

He could hear commotion in the alleyway below, the crunching of boots on glass and someone yelling at Sam's shooter for information.

The distraction was enough, and Sam reached down and lifted the gun from the floor. As another few bullets hit the frame, Sam took a breath and then spun from the wall, swinging his arm out of the window, and levelling the gun towards the men in the alleyway.

Two squeezes of the trigger.

Two men hit the ground.

As Sam turned back into the room, he could hear the thundering of boots on the staircase that ran through the building like a spinal cord, and he slid the mag from the Glock, checked the number of bullets, then slammed it shut as he approached the doorway. Holding his step, he waited until he heard the boots slam down on the landing, and he could hear the unmistakeable sounds of someone drawing their weapon.

With a gun in one hand, Sam reached back and retrieved his own Glock from the back of his jeans.

The corridor was narrow, the dank dreary walls offering nothing but shadow, and the window at the far end was thick with grime. Taking a deep breath, Sam held the guns up to his chest, then spun out, unloading both guns as he moved through to the open doorway to his own room.

As he swivelled through the door, he heard the first man drop, blood gurgling in his throat as his chest began to fill with blood.

The man behind him screamed something in his native tongue, and charged forward, and as he emerged in the doorway, he drew his weapon, only for Sam to pull the trigger on his own.

The man's kneecap blew out in a burst of blood and bone, and as he dropped to the ground, he scrambled for the gun that had fallen from his hand.

Sam put a bullet through his skull to save him the effort.

Through the thin walls, the wailing of sirens began to pierce the air, and Sam hurriedly gathered his belongings from the room. In the corner, the owner was cowering, his eyes swollen with tears. Sam dropped a few hundred Euros on the bed for his trouble, before he swiftly slid the magazine from the Glock and slammed in another. With his rucksack swung over his shoulder, Sam stepped out into the hallway, gun drawn.

It was eerily silent, and Sam tried to lighten each step that he took. He'd killed five men in less than five minutes, but he knew that none of them was the shot caller.

Which meant he still wasn't in the clear.

He stepped over the fallen mercenary in the hallway, who was painstakingly wheezing through his final breaths. Blood had pooled around him, and Sam looked down at the wide, vacant eyes of a man entering his final moments. By the time Sam had swung out and cleared the stairwell, the man had given up the ghost. The front door to the hostel was swinging wide open, and the imminent arrival of the police echoed through loudly. Tentatively, Sam stepped off the stairwell, but one step later, and the bald, bearded man emerged in the doorway, his hands clasped around a Benelli Supernova Tactical pump-action shotgun.

'Shit'. Sam uttered, took two massive strides, and as he pushed off the third, he heard the room shaking blast of the weapon. Sam hurled through the air, launching himself over the desk, as the avalanche of bullets ripped through the wood behind him. Sam hit the floor hard, the wind shooting out of him, but he scrambled to his feet quickly as he heard the sinister clunk of the weapon being cocked.

'He wants you alive.' The voice boomed beyond the desk; the words laced with an unplaceable accent. 'But that doesn't mean healthy.'

Another blast blew out the frame of the desk, evaporating the spot where Sam had been sprawled. But Sam was up on his feet, keeping low behind the desk as he shimmied towards the corridor that led to the back entrance. Beyond the man who had him cornered, the sirens grew in volume.

It was now or never.

As the man cocked the gun once more and an empty shell rattled onto the floor, Sam exploded forward like an Olympic sprinter, his head down, but his gun up, and he blindly fired in the direction of his attacker, who hit the deck for cover. He covered the few feet to the corridor, ran as fast as his legs could carry him, and as he threw open the door to the alleyway, another shotgun blast took a sizable chunk out of the doorframe beside him.

Three bodies greeted him in the alleyway, one of them crumpled amongst the glass shards that crunched under Sam's boots as he turned and hammered as fast as he could down the alleyway until it connected with another.

Then another.

As the police descended upon the war zone that was now the hostel, all they would find was a terrified owner and a waiting line for the morgue.

The bald man would no doubt have made himself scarce, along with the van they'd arrived in.

The street would be shut down.

They'd be looking for anyone involved.

But as he made his way through the network of alley-ways that he had committed to memory, Sam caught his breath and remembered the other reason why he'd chosen that hostel for what he knew was going to happen.

Beyond it being empty and having no CCTV, he emerged through one final alleyway to the Metro station. With his head down and his hands grasping the straps of his rucksack, he headed back down into the underground, knowing that he had rung a bell that couldn't be unrung.

Glass had sent men after him, and Sam had put them down.

In all likelihood, Glass would send more.

So, when Sam emerged above ground again, and Ranjit had sent him a location, Sam decided to save Glass the hassle.

CHAPTER EIGHTEEN

Le Ciel de Paris, as always, was packed to capacity, with the one hundred and forty-five seats filled, and the well-trained staff working efficiently to cater to every need. Situated on the fifty sixth floor of the stunning, sixty floor Montparnasse Tower, the views afforded from the window seats of the restaurant were extraordinary. The entire city of Paris lit up against the spring night sky, with the Eiffel Tower shooting up from the middle like a volcanic eruption.

The city was certainly one of the most beautiful from a great height, and it was why Sebastian Glass always ensured his trips to the French capital included a dinner with a view. The food, prepared to Michelin standard, was only the silver medal to the stunning vista that was before him.

And it felt like he needed an evening where things went right.

It had been almost twenty-four hours since he had been sitting in front of the laptop on his Portuguese balcony, watching as Sam Pope tore a hole through not only one of the most prestigious Veilmont locations, but also through Glass' entire reputation. Since leaving his assistant, Charles Glover, in the capable hands of Tristan and the mercenary team he'd pulled together at short notice, Glass had been on a personal mission to cater to some of his higher profile clients. The rumours of Sam Pope's assault swiftly spread among Glass' clientele, many of whom were rightly concerned that their association with Veilmont was now a potential hazard. Reassuringly, Glass doubled down on his confidence in the highly skilled, well-paid team he had hunting Sam Pope through Paris as they spoke, all wrapped up in a thinly veiled threat of what would happen if they tried to walk away.

Membership to Veilmont was a lifetime commitment. If the members tastes changed and they no longer required access, Glass couldn't just allow them to walk away with what they would have been exposed to. Their annual payment was a reminder to them, and a consideration to him, that their silence was assured.

He needn't remind them how every room they had ever entered on his premises was equipped with a multitude of cameras, meaning their every sordid movement was accessible at the click of his fingers. That was the power he had over them, which was worth more than the endless number of zeroes that filled out his bank account. But those assurances were hard to justify when Glover updated him on the mission.

Five of Tristan's men were dead.

The police were at the scene, which Tristan and his driver had evacuated as soon as Tristan had introduced the owner of the premises to the business end of a shot gun.

The streets were shut down.

Investigations were underway, but Glover had already begun the necessary work and financial renumerations to ensure that trail went cold pretty quickly.

But it meant that Sam Pope was still at large.

And it also meant that despite Glass' promises to his clients, they were no closer to bringing him in.

By the time the waiter uncorked the most expensive bottle of wine on the list for him to taste and approve, Glass was drained and felt his anger towards Sam Pope swelling by the second. Nobody challenged him in such a way, nor had anyone riled him up to the point of exhaustion in years.

The wine was sunk in one swift tilt of the head, and he ushered for the waiter to pour another before he selected his dinner from the minimalist menu of the finest local cuisine. As the waiter scurried away, Glass sipped his wine and sighed as Glover scampered towards his table. Glass made a point of sipping his drink slowly before even making eye contact, before gesturing for Glover to take a seat at his table.

'I trust you have made the necessary calls,' Glass said.

'Yes, sir.' Glover stammered. 'Are you sure that this is the way you want to handle it? Surely just giving Tristan and his team a shoot-to-kill remit would handle things a little smoother.'

Glass chuckled.

'But that doesn't send the right message, does it?' Glass shook his head. 'Right now, that man has done more damage to my reputation than any disgruntled member going to the press could. Anything anyone leaks or tries to give to the media, we could squash it under our boot in an instant. But Pope? He's done something that makes a mockery of everything I have promised people.'

'And that is?'

'He proved we were breachable,' Glass said venom-laced. 'He showed every person who has shaken with fear when they have come face to face with me, that what I have promised them isn't true. That Veilmont is not the whisper that we pride ourselves on being. And for that, my dear Charles, for that…he needs to be made an example of.'

'I understand it's just…it's short notice.'

'Did you say who was up for auction?' Glass snapped a hard glare at his assistant who nodded meekly. 'Then I have no doubt we will have a full house. Where is Tristan?'

'He's in the lounge.' Glover nodded across the restaurant to the door that connected through to the classy bar area, lined with leather sofas, and stocked with some of the most expensive liquors in the country. 'Shall I call him through?'

Glass waved him away.

'He can sit and stew on things for a while longer.' Glass smirked. 'Besides, I'm never shy of a gun or two, am I?'

Before Glover could force a response, a panicked scream echoed through the doorway into the lounge, and frantic footsteps shook the building, as dozens of patrons scuttled through the restaurant. The anxiety spread like wildfire, and the volume erupted as Tristan emerged in the doorway, walking backwards with his hands held up in surrender. As he stepped back between the tables, the fear exploded within the room as the Glock 17 that was pressed against his forehead came into view.

Glass scoffed.

It was hard not to be impressed, as the hand on the other end of the gun belonged to Sam Pope.

When Sam's eyes locked his own, Glass gestured to the seat opposite him, and took his own, as Sam marched Tristan towards the table. He sat Tristan down opposite Glover, and then, with the gun still trained on the hitman, Sam took the seat opposite Glass.

The most powerful man in Europe opposite its most dangerous vigilante.

Glass smiled, as he was certain that the look in Sam's eye was of the same acceptance he felt. That this was only going to end it one of two ways.

It just remained to be seen which one of them would kill the other.

Paris was an easy city to go missing in, and as soon as Sam had disappeared underground, he was in the wind. He'd rode the train a few stops before switching to another line, and thirty minutes after killing the majority of a hit squad, he was halfway across the capital. Eventually, they'd track his steps, but with the chaos he'd left behind, it would likely take the police a few days to trace his steps and by then, he was hoping to be long gone.

But there was just the matter of bringing down the most powerful man in Europe first.

Within hours of infiltrating and exposing one of Glass' main sites, Sam wasn't shocked that a hit squad was sent his way. What was surprising, was that they weren't shooting to kill. He had been on too many missions during his decades within the military and spent too many hours behind the scope of a rifle to know when someone is pulling the trigger with intent. The team that he'd put in the ground were trying to capture him alive, which meant Sebastian Glass had other ideas for him.

Other plans.

And Sam wanted to know what they were, and considering he wanted to give the man the opportunity to dissolve his organisation and face the consequences of his crimes, there felt like no time like the present to meet the man face to face. Ranjit was able to trace the man's movements and located the booking at *Le Ciel* for that evening.

Despite Ranjit's pointing out the obvious that Glass would have security, Sam was adamant that he was going to walk into that restaurant, look the man in the eye, and give him one chance to do the right thing.

If he said no, then Sam was ready to declare war.

That night, just as the sun touched down behind the horizon and bathed the sky in a haunting, red glow, Sam made his way into the Montparnasse Tower and rode the elevator all the way to the fifty sixth floor. As the doors pinged open, he marched through, bypassing the maître d' who was standing, pristinely dressed, by the altar near the front of the restaurant. The man angrily called out for Sam to stop as he stormed past, and as the heads in the lounge began to swivel, Sam had already locked his eyes on the man who earlier that day had unloaded a shotgun in his direction.

The man followed the ruckus, saw Sam, and his hand instinctively went to the inside of his jacket.

Sam's was quicker.

The appearance of the gun sent the room into a tail-spin, but both he and the hit man remained calm.

'Up.' Sam commanded, and the burly, bearded man obliged, and Sam casually stepped forward and pressed the gun against the man's shiny forehead. 'Move. Slowly.'

The man obliged, taking careful steps backwards as Sam guided him with the pressure of the gun steel against his skull. As they emerged into the decadent restaurant, the panic spread like a lethal virus through the room, and Sam kept his grip tight as he scanned the room.

It didn't take long to spot Glass.

The man stood swiftly, a monument of composure, as the rest of the room was transfixed with fear. It was also easy to spot the two other men in the room who were clearly Glass's paid security. Glass gestured to the seats surrounding his table, and Sam led the gunman across the room before shoving him down into the seat. Then, keeping the gun trained on the only other trained killer at the table, Sam sat down opposite the man behind Veilmont, and a broken looking man who Sam assumed was an assistant.

'Very impressive,' Glass said. 'A little theatrical for my tastes, but, impressive none the less.'

Glass made a show of pouring out a glass of wine, as if everything was normal.

'Well, they were fully booked tonight.' Sam replied, drawing a grin from Glass.

'They usually are. The seafood here is to die for. You should try it.'

'The seafood or dying?' Sam asked with a shrug. 'Because this man here and his team weren't trying to kill me earlier. They were trying to capture me.'

'Quite right.' Glass nodded approvingly toward Tristan. 'I made that clear. I told you I'd be seeing you, didn't I?'

'Well, here I am,' Sam said firmly. 'And I don't have too long until the police show up, and right now, I reckon I'm a pretty popular guy. So let me make this quick…'

'Oh, please do,' Glass said mockingly, sitting back in his chair and crossing his leg over the other.

'Shut it all down.' Sam's words were full of menace. 'Every single outpost you have. Shut it down. Anyone who you have in captivity. Any man, woman or child that you are putting through hell. You let them go. And then you take yourself, along with the long list of names that use your service, and you march yourself straight to the police and hand it all over.'

Glass held Sam's hate-filled gaze for a few moments, knowing that the smug look on his own face was dissolving into one of repulsion. People didn't make demands of him.

The very thought of it flipped his stomach.

'Is that it?' Glass finally said before he took a sip of wine. 'It doesn't seem like I get much out of it.'

'You get to live.'

The words cut through Glass' composure, and he slammed his fist down on the table.

'Do you understand who I am? Huh?' Glass took a breath and straightened his tie. 'The men you have taken down before, Sam. Men like Harry Chapman or Frank Jackson. Balikov. The Munroe family. All of these untouchable people…they all belonged to me. Do you understand? These seemingly imperious figures that you went to war with…they were in my pocket. What you think you know about power, Sam, is only half right.'

Glass clicked his fingers, and the two men that Sam had clocked on his way in rose from their seats amongst the terrified civilians, their own handguns drawn and locked onto Sam. Glass smirked and continued.

'I can have you killed, right here, in front of all these people, and nobody would even think about knocking on my door.' Glass finished his drink. 'So, allow me to reject your offer, Sam, and make one of my own. Lower your weapon. Come with me. And I'll make sure that the people who you hold dear, and trust me, I will find out who they are, end up as fucking instruments of pleasure in my Havens. Do you understand me?'

'I do,' Sam said calmly. 'Which means we're at an impasse. Which means, you have chosen the second option.'

Glass laughed.

'Which is?'

'War.'

The word hung in the air between them for a few moments, and Glass' mask slipped again into a vicious snarl.

'You don't want to go to war with me.'

Sam ignored him and continued.

'Like I said. Brick by brick. Haven by Haven. I will tear down everything you have, until you are put in front of the world, and made to face the law for your crimes.'

'I've had enough of this…'

Before Glass could signal to his men to fire, Sam cut him off by pulling his other hand up from under the table. His fingers had been wrapped around the live grenade ever since they'd taken their seats. The panic in the room melted into genuine terror as Sam held the explosive up for everyone to see, and he placed his gun down on the table and slid a finger through the pin. Glass held up his hand to warn his men.

'You can't be serious?' Glass snapped. 'You wouldn't dare.'

'Try me,' Sam said, stepping away from the table and taking slow steps towards the door, his hands still ready to detonate the grenade with a simple pull. 'You drop me and I take this whole floor with me.'

Glass ground his teeth with frustration, and he stood and stared down Sam as the man made his careful way back towards the entrance, the entire restaurant now ducking for cover.

'This isn't over, Sam.' Glass warned. 'Not by a long shot.'

Sam looked Glass dead in the eye and responded.

'I know.'

Then Sam ducked out of the restaurant and hit the button for the elevator. As it arrived and he stepped through, he heard a gunshot ring out, a cacophony of screams echo behind it, and a bullet thudded the wall beside the elevator.

The doors closed before another bullet could follow, and Sam made it all the way to the ground floor before he broke out into a sprint, bursting out through the glass doors to the impressive tower, before once again being welcomed into the embrace of the mazy city.

The battle lines had been drawn.

It was just a matter of who shot first.

CHAPTER NINETEEN

Sam pushed open the door to Theo's house, the wooden frame shaking against the rickety brickwork that had been obliterated by the blast. The howling wind accompanied the wind that lashed against his spine, and Sam was soaked to the bone.

Somewhere, he could hear the roar of a car engine, but when he turned and looked back down the street, there was nothing but darkness.

No other houses.

No road.

No pavement.

All that existed was the broken house before him, thick smoke pouring through the shattered windows. Taking a deep breath, Sam stepped over the threshold and into the hallway.

There was no smoke.

Surprisingly, his view was clear, and he could see the trail of blood from the front door to the living room, which he followed with careful steps. He looked down in his hand, his fingers acquainting themselves with an unfamiliar handgun that he didn't remember acquiring. None of it felt real, but the pain that thumped through his chest felt harder than anything. It was a familiar feeling.

Not pain.

Loss.

Sam lifted the gun expertly in his hand, took a few steps across the hall and pushed open the door to the living room, clearing each corner with precision that was as natural as breathing.

It was clear.

As he lowered his weapon, he heard a gasp from the corner of the room. As he spun and raised the weapon, he startled as Amy Devereux, his therapist, was seated in the chair, her legs neatly folded and a pad on her lap.

'Sam. Please. Put the gun down,' She said with the strictness of a headteacher. 'This isn't how these sessions are supposed to go.'

Sam looked around, the harsh smell of burning began to filter through the hallway from the kitchen. The house shook violently, as if hit by a wrecking ball. Plaster clattered to the ground beside him, and Sam looked up at the hole in the ceiling. He then turned back to Amy.

There was no furniture in the room anymore.

No decorations.

Just the remnants of a room, obliterated by an explosion.

'Sam.'

He heard her voice call out from the kitchen, and as Sam turned to the door, it slammed shut on its hinges, and the rising heat melted it in its frame. Sam slammed his shoulder against it, over and over, and pulled as hard as he could on the handle.

It wouldn't budge.

Loss was a hell of a feeling.

But it was the guilt that hung heaviest, and with every strain of the handle, and every slam of his shoulder, Sam knew it was guilt he would never budge.

Guilt that would stay with him until his dying day.

'Dad.'

A voice echoed behind Sam, and he froze. Both hands were planted against the splintered wood of the unmovable door, and he hung his head. Jamie's voice was a distant memory now, and that fact drove Sam's mission more than anything else. What had started as a release of his grief had evolved into a necessity that had saved countless lives. That purpose should have been enough.

But forgetting the sound of his son's voice only added gasoline to the fire that burned within, and Sam begged himself not to turn round.

Not to face his dead son.

Because he couldn't remember him correctly, and Sam knew he was dreaming. Knew he was getting locked inside his own guilt once more, and he knew that the passage of time had begun to rub away at the edges of his beloved son. The finer details of the face would be missing, and the colour of his son's hair would be ever so slightly off.

Like looking at an echo.

A reverb of an image that once existed.

'Dad'. The voice cried again. 'Please. Just let us go.'

'Us?' Sam said, his head down and his voice breaking.

'All of us.'

Jamie's words carried a sadness that a father couldn't ignore, and Sam turned and dropped to his knees. The living room had been transformed into a kitchen, which had been blown to smithereens by a hand grenade. Amongst the wreckage on the ground, Jamie's lifeless body stared up at Sam, the bones contorted from the impact of the drunk driver.

Beside his dead son, Sam laid his eyes on Carl Marsden, who was clutching the bullet hole that had ripped open his stomach. He gurgled one final time and then passed.

Beside him, Matthew McCoughlin lay riddled with bullets, his disfigured face a monument to the torture he'd suffered during his time as a prisoner of war.

Left behind by Sam.

The back wall of the kitchen was missing, and Sam watched as both his ex-wife, Lucy, and Mel Hendry were both walking away, tears in their eyes as they knew they couldn't be part of what Sam had become.

All the people Sam had loved.

All the people Sam had lost.

Flickers of flames began to ride up the walls, and Sam could smell the burning before he re-opened his eyes. Ash was falling like dark snow across the room, and leant against the wall, his body blown half to bits was Theo Hunter, Sam's best friend and a man he had served with for years during the army.

The man who had stood beside him when he'd married Lucy.

A man who, if Sam had been the religious type, would have been Jamie's godfather.

And a man who, despite not knowing her, had laid down his life to protect Amy Devereux at Sam's request.

With his limbs missing, and his flesh peeling back like lit paper, Theo coughed and smiled at Sam.

'You've given them everything, Sam.' He coughed some more. 'How much is enough?'

Sam closed his eyes and took a deep breath. All he could see were the broken children he'd salvaged from the Haven's basement.

His jaw set, and his now empty hands balled into fists.

'It's never enough.'

And the ceiling creaked and cracked before it collapsed upon them, snapping Sam out of his nightmare.

The terror rating in Paris had been raised from substantial to critical, and every news outlet on television and online was running through the series of events of the past twenty-four hours. Politicians from both sides of the political divide were weighing in on the sudden outburst of violence that had hit the capital city over the past few days, using Sam Pope's war against Veilmont as a way to score points with the voters.

The streets weren't safe.

Those in power weren't doing enough to protect the people.
Those wanting power would lean too far the other way.

It was a media circus, with the narrative being wrestled away from the truth by those who stood to gain from a public who were scared at the potential threats that now waited for them on their own doorstep.

Sam wished he could tell them the truth, but a public announcement that he was behind the incidents that had rocked the city over the past forty eight hours as he went to war with a billionaire with ties to every powerful government in the continent, would just end with a bullet placed firmly between his eyes, and his mission buried with him.

So, as he sat on the reasonably comfortable bed of the motel room he had booked, he read the subtitles that rolled along the bottom of the small screen that the room afforded. After leaving the Montparnasse Tower the night before, Sam had switched between trains before hopping on a coach that took him beyond La Francillienne to a small commune called Bondoufle. South of the capital city, the quiet town had just over ten thousand residents, and Sam headed to the taxi rank near the coach station and simply said *'motel'*.

Fifteen minutes after that, the driver pulled off the motorway and into a layby, where a dingy motel welcomed Sam with it's flickering *'vacance'* sign and a promise of a mediocre night's sleep.

It had been just what he needed, and he was surprised to find a burger van parked just beyond the motel grounds in the morning, and the greasy bacon baguette he devoured for breakfast was the tastiest thing Sam had eaten in what felt like days.

Given the choice between another one of those or anything off the *Le Ceil* menu that Glass had ordered from, Sam knew what he'd choose. As he sipped the bitter coffee he'd made from the machine in reception, he watched as the news reader once again announced that five men had been killed in a hostel in Paris, a day after a terrorist attack on a jewellery store in the 'diamond district' that saw DGSE and local law enforcement open fire.

Along with the reported incidents in a nondescript building outside of the city, and the reported suicide bomber at *La Ceil*.

'Finesse isn't exactly your strong suit.'

Corbin wasn't wide of the mark when she'd said that, and when Sam had made contact with her that morning, she warned him how her boss and the head of the DGSI were now pulling their resources to build a brand new counter terrorist unit, with the express purpose of tracing through the incidents of the past few days and holding those responsible to account.

In essence, it meant the net was about to get pulled in tight, and when they eventually made their way to Sam, there would be nothing she would be able to do from stopping his inevitable execution. Although France had abolished the death penalty over forty years ago, they would both be naïve to think that Sam would walk away from his capture alive.

Especially when a man like Sebastian Glass was presumably pulling some of the strings.

Corbin was thankful he was alive, warned him to behave himself and once again suggested he just walk away. When that was met with usual rejection, she had sighed, lit a cigarette and told him that Cheyrou had been reported missing. They were following his movements from when he was collected from the hospital, as "decisions" were made to drop the potential charges.

No one had seen him since.

Sam hung up the phone, wondering what state they would find the man's corpse in, when he then took a call from Ranjit, who seemed a little more appreciative of Sam's actions.

'*Fuckin' hell, mate. You should see the news back here.*' Ranjit had chuckled over the phone. '*They think a terrorist cell is planning to take down the government since it's still in a spiral after what you did a year ago. Tell me, Sam…do you just hate France?*'

Sam had found that amusing and then pushed Ranjit for an update on the encryption. Syphoning the contact list from Glass' phone was proving to be tricky, as the encryption software was beyond anything Ranjit had ever seen before. It wasn't a dead end, but it was requiring a multitude of programs to run at the same time, at a high bandwidth, and he'd already invested in two external hard drives to speed up the process.

'Just take it out of the account,' Sam had said as he motioned to hang up the call.

'*Will do, Sam. Oh, and Sam…*' Ranjit's voice squeaked up to him.. '*Just try to stay alive, okay?*'

Remnants of Sam's dream flashed through his mind's eye, and he shook them clear before responding.

'You, too, Ranj. Just stay alert.'

'*Come on, now.*' Ranjot chuckled. '*I'm not the one blowing up Paris.*'

Ranjit hung up, and Sam took the opportunity to take a walk through Bondoufle to clear his head. Guilt was beginning to seep through the cracks in his psyche, and speaking to good people like Corbin and Ranjit just reminded him of the good people he'd lost along the way.

Lost to his fight.

And he didn't want to lose anymore.

It always baffled Ranjit how calm Sam was, despite the situation. He'd seen it first hand when Guardian had tried to pin the murder of former Deputy Commissioner Ruth Ashton on him, and he'd systematically taken down the entire operation. People seemed to deem several other characteristics as vital to getting ahead in life.

Intelligence.

Strength.

Resilience.

But Ranjit was certain that composure trumped them all, and even if you took away Sam's lethality with his bare hands or behind the scope of a weapon, it was his ability to slow himself down and control any situation that made him so deadly.

Ranjit was a little less calm, but he knew he had his own strengths that were now a vital cog in Sam Pope's fighting machine. He was able to open doors, both physical and digital for Sam, and working at arm's length from the firing line meant the risk he was taking was minimal.

Every digital footprint he left was covered, and every avenue he ventured down was untraceable to the standard issue tracking software of the British government and law enforcement.

Even though he was sitting in an office in the middle of Kings Cross, one of the busiest parts of London, Ranjit knew he had never been more untraceable in his life. The only people who knew where he was, were Sam, and his wife and kids.

And Ranjit turned and looked at the photo of his family that he had on his desk and allowed the reminder of why he wanted a safer world to hit him once more. It would help him push on, keep trying his best to unlock the list of names for Sam, and help him bring down Sebastian Glass and Veilmont.

Looking at the photo also meant he wasn't looking at his screen, meaning he didn't see the reflection on the glass of the door to his office being silently opened behind him.

And it meant, as the piano wire was wrapped over his throat and pulled tightly, Ranjit's eyes were locked on his family's faces as they bulged during the struggle.

It meant, as he was strangled to death, Ranjit was thinking of his family, and ironically, how he was making the world a safer place for them.

CHAPTER TWENTY

'You sure that's him?'

Vivier called up from the floor of the printing press, a hint of resignation already in his voice. The *experts de la police scientifique* were already working their way around the factory, running over everything with a fine-tooth comb. On the metal walkway over the pulping machine was Corbin, who had been guided up there by the lead detective from the *préfecture de police de Paris* who had been handed the case.

Corbin nodded glumly, looking over the metal railing to the blood-soaked metal rollers of the printing press below.

Cheyrou had been disposed of, that much was evident, but what was worse was the fact that no effort was made to hide it.

This was a message.

The city had been sent into a spin when Cheyrou had been abducted two days prior, and when news began to spread that he was in custody, the rumour mill kicked into overdrive. The internet was a dangerous place to rely on for actual information, and rumours of his arrest were heavily linked towards the illegal trafficking of blood diamonds. Cheyrou was a well-known, well-regarded man of influence in the city, and Corbin had been aware that moves would be made to see him released from custody as soon as possible. When Vivier had told her that the pressure had been applied, and the man was walking free after less than twenty-four hours, she had felt sick to her stomach.

What they had found at the Haven had been truly disturbing, and she implored Vivier to stand up to the inevitable protection that Cheyrou would be afforded.

But they'd let the man go, and Corbin had clenched her fists until her nails drew blood to stop herself from smacking the smug look off the man's face.

Now, his face, just like the rest of him, had been rendered to paste, all apart from the severed finger that had been presented on the control panel of the apparatus that had crushed him to death. Corbin left that for the *experts de la police scientifique* to bag up and put through the appropriate channels, but she was certain that the print that had been gift-wrapped for them would identify the red staining and the squishy remnants of flesh and bone as Cheyrou. She thanked the detective and then headed back down the metal steps, where Vivier was now on a call. As always, the Director of the DGSE was in high demand, even more so when the country was on high alert. Vivier was aware that Corbin had someone who was rattling the cages, and she did wonder how much rope he'd give her or Sam before he needed to hang one of them with it. As she stepped off the final step, she took one more glance towards the large, blood-soaked equipment, and shuddered at the thought of a human being passed through it. When she turned back, Vivier hung up the call and took a deep, resigned breath.

'Everything okay, sir?' She asked, knowing it was a

pointless question. Vivier looked around at the law enforcement who were working their way through the scene, and he headed for the door of the factory, encouraging Corbin to follow. She did, and when she stepped outside, Vivier was already pacing.

'Just orders.' He huffed. 'Do you happen to have any cigarettes on your?'

Corbin nodded and dipped her hand into her jacket and pulled out the pack. She handed one to her boss and then took one for herself.

'I don't think I've quite got the hang of quitting,' she joked. Vivier took a long drag and frowned.

'I've been quitting for years.' He exhaled. 'This is the best I've done so far.'

The two stood in silence for a moment, watching as the *préfecture de police de Paris* continued the process of closing down the crime scene and obtaining everything they needed. Young officers stood on the cordons that held back the interested public, many of whom were showing a lack of class by holding their phones up to try and use the serious situation to garner a sliver of attention online. Corbin shook her head with disdain, and Vivier stubbed out his cigarette and watched as the black Citroën C5 Aircross made its way through the traffic and was waved through by the officers. Vivier patted Corbin on the arm and began to walk towards the vehicle.

'With me, Renée,' he said calmly, although the order was clear. Corbin swiftly took a final puff, flicked the butt, and scurried after her boss.

'Where are we going?' She asked, as Vivier opened the door for her. She got in and he joined her in the back seat.

'We've been called in.' Vivier looked solemnly out of the window. 'It seems your guy on the inside has upset one too many people with his little stunt in *La Ceil* last night.'

'They don't know it's…'

Vivier held up a weary hand to cut her off, as the car pulled out of the car park, and the driver carefully guided the vehicle through the throngs of interested spectators.

'Please, Renée. There was CCTV and plenty of eyewitnesses. We now know that Sam Pope held a man at gunpoint and threatened an entire building of people with an explosive device.' Vivier blew out his cheeks. 'The time for making excuses is over. So please, not just as your superior officer, but as your friend…when you get asked for what you know, just give them what you know. Your loyalty to Pope is not worth what will happen next.'

'But what if what he's doing is important?' Corbin snapped back.

'Then you'd better hope he gets it done before they catch up with him.' Vivier sighed and cast his eyes on the city as it sped by. Sensing the conversation was over, Corbin turned away and lost herself to her thoughts. They had found horrors at the Haven that Sam had taken down, and wherever Sam ventured next, she was certain he'd find worse.

He'd try his best to bring it all down and ensure those responsible were taken to task for their crimes.

But how did this all end?

Was Sam really going to walk away from what was looking like a powerful organisation with ties to the upper end of the French government?

Would they let a wanted terrorist walk off into the sunset?

Would the remnants of her career be thrown on the fire also?

It was only as the car began to roll to a stop that Corbin finally snapped out of her thought process, and when she did, her eyes widened with a shocked realisation that they were not back at the CAT. The building before them was a derelict factory, with shattered windows replaced with flapping tarp, and rusty, corrugated iron plates hanging from the walls. Through the window of her door, Corbin could see the black van and the Hyundai Santa Fe with tinted windows parked across the vacant lot. Several burly men were stood, clad in black, arms folded, their eyes locked on her vehicle, and standing in front of all of them was a well-groomed man in an immaculately fitted, pin-stripe designer suit. The driver killed the engine, and Corbin spun to Vivier who was already exiting the car.

'Sir?! What did you do?' She barked, but Vivier stepped out and turned back.

'Just, make this as easy as possible, Renée. Please.'

Before she could respond, her door was wrenched open, and a bald man with a thick beard hooked a powerful arm around her neck and hauled her from the back seat. She kicked and thrashed a few times, but he simply threw her to the hard concrete below and then drove a boot into her ribs for good measure. The air rushed from her lungs, and as she heaved and gasped for her breath, the man snatched a handful of hair and crudely dragged her to her feet.

Vivier stood a few feet away, unable to make eye contact with her.

Beyond him, the heavily armed men looked on with disinterest.

But right before her stood Sebastian Glass, and his eyes twinkled with excitement. His fair hair was slicked back, and his cleanly-shaved jaw broke into a perfect smile.

'Agent Corbin,' he said softly. 'There are two ways this ends for you. The first way is what I call the path of least resistance. Meaning, you call Sam, you tell him where to meet you, and we end this little issue we have as soon as possible. Comply without fuss, and maybe…just maybe, I will let you live.'

Corbin didn't respond to him.

Her eyes were locked on her feeble boss, who shuffled uncomfortably on the spot.

'You coward.' She snapped. 'Look at me, you fucking coward.'

Tristan yanked her head back harshly, cutting off her tirade, and Glass chuckled as he turned to Vivier, who was damp with nerves.

'Does she always speak to you like this?' He took a step closer to her. 'Or there is option two.'

Corbin spat in Glass' face.

The responding fist rocked her jaw so hard, she thought it would shatter. Tristan let her drop to the floor, and she spat a mouthful of blood across the concrete. She turned back, and the handsome, composed man was now looming over her, his eyes wide and his face contorted with rage.

'You disgusting bitch!' Glass roared, but then took a beat, ran a hand through his hair, and took a calming breath. As he straightened his tie, he seemed a man transformed once again. 'Allow me to tell you what option you just selected. You will now accompany me to an event where I, and a select number of my customers, will bring your friend, Sam Pope, to an end. You will watch him fight, my dear. You will watch him fail. And you will watch him die. And you will sleep every night with the knowledge that he was only there because of you. But then that means, you are responsible for the debt that he has yet to pay.'

'You don't scare me,' Corbin said as she bravely pushed herself back to her feet. 'Do what you want to me, but I won't bring you to Sam.'

Tristan swiftly locked her arms behind her back with one powerful arm and then fished her phone from her pocket. He tossed it to Glover, who immediately scurried off, and Glass took a step back and wrapped an arm around Vivier's shoulder. It was a belittling power move, one designed to inform both Vivier and Corbin how little of it their badges actually wielded.

'It's a shame to lose her, huh?' Glass said, before patronisingly patting Vivier on the back. 'Still, the fight she has in her, she will be just fine working off that debt in one of my Havens. And trust me, Agent Corbin, I have *plenty* of members who will pay good money to literally fuck the justice system.'

As the smug grin began to spread across Glass' face, Corbin tried to launch forward, only to be held in place by the towering Tristan. Glass looked her up and down a few times, nodded with appreciation, and then patted Vivier on the shoulder and sent him on his way. As he took a few steps back towards his car, he stopped and turned back to Corbin, finally meeting her hateful stare with bloodshot eyes.

'I'm sorry, Renée. I told you to leave it alone.'

Corbin spat a wad of blood at his feet.

'I was just doing my job. Sir.'

Vivier ducked into the back of the Aircross, and was soon a distant spec, hurtling through the wasteland that surrounded the abandoned factory. Corbin had been abandoned, left in the hands of the murderous Sebastian Glass, with the promise of a fate worse than death. As Glass clasped his hands together and told his crew to move out, he took one last look at Corbin and smirked.

She responded with the only thing she had left.

Defiance.

'Sam will kill you,' she said through blood-stained, gritted teeth.

Glass flashed his spotless veneers in response.

'My dear. I'm betting he's willing to die for you.'

Then everything went black, as a hood was roughly pulled over Corbin's head, and as she stumbled through the darkness, she was slammed into the side of the van.

Cable ties were wrapped around her wrists, the plastic piercing the skin, and then she was tossed into the back of the van. Before the door slammed shut, she heard Glass' voice one last time.

'Not too rough.'

The door slammed shut, and moments later, the van pulled away, and Corbin knew that wherever they were heading, it was unlikely she'd be coming back.

CHAPTER TWENTY-ONE

Something didn't feel right.

It had been a few hours since Sam had spoken to Ranjit, but something felt off. That nagging sense of guilt that had infiltrated his sleep was now clawing at the back of his mind, and Sam knew he was putting an innocent man in harm's way. Sure, Ranjit might have been breaking several laws to aid and abet his quest for justice, but Sam knew that Ranjit was a good man.

A good man who was working to provide for his family and make the world a better place along the way.

So why did something feel off?

Sam had left the motel and taken in what passed as the sights of the small commune of Bondoufle, and the sports centre and golf course were hardly streaming with tourists. As the guilt and the worry collided in his mind, Sam pulled out his phone and called Ranjit.

No answer.

With a frustrated sigh, Sam pocketed the phone once more, telling himself to keep his head straight.

Stay focused.

Ranjit was most likely chained to his desk, his eyes

scanning the bright screens before him as chill-hop music pumped through his noise cancelling headphones. It was a waiting game right now, and all Sam had to do was wait for his associate to work his magic, crack through the encryption software that was protecting Glass' contacts, and then Sam would have enough leverage to take down Veilmont.

But by the time Sam had returned to the motel, that nagging doubt had blossomed to a fully formed concern, and he once again called Ranjit.

No answer.

He tried again.

No answer.

Sam tossed the phone onto the bed and paced the room. To occupy his mind, he pulled out the two Glock 17s he had in his possession, dismantling the weapons with ease and cleaning each component thoroughly. The difference between life and death could come down to the state of the weapon, and Sam had spent his entire life treating his armoury with the respect it deserved.

When he'd put the second gun back together, he had killed over an hour, and there was still no contact. It had been hours since Sam had tried to make contact, and Ranjit was a frequent smoker, meaning he'd have had ample time to respond.

Something was wrong.

Then the phone pinged.

Ranjit: Photo Image Attached

Sam breathed a sigh of relief and tapped the open button and then felt the lump catch in his throat, and his blood slowly start to boil. The image was of his friend, laying motionless on the floor of his office, his eyes wide open but the life having long since left them. The whites of his eyes were strewn with burst blood vessels, and the thick, purple bruising around his throat, which surrounded the harsh, red burns of a piano wire, told Sam all he needed to know.

Ranjit had been murdered.

Strangled at the desk where he sat, by the men Sam had ordered him to track down.

'Fuck.' Sam uttered, and dropped down onto the bed, his hand locked around the phone like a mechanical vice.

Ranjit wasn't a soldier.

He wasn't born to fight, nor was he trained or prepared for the idea that he could die in the line of duty.

He was an IT technician turned hacker, who's only real exposure to danger was navigating the London Underground on a daily basis.

He was a husband.

A father of two.

An innocent man.

And Sam could feel the guilt hanging from his neck like a weighted chain, and as he dipped his head, he gave a guttural roar of anger. It reverberated off the thin walls of the motel room, the echo of his fury bouncing around the room and shaking the entire facility to its foundations. Sam blinked out a few tears, both of them a combination of his grief and his rage, and he hit Ranjit's number once more and lifted the phone to his ear.

Still no answer.

The photo was the only communication he would get, and it was a notification that they could get to Sam as quickly as he could get to them. But now, they had cut off his intel, meaning Sam was now stranded in a small village outside of Paris, with the most powerful organisation in the world plotting his downfall.

He was on his own.

His phone buzzed.

Corbin.

Sam wiped away the tears of anger and took the call.

'Renée. Things just got…'

'Sam, just run. Okay? Just…'

Corbin's panicked voice cut off, as the phone was clearly pulled away from her face. Sam stood and every muscle tightened in his body, as he heard her struggle before a familiar voice crackled in his ear.

'Mr Pope.'

'Glass.'

'I trust I have your attention now, do I?' Glass made no attempt to hide the enjoyment in his voice. 'So why don't we discuss what happens next.'

Sam was already lifting the gun from the table of his motel room and stuffing it into the back of his jeans.

'I'll tell you what happens next. First, you're going to let her go. And then I am going to kill you for what you did to my friend.'

The sound of Glass' defiant chuckle sent a surge of anger coursing through Sam like a second pulse.

'Your friend died because he was digging around where he wasn't welcome. And who advised him to do that? You did, Sam. So don't look any further than a mirror if you want to know who orphaned that man's girls.' The mention of Ranjit's family froze Sam on the spot. Glass could clearly sense it. 'Rita Siddique. Their children, Minal and Heena. Do you want me to continue? Shall I read you out their address?'

Sam felt a tear roll over his eyelid and slide down his cheek, and the bass in his voice deepened with his anger.

'If you lay a fucking finger on them I swear…'

'Oh, enough. Please.' Glass snapped with an over-the-top sigh. 'We could do this all day long, but neither of us wants that. I told you yesterday, this isn't over. It will never be over until you pay for the damage you have done to my business and the reputation I have spent years building. Now, I appreciate you think there is a way out of the situation for you and your friend, but allow me to assure you the only thing you have left to control is how painless I make this for you.'

Sam heard the crunch of tyres on the gravel of the motel forecourt, and as he peeped through the dusty shutters that hung across his window, he saw two black 4x4's pulling to a stop, and half a dozen armed men stepped out. Glass was clearly being updated, as he continued.

'Now, my men will take you, unarmed, and escort you to me. If you refrain from this in any way, if you raise a hand or a weapon to any of them, I will take off one of Agent Corbin's limbs. If you continue to fight back against what is going to happen, I will take her apart, limb by limb until she is just a body and a head, and I will strap her into a harness in the darkest fucking room I have and let the worst people have at her until she begs to be put out of her misery.' Glass' stopped, calming himself down. *'Am I clear?'*

Sam took another look through the window, weighing up his chances. Three of the men made little attempt to shield their FAMAS assault rifles from view, and Sam didn't fancy the chances of the cheap plasterboard keeping the bullets out. They could rip the room to shreds with one magazine and then Sam would be leaving Corbin to the horrors that Glass had promised.

Sam's silence irked Glass, who spoke again.

'Am I clear, Sam? Or do you need another photo, maybe of Ranjit's youngest fucking daughter before you realise that this is now out of your control?'

'Okay.' Sam responded calmly. 'I'll come easily. But I swear to God, if you hurt her or Ranjit's family in any way…'

'I think the time for your threats are over, Sam. Step outside, go with my men, and then face your consequences like the good little soldier you are.' Glass paused for a moment. *'Do that, and all I'll do is put a bullet through the bitch's skull.'*

The phone cut out, and Sam stood on the spot. For his entire life, he had never believed in no win situations. His former commanding officer, Sergeant Marsden, had chastised him countless times during his storied career in the military for never backing down when the odds were stacked.

Sam had been built for survival, and that had continued through his war on organised crime.

From the underbelly of London to Berlin, to the streets outside the Vatican. From South Carolina to a deadly prison in Serbia.

Sam had faced everything head on, knowing that, no matter how slim, there was always a chance of survival.

Always a way to win.

But as he pulled open the door, and saw two assault rifles sweep up and focus in on him, he couldn't see it.

Couldn't see any way out of this one.

Couldn't understand how, once he got into one of those vehicles, he ever came back from where he was going. The smart money would have been to bring out the gun, take his chances against highly trained killers, and try to disappear for good.

But that would leave Corbin at the mercy of a man without limits.

It would put Ranjit's family in danger.

And if there was even a whisper of a chance of stopping the worst-case scenario, then Sam would face it head on.

It was a no-win situation.

But he refused to walk away from it.

With the guns trained on Sam, he cautiously stepped out, his hands raised in surrender, and he approached the mercenary team. One of them stepped forward, pulled his own gun, and fell in behind Sam, prodding Sam in the spine as they approached the car. Another one of the men yanked open the back door for him, and as Sam went to climb in, he felt the sharp impact of metal, as the man from behind pistol whipped him in the back of the skull. The blow was like lightning, sending a crack of pain echoing through his skull, as his vision flashed erratically. Sam slumped against the car, and as the man roughly snapped cable ties to bind his wrists to the base of his spine through the loops of his jeans, Sam could feel the trickle of blood weaving through his hair and down the back of his neck.

Then they dumped him in the car, saddled up, and hit the road as fast as they could. Sam arched his neck to look out of the window, but the drowsiness began to take control, and as his consciousness began to slip away, he had no idea where he was being taken.

All he knew, as his eyes finally closed, was that it was likely to be the place where he would die.

CHAPTER TWENTY-TWO

The only consolation that Corbin could draw on was that they hadn't struck her again. The imminent threat of violence was balanced on a knife's edge, and every time one of Glass' men approached her, her body tightened both with fear and bracing for a potential impact. One of the men had intimated his attraction to her, and had even questioned why, if they were going to kill her anyway, he couldn't at least have some fun with her first, and the response had been a savage right hook from the bearded man who had struck her previously.

Judging by how hard the man hit the ground, and how long it was before he got up, Corbin realised that the man had certainly pulled his punch with her.

After Vivier had fed her to the wolves and slunk away to live with his guilt, they had loaded her into a van and driven for a few hours, and with a bag over her head, Corbin had no way of knowing where or how they got there. When they finally stopped and she was hauled from the back of the van, she realised they were at Paris Le Bourget private airport, and the private hanger that belonged to Sebastian Glass was a hive of activity.

The bearded man was clearly Glass' second in command, ordering the other hired guns to begin the process of packing up their armoury for whatever trip was being planned. When Corbin asked whether she was coming as a passenger or cargo, the man just smirked and told her it would depend on what her friend did next. Glass arrived, driven in his luxury car, and he welcomed Corbin to his hanger before turning to his weasely little assistant and demanding the swift turnaround by ensuring the roads in Stockholm were clear.

All Corbin heard was that it had been expensive, but there would be no issues for their guests.

Stockholm?

Guests?

Whatever Glass was planning, it was as decadent as the private jet that was stationed just outside of the hanger, and a couple of the armed thugs were loading crates of weapons into the cargo hold. The assistant, who stood out like a sore thumb amongst the rest of Glass' help, then took a phone call, and then handed the device over to Glass himself.

Whatever was said put a smile on his face, and then Glass pulled the phone away to check a photo that popped up on the screen. Corbin couldn't make out the finer details, but she knew a dead body when she saw one.

'Send it to him. When they are two minutes out.' Glass chuckled. 'Then we'll make the call.'

Corbin stayed quiet, strapped to a chair in the corner of the hanger, watching as the operation went about it's business. Besides the odd look of intrigue from the man who seemingly hadn't learnt his lesson, everyone went about their business, with the bearded man overseeing the successful transportation of their arsenal, whilst the bespectacled assistant hammered away on his laptop.

But it was Sebastian Glass who drew Corbin's attention.

And not only that, he also commanded her fear.

The composure with which he conducted himself was alarming, especially in the face of a battle to the death with Sam Pope, who Corbin had witnessed bring down a potential President. Glass was treating the whole ordeal like a mild inconvenience, akin to swatting a pesky fly at a picnic, but when he snatched the phone from her to confront Sam, she saw the mask slip.

His voice cracked.

The vile human snuck through.

Disgusting threats were made to her, all of which she was prepared to face head on so long as Sam turned and ran the other way.

For once, putting himself first.

But she knew that would never happen, and her heart broke slightly when Glass confirmed to the bearded man who she learned was called Tristan, that Pope was being escorted to them and would be there in under two hours. The jet was packed.

What remained of Tristan's team was on board, and the rest would join them when they arrived with their guest of honour. Glass took a seat on board with a cold drink, leaving his assistant and Corbin in the hanger.

Neither one of them spoke.

Both of them were effectively prisoners to the man, and although their circumstances couldn't have been more different, neither one had any other option other than to sit and wait for what happened next.

When Corbin heard the sound of approaching engines, her heart shattered in two.

She was about to be reunited with Sam.

And both of them were going to die.

At some point in the journey, Sam's eyes began to flick, and his stream of consciousness began to wash back through his mind. His vision was blurred, peppered with twinkling dots, as the throbbing at the back of his skull felt like a clamp on his retinas. Eventually, he blinked himself back to clarity, and the view from the window was of a rolling sky, dotted with greying clouds.

An hour later, amidst the heavy, inner-city traffic, commercial aeroplanes began to cut through the sky, and the increase in rumbling told him they were near the airport. When the car finally came to a stop, Sam had pushed himself up to a seated position, his hands still firmly clamped to the back of his trousers, and he could see the private jet that was waiting for them outside of Glass' hanger. Three armed men stepped out from the hanger, their fingers ready and most certainly willing, and they clasped hands with the men who filtered from the car in front.

The man who had caused the gash on the back of Sam's skull opened the door and demanded Sam step out. He obliged him, and as they walked towards the hanger, the man needlessly shoved Sam forward a few feet in a pathetic attempt of intimidation.

There was no need.

Sam wasn't afraid of what awaited him.

His only fear was that he'd drag Corbin down whatever hole Glass decided to push him down.

As he emerged into the hanger, Sam's eyes immediately fell on Corbin, who struggled against the restraints of her chair.

'Renée.' Sam called out, and as he burst towards her, Tristan's fist collided with Sam's stomach with such force that it took him off his feet and he collapsed on the floor, gasping for breath.

A few of the other men chuckled, but all that Sam could hear as he drew as much air as he could back into his lungs, was the patronising sound of tutting.

Sebastian Glass stepped between his hired guns, hiked his expensive trousers up, and then squatted down beside Sam.

'This doesn't seem very dignified now, does it?' Glass shook his head and then clicked his fingers. As soon as they snapped, two men hauled Sam back to his feet and stood him a few feet from Glass. The billionaire cockily smirked at Sam and then nodded to the nearest henchman. 'Cut him free.'

'Sir?'

'It's okay. He's not going to do anything, are you, Sam?'

Sam stayed silent, and the man stepped behind him, flicked a knife, and Sam felt the blade slice through the cable ties. Without hesitation, Sam threw a brutal haymaker, catching Glass clean across the mouth and sending him sprawling across the now cleared table and a spatter of blood across the floor.

The henchmen were on Sam like a rabid horde, pinning him down to the ground, and a few errant boots stamped down on his unprotected body, crunching him underfoot. Tristan barged his way through, hauled Sam up by the scruff of his t-shirt and drove his thick, shining forehead into Sam's face. The blow made a sickening thud, and Sam's knees buckled, but Tristan held him steady like he weighed nothing.

'Are you okay, sir?' Tristan asked, keeping his eyes on the dazed Sam in his grip. Glass stood, holding his jaw, and running his tongue across the split lip he now owned.

'Quite the arm.' Glass chuckled. 'Hold him steady.'

Tristan turned Sam towards Glass, who charged

forward and drove his knee into Sam's stomach. Sam doubled over in pain, and Tristan let him drop to his knees, and Sam had to throw his hands out to stop himself from hitting the ground.

'Now that we've gotten that out of our system, Sam, allow me to explain to you the decision you have made.' Glass stood over Sam, basking in the superiority.

He had won.

He always won.

As Sam rocked back on his knees, he looked up at Glass, squinting as the concussion from the blows to the head began to take effect. Blood trickled from the opening in his right eyebrow, and his breaths were deep and desperate.

Glass smirked.

The most dangerous man in the continent, rendered helpless before him. With a glint in his eye, he leant down to speak to his captive.

'I could have had you killed the second you stepped out of the car. Or had you thrown from the car. But I am a businessman, Sam, and unfortunately for you, you have cost me business. Now, I am a man of my word, so consider your friend's debt paid. She will not face a lifetime in Veilmont. No. We will just kill her when we're done with you.'

Sam's muscles tightened, and he looked up at Glass with hatred in his swollen eye, and he gritted his teeth.

'Just let her go.'

Glass sucked air through his teeth and shook his head.

'I'm afraid I can't. I have certain people in certain divisions of governments that need her dead. Good news, I'll make it quick. Bad news, Sam…is you're going to have to earn your death. I have a lot of people paying a lot of money just to have a chance at putting a bullet in your skull.' Glass squatted down and met Sam's eye level. The hatred between the two men was palpable. 'So, the longer you stay alive. The more money I make. How does that feel, Sam? Knowing that just fighting for your survival is funding my organisation.'

A smile cracked across Sam's battered face, and Glass sneered in anger.

'What's so fucking funny?' He demanded as the mask slipped once more.

'You stand here, with all this money, and all these men, making all these threats.' Sam shook his head slightly. 'But if you had the guts, you'd have a smoking gun in your hand and a bullet between my eyes.'

Glass took a deep breath, swallowing the rage that had roared up from his stomach, and he stood, looked down at Sam, and then cracked him across the face with the back of his hand.

'Put them on the plane.'

Glass' order was curt, and he turned on his heel and stomped up the steps that would welcome him to the luxurious cabin that would take them to Sweden. A few of the armed guards stayed behind to remove the final traces of their stay, before driving off in the blacked-out 4x4s to burn them from existence. Tristan lifted Corbin from her chair, and she flashed Sam a concerned look as he dumped her into the cargo hold. Then, he drove a boot into Sam's gut, rolled him onto his belly, and bound his wrists together once more. He then ordered two of the other men to lift Sam from each end, and moments later, he was dumped into the cargo hold beside Corbin, who quickly shuffled towards him. Before the two of them could say anything, the door slammed shut, concealing them inside the cold, pitch black storage compartment of the plane. The sound of the engine roaring was close to deafening, and as the plane hit the runway, the sound was so severe, that it shook Sam's concussion so hard, he almost passed out.

But as they lifted from the ground, and as the plane rose higher and higher into the sky, both Sam and Corbin adjusted to the dark, and to the sound.

They had also made peace with one final thought.

There was no coming back from this.

Not this time.

CHAPTER TWENTY-THREE

'You should have just left me, Sam.'

Corbin called from the darkness, as the jet hit a small patch of turbulence, and the contents of the cargo hold was thrown around with reckless abandon. With their hands still bound, both Sam and Corbin were at the mercy of the private jet, and as it jolted through the evening sky, the duo collided hard with a solid, metal trunk, and then slowly leant against it to catch their breath.

They were a few inches apart, their noses nearly touching, and as their eyes had adjusted to the darkness of the hold, Corbin could see the blood that had now plastered itself to Sam's handsome face. She wanted to reach out and comfort him with a tender hand, but like Sam, her hands were bound behind her back.

'I was never going to do that.' Sam uttered, wincing at the pain. 'I don't leave people behind.'

As the jet levelled out, Sam and Corbin both shuffled round, pressing their backs against the trunk for stability and they sat shoulder to shoulder. With a hint of sadness, Corbin lowered her head and rested it on Sam's round shoulder.

As she sighed, Sam felt a shudder of guilt echo through his body.

'I'm sorry I got you into this, Renée.'

Corbin pushed her head off of Sam's shoulder and fixed him with a glare. Even in the darkness, he could feel her eyes burning through him.

'Don't you dare try to take the blame for this, Sam. Don't even think about it.'

'If I hadn't…'

'I am an agent of the *Direction Générale de la Sécurité Extérieure*. It is my job to protect my country.'

Sam turned to Corbin, impressed by her bravery.

'I brought this to your door. Literally,' Sam said, shaking his head. 'I put you in the firing line, and now here you are. This isn't part of your job description.'

'I am here, Sam, because my boss betrayed me.' Corbin's voice trembled with anger. 'Director Vivier is either on the take or under the thumb. Either way, he handed me over to Glass like I was a dog needing to be put down. The fucking coward couldn't even look me in the eye.'

'Not many people can.' Sam shook his head. 'Not when they know they are sending someone to die.'

The defeatist tone in Sam's voice drew Corbin's attention, and she shuffled around in the small spacing between the packed-up arsenal until she was facing him.

'Sam, look at me.' He didn't listen. 'Look at me, Sam.'

Sam turned his head to face her.

'I need you to fight, Sam. Do you understand?' Corbin spoke with clear desperation.

'They killed my friend,' Sam said before he pursed his lips. 'Ranjit. His name was Ranjit. Only worked for me for the past few months. He was in with Murray, you know the one I told you about? He came to work for me when Guardian shut down. Good guy. Bit cocky. But a good guy.

Believed in what we were doing. Had two young girls…left behind a loving wife…all because of me.'

'You didn't kill him, Sam,' Corbin said sternly. But she knew the words weren't getting through.

'No. But I led them to his fucking door.' Sam sighed. 'Good people die when they fall in line with me, Renée. I've killed more people than I can remember. When I served in the army, I remembered every face that I saw through the scope of my rifle. Every person I killed in the line of duty. They stayed with me. Always right there, just in the corner of my mind, ready to surprise me when I closed my eyes. But now? Ever since I lost my son, the only faces of the dead that I remember are the ones that I lose along the way. That's why I couldn't leave you here, Renée. I don't want to add your face to that collection. I'd rather die trying than walk away.'

'I don't want you to die for me, Sam.' Corbin shuffled back beside him and rested her head again.

'Then I'll fight for you.' Sam nodded firmly, seemingly swallowing his guilt and finding his fire again. Corbin's next words caught him off guard.

'Tell me about your son.'

'Jamie?' Sam swallowed an unexpected surge of sadness. 'What do you want to know?'

'Just, everything,' Corbin said softly. 'Tell me about your boy.'

Sam chuckled a little, his eyes moistening as the memories he'd held dear began to flood his skull. As soon as the first words came to his lips, the floodgates opened, and Sam began to ramble on about his beloved Jamie.

How he always had his head in a book.

How he would often think twice before any jump, no matter how far.

How he would hum songs from the radio but not know where he knew the songs from.

How he was the most precious thing in Sam's world.

And how everything he has done, since that fateful night when he allowed Miles Hillock to drunkenly slide behind the wheel of the car, and minutes later, found the same vehicle on the pavement, and his son lying crumpled on the concrete.

With his hands bound, Sam couldn't even wipe the tears from his eyes, and as they slithered down his cheeks, they fell onto Corbin's hair. She shunted onto her knees and drew herself level with Sam's watery gaze.

And she kissed him.

A long, passionate kiss.

One that revealed every abandoned thought, and every held back word.

One that told Sam that in another life, maybe something else could have been waiting for them.

And one that told him, he wasn't alone.

That she was there with him.

And that her only hope of ever making it back to France, was if he could find that fight within himself one more time.

After the kiss, the two of them sat in silence for almost an hour, the roar of the engine and the vibration of the cargo hold put Sam in a dreamy state, which wasn't the best path to follow with a probable concussion.

'Thank you,' he replied. 'Most people don't want to talk about my Jamie, but…'

'It's good to remember the good.' Corbin smiled. 'People usually just hold onto the bad.'

The jet let out a deafening clunk, and then the sound of the wheels extending from the plane followed. The flight path changed, and Sam could feel the private jet dipping, and fifteen minutes later, the pilot navigated a smooth landing and gradually, brought the plane to a complete stop. As the engines and fans powered down, Sam and

Corbin sat patiently whilst Glass and his men disembarked and went into what Sam assumed would be another private hanger. Soon, the door would open, and they would be taken to whatever fate Glass had in store for them.

Corbin shuffled nervously. Sam called out to her.

'Renée. Just stay calm.' He nodded. 'Do whatever he asks, and I will find you. Okay? I promise you.'

Corbin took a deep breath and then nodded in agreement.

The lock to the cargo hold snapped open, and Corbin waited for the door to follow.

'And what about you, Sam?' she whispered. 'What are you going to do?'

Sam's eyes narrowed.

His bound hands flexed into fists.

His voice was laced with purpose.

'What I do best.'

Despite a career that saw him travel the world, Sam had never been to Sweden. The spring evening carried a briskness that was absent from France, and the air felt crisper.

Cleaner, somehow.

The plane had landed at Brumma Stockholm Airport, just a few kilometres outside of the capital, and Glass had clearly paid big money for his privacy. The entire business aviation terminal had been closed off, and a small, skeleton crew of workers were on hand to ensure the safe landing and disembarking of the jet. When the cargo hold had been pulled open, Sam and Corbin were greeted by the heavily bearded grin of Tristan, who warned them that any false moves would equate to unattended broken bones. When the head guard had beckoned Corbin forward, Sam had given her a reassuring nod and watched as she shuffled to the doorway. Tristan, with a surprising delicacy, helped her down and then led her away. As Tristan returned, Sam could hear the faint sound of a car engine, and then Tristan locked eyes with him.

'If I had it my way, we'd have dropped you out of the fucking plane over the Baltic.' Tristan turned and spat onto the ground. The chill revealed itself in white puffs from the man's mouth. 'But Mr Glass wants you in the best condition possible. So, the medic is going to look you over. He's going to patch you up. And then you are going to get in the car with me, and you're going to sit nicely. Is that understood?'

Sam didn't respond. His silence was enough. Tristan nodded.

'Good. Now let's get going.'

The following events played out as Tristan had demanded, and Sam had been led into the hanger to be checked over by a nervous paramedic who was clearly uncomfortable with the situation. Sam had stayed silent, beyond a few responses to basic questions, and the medic wiped the blood from his face, applied a few strips of medical tape to the gash in his eye, and then slapped a wedge of Vaseline on the gash that now dominated the back of Sam's skull. A couple of painkillers later, and the young man gave Sam the all clear, took an envelope of cash with a shaking hand, and was escorted away in the back of a black car.

Sam wondered if he'd even make it past the perimeter before they put a bullet in his brain.

Tristan shoved Sam to the 4x4 that awaited them, and strapped him in, before joining him in the back seat, gun drawn and told the driver to move. Soon, they were speeding away from the glorious city of Stockholm, heading north towards the more rural plains of the country. Rolling hills were silhouetted against the brightness of the moon, and the further from civilisation they travelled, the narrower the roads became. Every road was lined with thick trees, illuminated by the headlights of the car, and Sam watched lazily as the darkness sped by the window.

No words were spoken.

Just a silent promise that if Sam did make a move, the gun Tristan had trained on his stomach would open it up for him. The driver began a perilous ascent up a winding road that wrapped around one of the larger hills, and Sam could only imagine how stunning the unspoiled valley below would have been. If this was the final car journey of his life, he'd have appreciated a better view, but then he caught his reflection in the window of the car, met his own line of sight, and gave a slight nod.

This wasn't going to be the final time.

Not when he still had an ounce of fight in him.

Tristan pulled out his phone, scrolled slightly and then lifted it briefly.

'We are approaching. Gates.'

He hung up, and sure enough, through the windscreen, Sam could see the thick, iron gates drenched in the bright beams of the headlights. Two armed men were pulling the gate open, and the driver was waved through, and Sam counted another couple of armed guards waiting on the other side. The road began another climb, and Sam could see the extraordinary stone box that was built upon the top of the cliff, the white stone shimmering in the moonlight. It stood on colossal stone pillars, and had numerous strips of glass cutting through it, providing those within the most stunning views of the area.

It shot out over the cliff edge, overlooking what looked like an enormous animal enclosure beneath, and as the car continued it's climb, Sam watched as the huge floodlights fitted in all four corners of the enclosure burst into life like an evening football match.

Inside the brick walls were stretches of flat land, interspersed with spatters of woodland, various lengths of brick wall, and a few run-down, old buildings.

It was a curious sight, and Sam frowned, the medical tape pulling tightly on the opening in his skin.

Another round of security, and then Sam watched as the car was waved round to the far side of the incredible structure, rolling past over seven million pounds worth of luxury vehicles that had already arrived. It reminded Sam of *Boytsovskaya Yama*, when he and the other criminals had been driven to a secure location in Budapest to fight to the death for the entertainment of the elite. It was a cruel and sickening place, but Sam had survived and brought the entire structure crumbling down to its foundations.

But this felt a little different.

This felt more contained.

Better prepared.

Fortified.

There was no hint of desperation or competitiveness. All Sam could feel as the car came to a stop, was a sense that this was a situation completely out of his control.

Glass clearly had something in mind, something that he had told Sam would earn him back his money.

As he was hauled from the car by Tristan and then hurried into the back entrance at gun point, Sam could only think of two things.

Was Renée Corbin still alive?

And just how hard was he going to have to fight to survive?

CHAPTER TWENTY-FOUR

There was a lot riding on the night ahead.

It wasn't often that Sebastian Glass felt even a shred of anxiety, but this wasn't a normal situation. Never had he faced a threat to what he had built quite like the one that Sam Pope had posed, and even when the night was done, and Sam's death would have made him over one hundred million pounds, there was still a doubt in Glass' mind that things would ever go back to the way they were.

His bulletproof reputation had taken a few hits, and although offering the most dangerous man in Europe up on a platter for his members, the fact that he'd breached Veilmont and brought such attention to matters would echo for years to come.

Tonight needed to go off without a hitch.

His members needed to be satisfied that he, Sebastian Glass, was still the man who controlled everything.

And Sam Pope needed to die.

Glass had been taken straight from the airport into the centre of Stockholm, where his assistant had arranged for a haircut and wet shave at the most prestigious barbershop in Sweden. After that, he was driven to a well-regarded tailor, who fitted him for a new suit and made the necessary adjustments whilst Glass went for an early dinner in a nearby restaurant. Glover was permitted to sit with him, and Glass made no effort to hide his enjoyment at belittling his assistant throughout. Whilst Glover could see the sense in Pope's death, the man's conscious seemingly drew the line at the murder of a female DGSE agent.

Glass assured him that Agent Corbin wouldn't be murdered.

He had something else planned for her, despite what he had promised Sam Pope.

After paying for what was a pretty meagre meal, Glass collected his suit and then dismissed Glover for the evening. Despite his near constant anxiety, Glover was a capable assistant, but he didn't belong in the same room as the men and women Glass had invited to the 'Sanctuary.' Glover had put the word out, that tonight, there would be an auction for the biggest prize that could be offered.

Something that only *he*, Sebastian Glass, could provide.

It was twenty million just for a seat at the Sanctuary, and those who could afford the ticket could afford the necessary travel at such short notice.

Events at the Sanctuary were a rare occurrence, and with more Havens being opened across the continent, it was easy for Glass' customers to get what they needed at a greater convenience.

But something like this needed the majesty of the Sanctuary, and as the car passed through the security guards and the thick, iron gate, Glass peered through the window of the car and a smile spread across his chiselled jaw. The white, concrete structure loomed large over the contained area below, and Glass couldn't wait to peer out over the evening's proceedings.

There would be plenty of alcohol. Whatever drugs people requested.

Women.

Men.

Children.

All shipped in to provide whatever Glass' customers wanted, as they prepared for the evening's event. And when he stood before them all, his hands behind his back, and he gazed out across the hunting grounds beneath, he would watch with pleasure as someone finally brought this issue with Sam Pope to an end.

Whoever pulled the trigger would claim the life.

But it would be Glass who took the plaudits.

As he arrived at the Sanctuary, a few members of the staff greeted him, informing him that a few of the guests had arrived early. Those able to pay the twenty million were not people whom Glass would second guess, and he was pleased to know that they had already been welcomed into the stone structure and taken to private chambers for 'light entertainment and refreshments.' Glass didn't care to know what the requests were, nor did he judge anyone for their proclivities, he was just pleased that his operation was still working like clockwork.

That he could still provide everything he had originally promised.

The staff also informed him that Agent Corbin had been taken to a private room, where she would be fed and left alone until Glass required her presence, and that Tristan had delivered Sam Pope as promised, and that he was being held in the cells beneath the decadent building. Glass thanked his staff, implored them to return to work, and then made his way through the incredible structure, with its modern furnishings, until he came to the bar. The smooth, dark marble ran across the entire side wall of the viewing platform, which had been laid out with ten circular tables, all set for a grand meal. At the far end of the room, the entire wall was clear glass, offering anyone who stepped forward an incredible view of the surrounding hill tops, as well as the grounds beneath, which were now illuminated in the stunning brightness of the floodlights.

Glass ordered the finest whisky in his possession, and it was served to him in a crystal tumbler upon a soft, navy napkin. He necked it in one, hissing as the liquor scorched the back of his throat in a fiery mouthful of Dutch courage.

Tonight needed to go off without a hitch.

And as another guest arrived and was promptly taken through to a luxury suite for whatever frivolities they desired, Glass reminded the staff setting the tables that speaking to the guests beyond their orders was forbidden.

Failure to adhere to the rules would see them sent out with Sam.

Sent out to die.

As the terrified staff hustled back to work, Glass demanded one more drink, sunk it quicker than the first and then made his way through the Sanctuary. As his pristine shoes clacked loudly against the marble flooring, he came to the stairwell that led to the less decadent bowels of the building.

To the holding cells, where the prey was usually kept.

He wanted to speak to Sam one last time before he put him on show.

Glass wanted Sam's final conversation to be with the man who had sanctioned his murder.

Despite the undoubted luxury of the building above, Sam wasn't too shocked to find his holding cell to be nothing more than a concrete box, with a dripping pipe and the stale smell of neglect. The walls were chipped, either from abuse or decay, and all that welcomed him in the room was a sizeable meat hook that had been affixed to the ceiling. The adjoining chain was pulled tight and fed through a pulley that was bolted to the ground, allowing the operator to control the height and slack of the chain.

Tristan marched Sam in, accompanied by two armed men, and when he cut Sam's cable ties, the two men trained their guns on Sam like he meant them harm. Calmly, Tristan pulled Sam's hands forward, bound them together again, and then lowered the hook and slipped it through the small gap of Sam's bindings. Then, with a sneer, he began to pull the chain through the pulley, wrenching the hook higher towards the ceiling and hoisting Sam's hands high above his head.

Just as Sam was lifted onto his tiptoes, Tristan locked the hook in place, leaving Sam swinging gently, his shoulders already aching under the weight of his muscular frame. The skin around his wrists had been chafed away by the ties, and blood trickled down his forearms.

Offering zero threat, the two men now lowered their weapons, and Tristan sent them on their way with a curt nod. They obliged, and as Tristan followed them to the door, he stopped at the threshold and took a deep breath. He took a step back, closed the door, and then turned to Sam, who calmly returned his gaze. Slowly, Tristan removed his black jacket, revealing sizable arms that stretched the polo shirt underneath. He folded the jacket and placed it carefully by the door and then pulled out his Glock and set it down beside it.

It was all a show, and Sam rolled his eyes.

'Can we get this over with?' He offered, drawing a chuckle from Tristan.

'For a man in such a bad situation, you are very calm,' Tristan said, rolling his shoulder. 'I'll give you that. However, back at the hostel, you killed several of my men.

Not my brothers, no, no, but men I had known. Men I had worked with. Men I respected. Now, Glass has put a hell of a price on your head, and I am to make sure I leave you with a fighting chance.'

Tristan took a step closer to Sam, his fists clenched.

Sam kept calm. There was nothing else to do.

No escape.

No chance of fighting back.

Just don't give them any satisfaction.

'That's very good of you.' Sam quipped. Tristan's nostrils flared.

'I don't have enough money to get to kill you.' Tristan stepped in close. 'But I will get my pound of flesh.'

Tristan's hand revealed a pocketknife, which he flicked open, but that split second of showmanship gave Sam the opportunity to fall backwards. As he did, the hook swung slightly, driving him forward and Sam caught Tristan flush on the nose with a sickening headbutt. The blow sent Tristan sprawling across the floor, his nose obliterated into a soft, bloody mess, and he roared with fury as he hit the ground. Sam grimaced in pain, the impact adding another layer of agony to his concussion, and as he swung help-lessly on the spot, the blood-soaked Tristan got to his feet, dabbed at his nose, and winced with pain.

'You are going to fucking pay for that.' Tristan spat, and as he collected the knife from the ground, the thick, metal door to the cell opened and Glass walked in. Against the dreary, haunting emptiness of the cells, he was an explosion of style, a world away from the beaten and scuffed man that hung from the hook before him. Glass raised an eyebrow at the bloodied Tristan, who's eyes bulged with fury and his hand gripped the knife with murderous intent.

'What on earth is going on here?'

'This piece of shit just broke my nose.' Tristan

snapped, although his urgency had evaporated. Killing Sam in front of Glass would have been the biggest mistake of his life, and all three men in the room knew it.

Glass looked back and forth between the two men again, surveying the situation.

'Whilst he was tied up?' Glass pointed to the hook. Tristan snarled. Glass clapped his hands and turned back to Sam. 'You are impressive, Sam. Defiant to the end.'

'Are we going to get this over with?' Sam asked. 'My shoulders ache.'

'All in good time,' Glass said, casting an eye over Sam. 'My guests, they need to eat first. Get their strength up for what's to come. I'd offer you the same courtesy, Sam, however I feel you at full strength would have an unfair advantage. See, this isn't just about killing you, Sam. This is about restoring the faith that you eroded. This is about showing the people who have put their faith in me, that I can deliver what nobody else can.'

Sam winced and tried to adjust his shoulder.

'If it's a boring speech, I hate to break it to you, but there are lots of people who can do that.'

Glass smirked.

'I could just let Tristan here gut you like a fish on a hook. I could put you in a dark hole in the far reaches of Eastern Europe, strap you to a bed, and let some very deranged men take out their frustrations on you in ways that can only be described as deeply pornographic.' Glass stepped closer to Sam, but then, after a glance at Tristan, took a smaller step back. 'But that's not how the world needs you to die. It's certainly not how I want you to go. No, I want the word to spread, and trust me, it will…that I, Sebastian Glass, served Sam Pope up to the highest bidder. And then all the people you have foiled, and all those who are hesitant because they know you exist, they will all come to me, Sam. They will all line up, they will all pay their fees, and they will all be filtered into my pocket.'

Glass let the words linger in the room for a few moments, and the only sound beyond the dripping pipe, was Tristan wheezing through what used to be his nose. Eventually, Sam spoke.

'For a guy who has everything, you are pretty needy.' Sam looked to Tristan. 'You don't fancy just killing me, do you?'

'My pleasure,' Tristan said, stepping forward menacingly. Glass held up a hand and then fixed Sam with a glare. He ran his tongue against the inside of his lip, clearly annoyed by Sam's lack of fear.

'You might not be afraid, Sam. But your friend, Agent Corbin is.'

'She has nothing to do with this.'

'Oh, but she does.' Glass chuckled. 'Because of you, she has something to do with this. Because of you, your little friend in London had something to do with this. And trust me, you might mourn that he is dead, but you should consider that a mercy for what I have in store for your little agent.'

Sam pulled against his restraints, shifting forward a few inches, and causing Glass to startle.

'I swear to a God I gave up on a long time ago, that you will die tonight.'

Sam's eyes were burning with rage, and his threat was spat with a ferocity that caused Glass to shuffle uncomfortably in his expensive, leather shoes.

'The only truth you need to believe in Sam, is that the legacy you leave behind isn't that you fought for good people.' Glass struck Sam with the back of his hand. Sam barely reacted. 'It's that you sent good people to their deaths.'

Glass locked eyes with Sam one more time, both of

them making a silent vow that they would ensure the other one would meet their end tonight. As the stare became a little too intense, Glass broke eye contact, and turned to Tristan.

'No knives. I need him fighting fit, otherwise they won't bid.' Glass turned back to Sam and sneered. 'But feel free to beat the shit out of him.'

Glass pulled open the door, as Sam stared down the eager looking Tristan, who's eyes sparkled like a wolf coming upon a wounded deer. As Glass stepped out into the dank, dark corridor, the final sound he heard before the door swung shut, was the brutal thud of Tristan's meaty fist rocking Sam in the ribs.

The door shut, and Glass headed up the stairs to his guests.

It was time to begin the evening's event.

CHAPTER TWENTY-FIVE

After being separated from Sam and driven to the Sanctuary, Corbin had been shown to a comfortable room, where she was freed from her restraints, but left with an armed guard who protected the door. Food and drink were brought in to her by a young woman who refused to make eye contact, and as Corbin finally ate, she tried to extract information from the guard.

He didn't respond with words.

He just wiggled the Glock in his hand and held a finger to his lips.

Corbin made herself comfortable on the chair by the window, looking out at the vast stretch of woodland that was slowly being swallowed by the darkness. Every so often, she could see headlights rounding one of the bends on the hill, as another guest ascended to the Sanctuary.

She had no idea which car had held Sam, or if he was even alive.

When Glass arrived with an expensive dress for her to change into, he offered her no information other than Sam had once again threatened his life.

That brought a smile to her face.

The back of Glass' hand wiped it away.

Corbin refused the dress, and Glass then presented her with the option of being marched out in front of her guests, naked, and being made to put it on in front of them all.

Minutes later, Corbin had changed in the privacy of the room and was then marched through the decadent corridors of the Sanctuary by her armed escort, who led her to the bar. As she approached, she could hear the roar of conversation over the live grand piano that somebody expertly played. At the door, she was handed over to another armed guard, who then marched her through the seemingly pleasant evening to the table where Glass was seated. As she approached, he stood, resplendent in his custom three-piece suit, and he ushered her to her seat as if they were meeting for an awkward first date.

'Agent Corbin.' He smiled. 'Please sit.'

She did, but only when the armed guard dug his fingers into her trap muscles and forced her down. A few glances emanated from the other tables, but everyone knew better than to speak up.

These people were paying Glass for the privilege.

Not one of them would dare challenge his actions.

As Corbin sat rigid in her chair, she cast her eyes around the room. She counted ten tables, all of which were occupied either by couples or by groups of people, all of them dressed to the nines in expensive suits or glamorous dresses. Everything was designer, and Corbin didn't need to be a senior agent at the *Direction Générale de la Sécurité Extérieure* to know that everyone around every table had a fortune larger than most first world countries. Delicious looking food was being enjoyed over open bottles of the finest wine, and Corbin couldn't even hazard a guess at how much money was in the room.

Glass could seemingly read her mind.

'These are some the richest people in the world,' Glass said. 'You probably recognise some of them. CEOs. Famous actors. Crypto billionaires. But in here, who they are on the outside doesn't concern me.'

'Their money does.' Corbin snapped sharply. Glass lifted his glass of wine and swirled it thoughtfully.

'It does indeed. With money comes power, Agent Corbin. Whether you like it or not, my bank balance trumps your crummy little DGSE badge ten times out of ten. Why do you think your boss handed you over to me?'

Glass flashed a grin as Corbin shuddered with anger.

'Because he's a gutless coward. And you have something on him.'

'Because he has access, Agent.' Glass shook his head and sipped the wine. 'He might not get the prestige package like my most treasured customers, but men like Vivier, we give them enough of a taste, so they allow us to keep the doors open. So that when the likes of Sam Pope take down one of my Havens, or when one of his own starts pulling at threads they really shouldn't, he can step in and make it go away.'

Glass clicked his fingers.

'And the world is none the wiser,' Corbin said with hatred.

'Oh, spare me.' Glass rolled his eyes as he poured himself and Corbin a glass of wine, which she refused. 'The world doesn't want to know the truth. That those with the money and the power, quite literally do whatever they want. That there isn't a law enforcement agency on this planet that has the means, the capability nor the actual desire to take us down. Every now and then, they chose a sacrificial lamb, someone with name recognition and throw them under the bus. Let the authorities rip their lives to pieces in front of the watching world to maintain the illusion of power. But that's all it is. An illusion.'

'And this?' Corbin looked around at the vast room overlooking the enclosure below, sweeping her hand at the rich and famous. 'All this is power?'

Glass shook his head, stood, and buttoned his jacket.

'No. But you are about to see what *is* power.'

Glass stepped forward, lifting his glass of wine and tapping it gently with a spoon, drawing everyone's attention like a best man at a wedding. The conversation died down, and the elegant young woman lifted her fingers from the piano keys. Glass smiled warmly, stepping casually out into the front of the tables, the glass wall behind him.

'Thank you all for coming at such short notice. I appreciate the ask was expensive, both financially and logistically, and to those of you who have been here before, you know it should be worth it.' Glass finished his wine and held out the glass, summoning one of his well-trained staff to scurry forward and collect it. 'By show of hands, who has never attended one of my events here at the Sanctuary?'

A few hands lifted into the air, with the only judgment coming from the fierce glare of Agent Corbin. Glass gestured to the newcomers.

'It is a pleasure to have you. And to you both, and to all my guests, welcome…to the hunting grounds.' Glass gestured to the window, and a few people looked out at the enclosure below which was bathing under the glare of the floodlights. 'Now usually, we would have four or five hunts, but tonight, we have just one. However, due to the nature of the prey, I will be allowing as many of you to hunt him as possible.'

Excited chatter broke out amongst the guests, and Corbin looked at them in horror.

They were going to hunt Sam. Like an animal.

And what was worse, based on Glass' speech, less capable people than Sam had been thrust into the enclosure before. As Glass allowed the excitement to grow, a voice from one of the tables called.

'Who is it?'

Glass held up a hand to slow the conversation.

'Ah, now that is the question. However, your twenty million fee only got you to the table. To compete in the hunt tonight, it will be ten million, per person. So, if you're entire group of four wants to partake, that will be forty million.'

Again, Corbin was mortified at the scene before her, as the privileged nodded along, as if forty million pounds was a reasonable price to pay for the opportunity to murder someone. She could feel her stomach twisting with disgust, and it took every fibre of her being not to vomit across the table.

Glass continued.

'The fee is non-negotiable nor refundable. If you pay and back out, then that is your prerogative. However, ladies and gentlemen, I am offering the chance of a life-time.' Glass beckoned his hand to a side door. 'Who will be the person to hunt and kill…the most wanted man in Europe…Sam Pope.'

A collective gasp echoed from the small crowd before him, and Glass stepped to the side as Tristan marched Sam Pope from the side door to the front of the room. Pope's eyebrow had been re-opened, and the blood on Tristan's knuckles made it easy to see how. His lip was also bleeding, and his left eye was already beginning to swell. With his hands bound before him, Sam was shunted front and centre, and then Tristan stamped a foot into the back of Sam's leg, dropping him to his knees. Sam took a breath and straightened up, looking out at the tables of excited faces.

His eyes landed on Corbin, and a tear ran down her cheek.

A few excited hands shot up.

'That's four of you,' Glass said, counting excitedly. 'Five. Anymore?'

A few more hands.

'Fantastic.' Glass clasped his hands together and then turned to Sam. 'You see, Sam? You're a popular fellow, aren't you? Would you like to say anything to your competitors before we begin?'

Sam looked up at Glass, who was basking in the moment. Sam held his gaze long enough to make Glass turn in discomfort, before Sam fixed the room with a cold, hard stare.

'Good luck,' he said. 'Because I am coming for each and every one of you.'

A sickening thud ended the threat, as Tristan drove the grip of his Glock into the back of Sam's skull, drilling him right across the bandage that had been applied earlier. With his hands bound, Sam hit the expensive tiles cheek first, and Glass mockingly put his foot on Sam's head.

'To our participants, please accompany Andreas to the armoury, where you can select the weapons of your choice.' Applying a little extra pressure to Sam's skull, Glass turned to Tristan. 'Take him down, drive him out to the back, and dump him. At least give him a few minutes to run before the hunt begins.'

As the excited, seven-strong hunting party left their seats, Glass removed his foot from Sam's head and gestured for Tristan to pull him up. He obliged, and the large mercenary held Sam steady as he swayed woozily on his feet.

'Remember when I told you this wasn't over?' Glass smirked at Sam, who gathered his marbles.

'You're right. It's not,' Sam said defiantly, and Glass's smug face contorted into a vicious scowl.

'Take him.' Glass ordered, not taking his eyes from

Sam's. 'And don't cut his ties. Let's see how he survives with his hands tied together.'

Tristan roughly hauled Sam off to the side, shoving him back through the side door to march him off to his impending death. As they exited the room, the piano music began again, and the excited conversation by those willing to spectate rose once more. Glass took his seat beside Corbin once again, only this time, that smug sense of self-satisfaction had been replaced by aggravation.

Only Sam could be looking down the barrel of a hopeless situation and make the one holding the gun feel nervous.

Corbin felt her heart break, only this time, with pride.

And Sam's defiance was infectious.

'He's going to kill them,' she said. 'And then he'll come for…'

Her taunt was cut off by a brutal slap that took her off her chair. A few guests turned, but quickly looked away, as Glass stood over Corbin, who pulled herself up by the table.

'Keep your mouth closed, you useless bitch.' Glass snapped. 'I have a contact in Dubai who wants to put you to work, and trust me, he will use you until the brink of death. Until then, sit tight, and watch as your friend dies.'

As Corbin wiped away a dribble of blood from her lip, she looked above the glass wall, where a series of monitors burst into life, all of them offering different views of the hunting grounds below through the various cameras that were dotted throughout.

The entire room would get to see everything.

There was nowhere for Sam to hide.

And Corbin would have to watch as he was hunted.

Sam had been dumped into the back of a Jeep, and Tristan slammed his foot down as it lurched forward and navigated the treacherous terrain. The Hunting Grounds were just a square mile, with the brick wall looming large as they drove alongside it. The only way in or out had been the metal shutter that Tristan had driven through, and a few of the guests were eager to see them off, wanting a glimpse of the most wanted vigilante on the continent before they took his life.

The price for his head was expensive.

But the thrill of being the person to put down Sam Pope was evident, and a couple of the young billionaires cheered as Tristan shoved him into the car and departed. Soon, they'd be entering the battlefield, and Sam didn't doubt that Glass' armoury would offer them whatever they wanted.

Chances were, seven people would descend on him with high powered assault rifles, empty their magazines at the same time, and blow him to Kingdom Come.

But until that happened, Sam had to keep going.

Keep fighting.

Survive.

Corbin was still in the clutches of the most vulgar man that Sam had ever come across, and as long as there was a breath in his lungs and a beat in his chest, he would fight to get back to her.

Fight to put Glass down.

Fight to put an end to Veilmont.

Tristan pulled the Jeep sharply to the left, following the wall as it curved and then he rolled to a stop. The bitterness of the nighttime welcomed a spattering of rain, as a thin drizzle fell across the windshield. They were at the furthest point from the Sanctuary, and Tristan pulled the handbrake, kept the motor running, and slid out the door.

Seconds later, Sam was hauled from the back seat and shoved him down onto the moist grass.

Without a word, Tristan got back into the Jeep, turned sharply, and thundered back towards the Sanctuary, his taillights fading and then disappearing behind one of the abandoned structures that lay between Sam and his potential killers. He rolled onto his front, and then pushed himself to his knees, just as an alarm sounded from the giant structure before him.

The hunt had started.

Somewhere across the battlefield, seven heavily armed rich folk were entering with unknown weapons.

Blood was going to be shed.

And as Sam set off to find the nearest wall to try to cut through the cables that bound his hands together, he was adamant it wouldn't be his.

There was nowhere to go but forward.

To face the hunt head on.

To fight.

CHAPTER TWENTY-SIX

There was a buzz of excitement emanating through the Sanctuary, and Corbin watched the rich and powerful start placing bets on who would be the one to make the kill.

It didn't matter that they were hunting a human.

To them, this was all a game, an opportunity to bask in the untouchable nature of their wealth, all of it provided by the man who was sitting beside her. Glass was casually pulling on a lit cigarette, his eyes fixed on the monitors above the glass windows, where they could see the hunting party taking tentative steps towards the open shutter. Corbin wasn't a weapons expert, but she knew what she could see.

High powered assault rifles.

What looked like a pump-action shotgun.

Someone had something strapped to their back like a rucksack, with a connecting wire to a device that looked like a jet washer.

One well-built, well-groomed guest was marching confidently towards the increasingly heavy drizzle, swinging a machete in his hand. Glass did take a moment to notice that the man also had a Glock 17 tucked into his jeans; he just enjoyed the thrill of butchering another human with his bare hands.

Corbin felt sick to her stomach. Not just with the fear for her friend, but from the thought of who had faced this horror before? And how many times had a guest of Glass' picked up that machete and butchered another human being. Glass motioned for the waiter to top up his wine, and then he leant forward towards Corbin with a cruel grin.

'Lighten up and enjoy the show.'

Through the glass, Corbin could see the downpour increasing as the floodlights dimmed slightly, and her eyes scanned the monitors above the glass. She could see some of the guests, huddled together, their weapons drawn, as if they were the ones in real danger. Corbin could see the fear in them all, and even though they were hunting an unarmed, restrained man, they still walked with the trepidation of people who were second guessing their decision.

On another screen, she saw the machete wielding psychopath, casually walking as he cut shapes into the air with his blade.

The one with the rucksack pulled the trigger of his hose and sent a shriek of excitement through the room as a flame erupted from the nozzle.

Another couple of guests were walking with a little more purpose, and one of them pressed against a brick wall and held his fist up, clearly having seen one too many military programmes. He motioned for the others to follow, and the two men scurried forward, guns drawn and their fingers ready.

The camera on the inside of the building, where the shutter had released the hunters, showed Tristan standing by, along with four other armed guards, all of them in a deep discussion over coffee and cigarettes.

Their guns were lined against the wall, ready to wipe out any threats should the worst happen.

All Corbin knew was there was no way out for Sam.

Even if he made it through the hunting party, Glass' private security would ensure he didn't make it out of the hunting grounds.

Glass' Sanctuary would be Sam's tomb.

And after what Glass had promised awaited her once the hunt was over, Corbin could only wish for the same fate.

Then a series of gunshots echoed, and all eyes turned to the screens, as whispers of excitement swept through the room.

A horrified scream echoed behind Corbin, one that was heavy with heartbreak.

A worried scowl took control of Glass' brow, furrowing it as he angrily yelled into the radio. A few of the guests echoed his concern, especially as they saw the reason the camera showing the horrors suddenly turned to static.

A grin cracked across Corbin's face, as for the first time in a while, she felt a flicker of hope.

———

As the drizzle began to lash down with a great hatred for the world beneath, Sam ran as fast as he could towards the broken wall a few hundred feet ahead. The downpour was skewing his visibility ever so slightly, which he knew he could use to his advantage. He'd looked out at everyone behind the tables of Glass' opulent dinner, and what he saw gave him hope.

He saw the eyes of sick people with ill intentions.

But what he didn't see was a true killer.

The floodlights that loomed over the hunting ground dimmed ever so slightly, but Sam just kept himself steady as he ran. His hands were still pulled together by a cable tie that had chafed away a layer of skin, but Sam put it out of his mind. As he approached the corner of the wall where the bricks had cracked and crumbled, he was stopped in his tracks by the explosion of a gunshot. A bullet whizzed past him and hammered into the wall, a burst of dust blasting out on impact.

Sam dropped to a knee, spun to the right and darted behind the parallel wall, just as another bullet shattered the brickwork behind him.

'He's here.' An excited voice called out, and Sam zeroed in on its location.

It had been a long time since he had been in the military, but he was still the most lethal marksman the country had ever known. The ability to read the situation, to ascertain the locations of his targets.

Reading the weather.

The terrain.

Sizing up how dangerous an opponent was, just by the laziness of giving away their position.

Making a logical guess on how many steps to the target, how quickly he could kill and disarm, and then turn the gun on the other hunter.

It was all second nature.

Killing these people would be as easy and as natural as breathing.

And there was still air in Sam's lungs, which meant there was still a fight to be won.

Sam pressed back against the wall, and shuffled alongside it, darting across an opening that led to another wall. There was no discernible layout to the brickwork. Glass clearly wanted areas of excitement in the hunting grounds and having a few corridors of chest high walls certainly encouraged a game of cat and mouse.

But whilst the two hunters were talking loudly, incorrectly using military jargon as they played out their sick fantasy, the reality was they were signing their death warrants.

'Move in.' One of the hunters called out, and Sam peered up from over the wall to track the location of the voice. The man was standing a few feet away, his back to Sam, as he scanned the opening between the walls with his rifle. Beyond him, Sam could see the other gunman, weapon drawn up in an amateurish grip, and he rounded a wall and disappeared from view.

Sam made his move.

Sam stepped out from behind the wall, and took a few careful steps, his footsteps cloaked by the falling rain. As the approached the man, Sam slowly lifted up his arms, and just as the man began to turn with his gun, Sam looped his arms over the man's head, drew his wrists back to the man's throat, and then dropped to the ground as quickly as possible. As he pulled the man down with him, Sam lifted up a knee and drove it into the man's spine, arching him back, as the sharp, taut cable ties cut into the man's throat. The hunter dropped his gun and clawed at Sam's hands, but the pressure was too much, and he quickly faded. Sam wrenched back with as much strength as he could muster, and he could feel the blood seeping from the man's throat as the cable tie cut in.

The man gurgled as his final breaths escaped him, and when he finally died, Sam dropped him to the wet grass beside him, and then quickly searched the body. With his hands bound, Sam couldn't operate the FAMAS that the now dead hunter had carried, but before Sam could pat him down for another weapon, a bullet struck the corpse, sending a spatter of blood up Sam's front, and Sam quickly rolled aside as another burst of fire shattered the wall behind him.

'Motherfucker.' The man roared, unloading more

bullets into the dark gaps that punctured every wall in sight.

Sam was somewhere amongst the bricks, but the man looked down at his friend and angrily unloaded an entire magazine into the unknown.

As he fumbled to release the mag, the man felt two hands press against the back of his head, and before he could struggle, his face was driven at full force into the jagged rocks of the wall. Sam gripped the man's dark, wet hair, peeled what was left of his face from the stone, and then drove it forward once more with all his might.

He felt the bones crack.

He heard a few gurgles of pain, and as he released the man's hair, he watched as the body limply slid down the bricks, leaving a trail of blood and skin behind it.

Two down.

Gritting his teeth, Sam approached one of the bloodied rocks jutting out from the wall and carefully looped the plastic cable tie over it. The binds were tight enough to pull his wrists together, but as he began to erode the plastic against the rock, he ignored the pain as another layer of skin was whittled from his wrists.

Blood poured down his forearms.

The bitter cold hitting the exposed wounds caused him to grunt with agony.

And then he was free.

Snapping the cable ties over the stone, Sam quickly rubbed his wrists, trying to ignore the pain, as he turned back to the bodies he had left strewn in the walled garden. The man he'd choked to death was still staring at him, his vacant eyes punctuated with burst capillaries. The other man lay hunched over, the remnants of his face tracing his journey across the brick to the wet ground below.

Sam felt nothing for them.

The men were no real threat. Just two rich people who believed they were above the law.

Who believed that they wielded enough money and power to literally hunt another human being and shoot them dead.

And they were dead wrong.

Literally.

Sam slid off his bomber jacket and tossed it over one of the walls, freeing himself entirely as he squatted down beside the man he'd choked to death. He ripped at the ground beneath him with his fingers, churning up the mud that had softened under the downpour. Then, as the rain battered the soil into a paste, Sam smeared it up his forearms, and then in streaks across his face. It was crude, and with the dim floodlights above, it wouldn't completely shield him from view.

But marginal gains would give him a fighting chance, and although there were five more hunters somewhere within the grounds, none of them had what Sam had.

A life of killing when it mattered most.

Sam hauled up the FAMAS the man had dropped and quickly slid the mag to check the ammo. Pleased, he slammed it shut and then pocketed the other mag that was protruding from the man's jacket. The other body offered nothing else other than another spare round of ammunition, and a detailed view of brain seeping through an obliterated skull.

As Sam turned to leave, he heard the dull thud of footsteps and hushed voices, and he ducked down against the wall for cover. Two more of the hunters were shuffling by, and Sam peered around the corner of the wall to watch.

It was a married couple, walking back-to-back, one with a pump action shotgun, the other with a FAMAS similar to what was resting in Sam's arms. They were clearly terrified, and Sam could even hear the wife admonishing her husband's lack of fortitude as he begged for them to turn back.

Unloading a couple of bursts in their direction would eliminate two more people.

Would make it two on one.

But it would also give away Sam's position, and beyond the walls where he'd taken refuge, Sam didn't know what awaited him beyond them. Pinning himself down in one location could lead to him being flanked, and taking fire from two different angles usually only ended one way.

He needed to do things quietly.

At least until there were only a few left.

And besides, there was a team of *actual* killers waiting in the wings, and the rest of Glass' dinner party that more than deserved the bullets in his rifle. Sam peered round the edge of the wall one more time, watching as the two silhouettes disappeared into the low settling mist spreading across the enclosure.

The rain was hitting the ground like it held a vendetta, echoing off the surrounding walls.

Covering the careful steps of the man behind Sam and bouncing off the razor-sharp machete he swung at his unsuspecting target. As the blade sliced through the air, the moonlight hit the metal, sparkling brightly in the corner of Sam's eye. Instinctively, Sam dropped forward, and the machete sparked as it clattered off the rock a millimetre from Sam's scalp. Sam rolled forward, lifted the rifle, but the blade swung upwards, and Sam had to relinquish his grip to avoid having his hand severed. The blade swished an inch from his chest as he fell backwards, and as he rolled over, he heard it embed into the mud seconds after.

'Fuck.' The man panicked, as he tried to wrench it clear, but just as he did, Sam was on his feet and darted, launching at the machete-wielding hunter and tackling him down to the mud.

He groaned in terror as the machete slid from his grip, and Sam drilled an elbow into the man's jaw, and then spread his fingers across the man's throat. As Sam's grip began to set, the man heaved and threw lame punches, but to little effect.

It was only when he pulled the Glock from the back of his jeans and blew a hole clean through Sam's left shoulder, did he take a full breath of air.

Sam rolled off in agony, the bullet ripping out the back of his shoulder and chipping the bone on the way through. The pain was unimaginable, but Sam pushed it away just in time to see the man pushing himself to a seated position and raising the gun again.

Sam kicked out violently, his boot crunching the man's wrists and knocking the gun out of his grip and sending an errant bullet into the downpour. Terrified, the man began to crawl after it, losing his balance as he slipped across the slick grass.

Sam stood, his fingers already gripping the machete, and as he marched through the downpour and his own pain threshold, he lifted the blade and grunted with agony as he swung it over his head.

Just as the hunter claimed his handgun and turned to kill him.

The thud of the machete hitting the man's skull was dull and final, and Sam felt the blade lodge itself into the bone as it split it cleanly. The man twitched a few times, and his eyes rolled inwards, as a thick trail of blood snaked out from his broken cranium. With the machete lodged deep within his skull and brain, the man shook violently and dropped to the ground.

Above, on the wall, a CCTV camera turned and focused in on Sam's position.

Sam leant down, picked up his FAMAS, and then took the Glock from the man's now motionless hand.

Without so much as a second to steady himself, Sam lifted the Glock and fired, blowing the camera clean off the wall.

As it toppled to the ground in a flutter of sparks and smoke, Sam tucked the Glock away and then reached down and ripped the sleeve off of the dead man's jacket. He wrapped it round the flesh wound that was pumping blood from his shoulder, and with the use of his teeth, he managed to tie a crude knot over it.

It was a poor attempt at a tourniquet, but it would have to do.

In the meantime, Sam hoisted up the FAMAS, ignored the searing pain as he drew it up, and kept low as he hurried out into the downpour.

Three down.

Four to go.

The hunt was on.

CHAPTER TWENTY-SEVEN

Grimacing with pain, Tristan glared into the mirror of the bathroom and pinched the bridge of his nose. The shattered cartilage gave a sickening crunch, and he grunted as the pain stretched across his face. But it wasn't the agony of breathing through the obliterated nose that hurt the most.

It was the embarrassment.

Tristan's reputation proceeded him, and to the remaining men in the room, he was still somebody to be revered. He was one of the most dangerous and efficient hired guns in Europe and had even been headhunted for jobs across the Atlantic. His Argentinian roots held him in good standing with some of the cartels in Buenos Aires, and people would often listen to him with their head down and their buttocks clenched.

He was a man to be feared.

Yet here he was, standing in the rest room, looking at a face he didn't recognise. His nose was visibly disjointed, covered in a horrific purple bruise that had spread like a virus around one of his eyes. Through his thick, dark beard, he bared his teeth and poked a tongue through the gap that Sam's headbutt had created.

All the men in the other room, waiting patiently for their orders, knew that it was Sam Pope who had done that to him.

What they didn't know, was that Sam had been restrained when he'd done it.

That fact sent a wave of anger through Tristan's body like a sonic boom, which erupted through his meaty arm as he swung a fist at the mirror, shattering it into hundreds of pieces.

Blood dripped from his slashed knuckles, and Tristan flashed an angry glance at the few remaining shards, catching the now disfigured reflection looking back.

He wanted Sam to survive.

He wanted Sam to teach those pathetic, rich pricks that their money didn't equate to fortitude, and that even when he'd dropped him at the far end of the hunting grounds, bound and unarmed, Tristan wasn't convinced it was the last time he'd see him.

The elite were a different breed, and many had built their wealth off the backs of the impoverished. To them, the common man was beneath them, and their money made them believe they were untouchable.

To them, Sam Pope was just a soldier.

A man paid a menial wage to put his life on the line to protect the institutions that had made them rich beyond reach.

They were better than him.

Therefore, they could pay a fee to have the honour of killing him.

Tristan hoped they were very wrong, and as he stepped back into the garage where he'd parked the Jeep, he glanced around at the remaining six mercenaries, all standing by to put the fire out. A few of them were playing cards, whilst a few others sat in quiet contemplation over a cigarette, all of them waiting patiently to cash the easiest cheque they'd ever get paid.

But Tristan wasn't happy with another zero being added to his bank account.

He had plenty of money. Enough to set his family up for life, and enough to live a life of luxury in between jobs.

Tristan wanted revenge.

He wanted to put to bed the doubts in his own mind and take down the man who had shattered his face. Take down the man who had either killed or incarcerated well known associates who swam in the same shark tank.

Roland Brandt.

Mendoza.

Dominik Silva.

Some of the most feared hitmen in the world that had all fallen at Sam Pope's feet.

Tristan wanted the scalp for himself and wanted Sam's legacy to be the foundation for his own.

And when the panicked voice of Sebastian Glass crackled through the radio, Tristan smiled through the pain.

'He doesn't leave the fucking grounds. Do you understand me? I want him dead.'

The order was clear, and Tristan sauntered over to the monitor that a few of the others had since gathered around. The screen was split into multiple windows, each one offering a different, black and white angle of the hunting grounds.

A few of them offered only static.

But Tristan could see the bodies.

See the rampage being left behind.

See the fight that Sam was putting up.

Tristan barked the orders, and the men began to arm themselves, casting expert eyes over their weapons as the adrenaline levels in the room began to rise. The men were of various backgrounds and spoke different languages, but they all understood what the mission was.

That when the shutter opened, they were to fan out, sweep through the enclosure and eliminate Sam Pope.

Tristan would take the position at the back, as he expected a number of them to take their final steps across the wet grass beyond the shutter.

They would give away Sam's position.

They would effectively provide Tristan with a human shield.

But when the shutter opened, all eyes widened with surprise, as a mighty fire erupted across the woodlands, the flames flickering like beckoning fingers.

Tristan gave the orders to proceed, and as he was about to follow behind, he lowered his weapon and batted one thought from his mind.

'What will it take to kill this man?'

Then he took a few steps back inside and decided that a change of plan was necessary.

Sam had kept low, allowing the downpour and the shadows of the glaring lights to provide him with enough cover as he weaved his way through the hunting grounds. As he approached a run-down outpost that had been erected near the far wall, he wondered how many innocent people had been let loose in here and hunted for sport.

How terrified would they have been, to have been locked within the enclosure whilst sadistic people with means to evade the law, butchered them for some depraved sense of superiority?

It filled Sam with even more venom and pushed him further.

The pain in his shoulder was gnawing away at him like a toothache, but he gritted his teeth and pushed open the door. He cleared the entrance way, but just as he stepped through, bullets sloppily hammered into the wall beside him, and Sam swung into the building and pressed against the brick for cover.

'You missed!' The woman barked at her husband, barely audible over the rain.

'At least I fucking shot.'

Clearly, the intensity of the situation was putting a strain on their marriage, and Sam used their argument as a way to pinpoint their distance from the door.

He had about ten seconds before they arrived, and given their inexperience, would burst through the door all guns blazing. Undoubtedly, the errant burst of fire that had pock-marked the concrete building would alert the others to his possible location, and Sam needed to act fast. He hurried through the outpost to the far wall, and with the butt of his rifle, smashed through the murky glass pane that offered no view of the outside prison. He cleared the remaining shards from the frame and then climbed through, dropping down into a thickening muddy puddle beneath. His boots squelched and struggled through the worn ground, until he made it back up onto the grass, and peered round the corner of the outpost, just as the married couple approached the door.

The husband approached the door, rifle raised but without the confidence of a true killer, and behind him, the regretful wife was struggling with the pump-action shot gun.

'Go on then,' She hissed.

The man stepped through.

The wife followed tentatively, and Sam moved.

He kept his back against the concrete until he came to the doorway and then steadied himself. He took a breath and then swung in, raising his rifle up, and drilled the butt of it cleanly into the wife's temple. She squealed as she dropped to the side, and as the husband spun, Sam had already pulled his FAMAS to his eyeline, and his finger to the trigger.

He squeezed.

A three round burst exploded forward, with two bullets hitting the man in the chest, before the third burrowed a hole through the centre of his throat. It took the man off his feet, and he hit the ground, gurgling as his final breaths were drowned out by the pooling blood.

Sam turned the rifle onto the wife, who woozily turned back to the commotion. Her eyes rested on her husband, and once the dizziness had cleared enough for her to connect the dots, her face dropped into one of heartbreak.

Then fear as she turned to face Sam.

Then blank as he unloaded a single bullet that blew out the back of her skull.

As her body clattered onto the floor with a thud, Sam turned to leave, only for a burst of fire to erupt through the doorway of the outpost. The blast caught Sam by surprise, and he launched himself backwards, and landed with a sickening crunch on his wounded shoulder. He roared with agony and turned to see the body of the wife now engulfed in flames, as a portly man with a crazed look on his face emerged through the doorway, the flamethrower hanging in his hands.

'Ready to die, Pope?' The man squealed with excitement and then pulled the handle back once more. Another eruption of flames filled the room, and Sam scrambled to his feet and then launched himself through the window he'd previously cleared and was grateful for the softer landing on the bog beneath. As he got to his feet, he pulled the Glock from the back of his jeans, just in time to see the other remaining hunter emerge round the corner of the outpost, a rifle in his hand.

He lifted it towards Sam.

Sam had already raised the gun, his muscle memory drawing and squeezing in one fluid motion. The man's head snapped back in a cloud of red dust and fell down into the mud. Sam hurried to the body, and relieved it of the FAMAS, and then made his way round the outpost, which was now engulfed in flames. Carefully, he rounded the corner, where the man responsible for the blaze was searching for Sam beneath the window.

Masked by the crackle of the spreading fire, and rain crashing against the mud, Sam approached the man from behind, who turned just a second too late.

Sam grabbed the man's hand before he could reach the level of the flame thrower, and in a sickening display of strength, snapped the man's fingers backwards until they pressed against his own hand. The man wailed like a child, collapsing to one knee as he begged for mercy.

Something that Sam had long since abandoned.

Sam pulled the backpack from the man's shoulders, dropping the weapon onto the grass verge, and then he hauled the man up to his feet.

'Please don't kill me.' The man begged, before Sam hoisted him up and shoved him back through the window into the blazing outpost. Harrowing cries echoed through the shattered window, as the man became engulfed in flames. A few moments later, like the man himself, the cries were reduced to ash.

Seven down.

All of them having paid eight figures for the privilege of their own death.

And no matter how hard the rain fell, Sam knew that it wouldn't be enough to wash the blood from his hands.

Especially as there was plenty more in the shed.

There was no way that Glass would allow Sam to make it back to the Sanctuary, that much was obvious. Soon, Tristan and his heavily armed mercenaries would take to the hunting grounds, and unlike the elite corpses Sam had left in his wake, they would know what they were doing.

Sam wouldn't stand a chance if they were able to get into formation.

The only defence Sam had, was to mount an all-out offence.

If he was going to die, then he was going to face it head on.

Sam lifted the backpack from the grass, and eased his brutalised shoulder through one of the straps. He then looped the other over, lifted the flamethrower, and broke out into a sprint.

The rain was lashing down, and through it, he could see the magnificent Sanctuary looming large and could make out the figures lined up by the window, watching the carnage below.

The closer he got, the more detail came into focus, and he could make out which one was Glass.

Beside him, Sam could see Corbin.

She was still alive.

Which meant beyond his own survival, he still had a reason to fight.

Tucked underneath the protruding building that hung over the enclosure like a storm cloud, Sam could see the flashing light above the shutter, its flashing signifying its imminent opening. Sam pulled the backpack from his shoulders and then ripped the pipe connecting the fuel to the thrower itself. Gasoline began to pour from the tube, and Sam held it down to the ground and then ran as fast as he could across the open field, praying that the ground wasn't too wet.

If this didn't work, he'd be a sitting duck, with a handful of rifles pointed at him.

It had to work.

As the shutter clattered loudly as it began to rise, Sam dropped the backpack to the ground and lifted the flame thrower. It still had the lighting mechanism, and Sam hoped, just enough fuel residue to ignite a flame.

With a clang, the shutter disappeared fully into its bracket, and sure enough, backlit by the lights of the garage, Sam could see the death squadron emerging into the rain, armed to the teeth and ready to put an end to his valiant attempts at survival.

Sam closed his eyes, took a deep breath, and pulled the lever.

The fire hit the gasoline on the grass and then spread at a terrifying pace across the entire hunting ground, entrenching most of it in its glorious dominance. As the flames roared forward, Sam watched as the five men drew their weapons, and a sense of panic gripped them. Slathered in mud, and hidden in the shadows, Sam drew his FAMAS up once more and then stepped behind the flaming wall he had created.

Through the relentless flickers, Sam could see the approaching squadron. They were slowly starting to fan out, and were scanning the area, ready to shoot at a moment's notice.

Sam would give away his position.

He had to.

As two men began to head directly towards him, Sam drew up his weapon, ignored the flames flicking at his forearm, and through the heat, he fired.

Two bursts.

Two heads snapped back, as the bullets hammered through their skulls, and they hit the wet grass along with their bone and brain matter.

Sam immediately swung down and dived behind a decrepit wall, which bore the brunt of the onslaught of bullets.

He needed to move.

The fire would act as cover, but a keen eye and a deadly hand could drop him the second he moved.

He had to risk it.

Sitting still was just waiting for death.

Especially as over the roar of flames behind him, he heard the engine of the Jeep come to life, and the odds stacked even more heavily against him.

CHAPTER TWENTY-EIGHT

Tristan watched as two of his men went down, their heads snapping backwards as the perfectly-placed bullets ripped through their skulls. The sound came from the left, and instinctively, the three other members of his team trained their guns on the potential point of fire and began to spread out.

One of them was likely to be killed, but it meant the others would get a clear shot on Sam's position.

It was just a case in seeing who drew the short straw.

Tristan watched from the driver's seat of the Jeep, still sheltered from the rain in the garage. The men were doing everything right. Taking careful steps, feeling their way across the wet terrain as the weather continued to be their enemy. The fire was still blazing, ripping across the open field of the hunting ground, and offering only a blurred, smoke-drenched view of what was beyond. As long as the fire blazed high and offered a layer of distraction, it gave Sam Pope a fighting chance. For his team to go round it, they'd spread themselves too thin, or cluster too close together, meaning Sam could either pick them off one at a time, or eliminate them in one burst.

The man didn't miss.

His reputation, quite rightly, preceded him, and Tristan knew that the only way to get to Sam was to either wait for the fire to die down, or drive him out himself. And considering that Sam wouldn't wait for the rain to extinguish the fire before he killed them all, Tristan pulled his pistol and rested it on his lap and brought the engine to life. The lights of the Jeep burst across the field, casting long shadows as the glare hit his men. They continued their slow movements forward, and Tristan floored the pedal, and the Jeep shot through the shutter and out into the rain, and he turned the wheel violently to the right to stick to the side of the enclosure.

The plan was simple.

Get beyond the fire and then alert the team to Sam's location. Either by his line of fire or by killing him.

Eitherway, as soon as Tristan made it past the flames, Sam was as good as dead.

And just a few feet from the inferno, Tristan's smirk turned to wide-eyed fear, as through the flames, he saw Sam rise up, rifle drawn, and the last thing Tristan saw was the flash from the end of the FAMAS.

Two bullets ripped through the front tyre.

The Jeep swerved violently to the right, clipped a pile of rubble, and lifted off the ground. The world spun before Tristan's eyes as his vehicle twisted through the air before it hit the ground with a sickening crunch. It rolled across the mud, panels and glass ripped from its body before it came to an abrupt stop as it slammed into a thick, concrete wall.

Smoke filtered from the debris.

It was the only sign of movement.

Sam didn't have time to admire his handiwork, as bullets hammered the wall beside him, the other three men locking into his position. Sam kept low, ducking behind the wall and running the length of it to try to get round the fire. The blaze was spreading from the original path he'd laid for it, as the flames were now engulfing the nearby trees. Smoke was falling across the entire enclosure like a thick, morning mist, and Sam took a deep breath, ran, and leapt through the blaze and landed with a groan on the other side. He quickly scrambled to his feet and lifted the rifle, just in time to see the rest of the squadron zeroing in on his previous position.

Cloaked by the smoke, Sam took a few careful steps around, lining all three of them in his deadly sights, and then he pulled the trigger.

The first burst ripped through the spinal cord of the nearest man.

The second burst ran up the rib cage of the man turning in panic.

The third hit the final mercenary in the thigh, dropping him to one knee, but the other bullets vanished into the flames. In response, the man swung up his rifle and sent an errant stream of bullets in Sam's direction. Using the smoke as a screen, Sam darted to the right, grateful to hear the bullets rip into the ground behind him. As the man scrambled to his feet, Sam lifted the rifle and stepped through the thick, dark smoke and sent a bullet through the man's other knee.

He dropped, roaring with pain as he clutched his shattered joint, and as he turned to defiantly curse Sam, another gunshot echoed, and he fell backwards.

The bullet had blown straight through the gap between his eyes.

Sam stood for a moment, covering his mouth with his t-shirt, as the fire spread and the smoke thickened. His left shoulder ached, and Sam shifted the weight of the rifle into his right hand to lessen the agony. With the hunting ground littered with bodies, which were engulfed by the flames burning the entire place to the ground, Sam turned to head towards the Sanctuary.

After a few steps, he heard the thud of a footstep. He turned, lifted the gun, but Tristan clattered into him, sending them both, and the gun sprawling into the darkness. Sam pushed Tristan to the side and both men scrambled to their feet, as the flames flicked beside them. The fire illuminated their battle scars.

Sam's eyebrow was wide open, as blood crept down his cheek. His left arm hung limp, the shoulder caked blood that still pumped through the makeshift tourniquet.

He was muddy.

Beaten.

Bloodied.

But standing.

Tristan's face was a crimson mask, with small shards of glass still embedded in the skin. Blood poured from his mouth in a constant stream, bypassing the now ruptured gums that had lost their teeth when he was slammed into the brick wall.

Two of his fingers were missing, severed in the barrel roll, and at least one bone in his forearm was cracked.

He was also beaten and bloodied.

Possibly dying from internal bleeding.

But the pure rage and bloodlust had pulled him from the wreckage, and now, as he stared down Sam, as the world burned around them both, that bloodlust boiled over. With a guttural roar of hatred, Tristan burst forward, eating up the distance between the two, and then swung the first blow. Sam weaved out of the way, and threw his own right hook, but Tristan blocked it with his forearm and then drove an elbow into Sam's bullet-ridden shoulder. Sam wobbled a little, the pain flashing quickly through his body, and Tristan zeroed in with a few clubbing blows to

Sam's ribs, before driving a solid teep kick that sent Sam backwards and to the mud.

'Let's finish this, Sam.' Tristan yelled, the flame flickering behind him like the devil incarnate. Sam pulled himself to his feet and cracked his neck slightly.

He didn't need another invitation.

Tristan lunged forward again, homing in on the shoulder, but Sam weaved to the side, and caught Tristan with an uppercut to the stomach. He grunted as he doubled over, and Sam lifted his knee, drilling it into the fleshy remains of Tristan's nose. The mercenary snapped back, blinded by the pain, and he threw a wild right that Sam bobbed under, and then Sam drove a hard kick into the back of Tristan's knee. He fell forward, throwing out his hands to catch himself before he fell into the flames, only for Sam to stamp his boot once more.

It came down at the midpoint of the already broken forearm, and Tristan let out a squeal of anguish as the radius bone snapped in two, with the sharp, jagged edges ripping through the skin.

Sam lifted the boot one more time and brought it down on the back of Tristan's skull, driving the man forward and face first into the blaze. The heat ripped up Sam's leg, and he staggered backwards, watching as Tristan's body spasmed as the fire wrapped around his head, and began to travel down the back of his jacket.

The man's screams were quashed as the fire scorched his vocal cords, and Sam watched as the man's final seconds were played out in absolute agony.

Then he stopped moving.

The pain was over.

Tristan was dead.

Gritting his teeth, Sam lifted the FAMAS from the ground and began his slow march back towards the Sanc-

tuary, estimating that Glass was already calling for rein-
forcements.

He also guessed that Glass wouldn't stick around much
longer.

Time was ticking, and as Sam stepped through the
smoke and into the bright lights beneath the Sanctuary, he
sent a glower of hatred up towards the viewing platform
where Glass was standing.

But then Sam's eyes widened with horror, and he let
out a violent scream of pain, and then hurried towards the
open shutter, ready to kill anyone who got in his way.

———————

The panic had turned to defiance, and Glass angrily berated
the other guests, who had begun to question his authority.
They had attended multiple events, either at the Sanctuary or
at one of the many Havens, all of which had gone off without
a hitch. But as the events of the evening were unfolding, and
the guests watched as Sam mercilessly ripped through their
friends and associates with brutal efficiency, all eyes had
turned to Glass, demanding to know how he would handle it.

He had snapped back at them, threatening to revoke
their memberships and ensure their lives were ruined
should they question his authority.

He pulled the radio and screamed at Tristan to deal
with things accordingly, and then stood by the window,
hands behind his back and a look of smug victory as the
screen showed the shutter opening, and Tristan's team,
armed to the teeth, preparing to take to the battlefield.

Even Corbin had a look of resignation, that not even
Sam could face what was coming.

Then the open ground beneath the window burst into
a wall of flames, and the panic once again spread

throughout the Sanctuary. The other guests charged to the window, watching in terror as the first two men of Tristan's team snapped backwards and were dead before they hit the mud.

'He's going to kill us all.'

'Do something, Glass.'

'I'm out of here.'

The cries were growing louder, and Glass' eyes bulged as he saw Tristan burst forward in the Jeep, only for the front tyre to blow out. The vehicle hit the rocks, flipped through the air, and then rolled across the ground until it made a devastating collision with a wall.

Tristan was gone.

Glass needed to be, too.

Glass pulled out his phone and sent a coded message to Glover, who would act upon it at once. A chopper was always on hand to evacuate Glass from the Sanctuary at a moment's notice, and within five minutes, Glass received his assurance that the helipad would be occupied within five more.

Just enough time for Sam to kill the remaining soldiers and then storm the Sanctuary to find both Glass and Corbin gone.

Glass turned back to the room, where a few gasps echoed from the remaining guests. Glass approached, taking his place beside Corbin, and they watched as Sam evaded Tristan's last stand, before shattering the man's forearm and feeding him headfirst into the flames.

It was barbaric.

Such a violence was usually celebrated by the room, when one of the guests was performing it on an innocent lamb sent to the slaughter. When it was the last line of defence, the room was a deathly silence.

Corbin finally spoke.

'Guess it's a bad day to be one of the one percent.'

Glass turned and re-introduced Corbin to the back of his hand. The impact sent Corbin sprawling towards the table, spilling over a few plates and glasses, and before any of the guests could speak up, Glass pulled a gun.

They all gasped.

'I am leaving to attend an urgent matter.' He warned them. 'Any attempts to follow me will result in me pulling this trigger. Do you understand?'

A few solemn nods were returned, and then Glass turned to Corbin, who wiped the blood from her lip and then nodded to the window. All eyes turned to the smoke-filled battlefield, where sure enough, through the dark, thick smoke, Sam Pope emerged. Caked in blood and dirt, and soaked through from the rain, Sam limped onward, his left arm limp, but his right one still clutching an assault rifle.

He looked up at the window, his eyes locked on Glass, before they shifted to Corbin.

They shared a brief moment as their eyes locked, that maybe, they might just make it out alive.

Then Glass shoved Corbin forward, pinning her against the pane. On the ground below, he could see Sam's horror, and Glass revelled in it as he pressed the gun to the bottom of Corbin's spine.

He pulled the trigger.

The bullet ripped through Corbin's spinal cord, through her intestines and then burst out of her stomach. It hit the bullet proof glass and sent an instant web of cracks throughout the pane, all of them thick with her blood.

The other guests screamed and ran in whatever direction they could.

Corbin collapsed to the ground, her hands feebly clutching her stomach as its contents spilled between her fingers.

Sam was already running towards the open shutter, as Glass stared down at him, then at the French woman who was gasping for her final breath.

He could have put one in her head, but that would have been a waste of a bullet.

Watching as Sam made his way to the shutter, Glass ordered the remnants of his security detail to put him down. He had little faith in them, but they could at least buy him the time he needed.

As Agent Corbin grasped to the last moments of her life, amidst a backdrop of bloodstained glass and a ferocious fire below, Sebastian Glass turned on his heel and hurried to the stairwell. The chopper would be a few minutes out, and as soon as he took to the air, he would disappear. With his money and connections, everything would be swept away, and then he would begin the process of ensuring everything that Sam Pope had ever held dear would be burnt in front of him.

Just like his Sanctuary.

Just like Glass' reputation.

Sam had taken it all from him, and as Glass took the stairs two at a time, he made the vile promise that he would do the same in return.

CHAPTER TWENTY-NINE

Sam squeezed the trigger as soon as the armed security stepped onto the stairwell, a controlled burst ripped through the man from stomach to collarbone. The man flopped down the steps, leaving a spatter of blood across them all, and as Sam rounded the landing and onto the next step, a gunshot rang out a floor above.

The bullet clattered off the dull brick behind Sam, and he returned fire, catching the shooter in the throat, and sending them stumbling backwards into the stairwell. As Sam cleared the steps two at a time, he rounded the final flight to find the man slumped against the wall, hand pressed to his throat, gurgling as the blood slowly drowned him. The man's lifeless eyes looked right at him, and the man feebly lifted the gun.

Sam put him out of his misery.

Beyond the stairwell door, Sam could hear the panic from the fancy room where he'd been presented for auction, and as he kicked open the door, a shriek of fear erupted from the remaining guests, who had been held in their seats at gunpoint by Glass' staff. There were only five of them left, a couple on tables on opposite sides of the room, and one lone woman, weeping, as she sat on the table nearest the door. Behind each of them, an armed guard was kneeling, using the rich, paying customers as human shields, reducing them in the same way they had reduced Sam.

Expendable.

The one nearest to the door to the stairwell opened fire, the bullets clattering the metal door where Sam had stood. Expecting the onslaught, Sam had swung back into the stairwell, and he grunted with pain as he slid the mag.

Only a few bullets left.

As he slammed it shut, he spun out into the doorway and sent the final burst in the direction of the shooter.

Sam hit both the shooter and the human shield and felt nothing but vindication as they both hit the ground.

More bullets rained in on his location, and he stepped back into the stairwell, dropped the rifle, and then relieved the dead mercenary on the steps of his Glock. The man had drowned on his own blood, and his lifeless eyes stared up at Sam as he stepped back into the action.

Sam broke out into a sprint, darting through the door as he opened fire in the direction of one of the shooters, one of the bullets snapping the head of the rich man at the table, and sending him spiralling in a spray of blood. Sam dived forward as the shooters returned fire, clattering onto the ground and upturning a table to use a temporary shield. Bullets thudding into the oak, chipping away at the smooth wood, and as Sam counted down their rounds, he spun up, drew the gun up with his right hand to his line of sight, and pulled the trigger before he steadied the gun.

With pinpoint precision, the bullet zipped across the decadent room and drilled a hole between the eyes of the security guard, sending him snapping back into the blood-soaked glass panel behind.

A second gunshot rang out across the room, and Sam

felt the burning sensation of a bullet running across the skin of his left bicep, as the scorching metal skimmed his arm. It was enough to spin him round, and he dropped back down against his cover, as a follow up bullet thudded the oak behind his head. One shooter left, and Sam gingerly tried to lift his left arm, but the pain was overwhelming. Blood trickled down from his bicep, and Sam cursed silently.

His left arm was failing.

His right arm was already useless.

Across the room, his friend lay dying, clutching her stomach as her life pumped through her fingers. Beyond that, the world was on fire, a flaming testament to his rampage.

Another gunshot rang out, followed by a weep of terror, and another bullet crashed into the table. Sam could hear shuffling across the room, followed by carefully placed footsteps. The shooter knew they'd hit Sam and was now clearly moving in for the kill.

The gun would be trained on the table, and the second Sam poked his head over the top, it would be met with the full force of a bullet.

Sam knew he had one shot. His arm was too damaged to line up a second shot. He glanced once more to Corbin, whose body was shuddering as it entered its final moments, and Sam rolled to the side. As he hit the ground, he gritted his teeth and thrust his arm out, the gun locked in his outstretched grip. The approaching shooter tried to adjust his aim, but Sam took his shot.

The bullet ripped through the man's jacket and through his ribcage, spinning the man through the air, and he hit the ground, gasping for air as the blood immediately began to fill his lungs.

He'd be dead in a few minutes, and Sam roared with pain as he pushed himself to his feet, and he stared down at the terrified guests who were locked to their seats with fear.

'Where is Glass?' Sam yelled, as the fire beyond the glass crackled as it absorbed more of the surrounding woodlands.

'U-upstairs,' one of the guests responded. 'The helipad. There is a helipad.'

Sam nodded and then hurried toward Corbin, ignoring the agony that was spreading throughout his body. None of that mattered, and he dropped down to one knee beside Corbin, who looked up at him with tired eyes. The vacancy in her eyes matched the pallid shade of her skin, and Sam felt his heartbreak as blood trickled from the corner of her mouth. Her hands were resting softly on her stomach, as the final remnants of her life pumped through, and Sam reached out and locked his fingers in hers.

There was blood on both their hands.

But only Corbin's was stained with her own.

Sam gently shushed as Corbin tried to speak, and the burning in his shoulder didn't even register as he gently stroked her hair.

'I'm sorry,' he whispered and then felt the tear trickle down his cheek as Corbin's body gave one last, pitiful jolt and then it was over.

Agent Renée Corbin was dead.

And with a heart-wrenching roar of sorrow, Sam lifted her hand to his lips, gently kissed the back of it, and then laid it down on her lifeless body.

He then stood, gun in hand, with the entire world behind him ablaze, and then marched towards the stairwell that led to the roof, with only one thought looping through his mind.

Kill Sebastian Glass.

And enjoy every fucking second of it.

Glass stumbled up the final steps to the rooftop door of the Sanctuary, whelping audibly as the echo of gunshots filtered down from the viewing platform. Sam Pope was ripping through the final lines of his defence, which meant Glass needed to get the hell out of there. Through the panic as he thundered up the final steps, he hadn't noticed the horrifying silence of the outside world, and as he pressed down on the bar to open the door, he stumbled out onto the flat, concrete roof of the Sanctuary and saw nothing but smoke.

Heard nothing but the fire that was reducing his hunting ground to ash.

And he shook with fear and turned his eyes to the brilliant, clear night sky.

All he saw was a multitude of stars, spread across the vast darkness like an army of fireflies.

There was no helicopter in sight.

No distant thud of the propellers.

No way out.

As the smoke from the inferno below filtered up and around the helipad like a thick, grey wall, Glass fumbled in his pocket and pulled out his phone. Frantically, he found Glover's number and made the call.

Glover answered on the first ring.

'You fucking idiot. Where is my chopper?'

The panic is Glass' voice spread to his expression as Glover calmly responded.

'An idiot would be someone entrusting their safety to someone they have treated like shit on the bottom of their shoe.' The audible sound of Glover taking a victorious sip of his beverage. *'I've been watching through the feed. Goodbye, Sebastian. It has not been a pleasure.'*

The call cut off before Glass could respond, and he

screamed a tirade of profanities at his phone before his rage saw him hurl it into the steadily rising smoke.

There was no escape.

The only way back was through the building, and Glass doubted the last vestiges of his security would put Sam down.

Glass looked at the Glock in his hand, the same one that had now snatched the life from Sam's friend, and the same one that had signed his own death warrant. Glass swallowed, trying to push down the fear, and as the metal door to the helipad was thrown open, Glass lifted the gun and wildly pulled the trigger.

He managed to squeeze off a few shots, none of them with any accuracy, before another gunshot echoed through the hilltop, and Glass felt his leg sweep from beneath him, and the overwhelming anguish as the bullet shattered his shin bone. He hit the concrete with a thud, his gun spinning from his hands that now clutched his bloodied leg. Through his wails of pain, Glass begged for mercy.

'Please. Sam. Please. You don't need to do this.'

Sam limped forward.

He was a mess.

His face was caked with a mixture of blood, soot, and mud, and both his arms swung by his side, his left arm now a sleeve of red from the wound that dominated his bicep. His clothes were muddied, torn, and soaked through, and as the rain began to ease off, Sam shuffled closer and closer to Glass, who was weeping with pain.

'Sam. Look...' Glass began, but Sam lifted his boot and drove it down on his obliterated shin, squashing the remnants of bone into dust. Glass howled like a wolf, the agony threatening to snatch his consciousness away, but before he could plead, he felt Sam's fingers grip the scruff of his designer shirt and haul him upwards.

As he did, Sam's other fist collided with Glass' nose,

destroying it in one clubbing blow and drenching the man's mouth and shirt in an explosion of blood.

Sam lifted him again and again and again.

Each time, he hauled Glass into another sickening right hook, which was pounding the billionaire into a bloodied, and beaten mess.

After the seventh punch, Sam let go of Glass's shirt and stood, shaking off the stinging sensation that was wrapped around his swollen knuckles.

They were drenched in blood.

Mostly Glass'.

Sprawled across the helipad, Glass tried to crawl away, but he coughed a mouthful of blood and spat it out with the last few of his teeth. He could barely see, as the swelling around his eyes began to press together, and Sam's avalanche of blows had fractured both of his eye sockets. He was a broken and beaten mess, and as he dragged his limp body across the concrete, Glass knew there was no way out.

No way back from this.

Despite all his vast wealth, and despite all the power and leverage he held over the richest and most influential people in the world, none of it was enough to stop what was coming.

None of it was able to replace what Sam wanted.

Revenge.

Incorruptible to his core, Sam stood over Glass, staring down at him with enough hatred to turn a man crazy. Glass finally found a shred of dignity, and pushed himself to a sitting position, and then tilted his disfigured face in the direction of his attacker.

There was one more chance to beg.

'You can have everything, Sam.' Glass struggled, his toothless mouth filling with blood. 'Every penny. Every building. Every name on my books. All of it. Just let me live.'

Sam looked out across the sweeping landscape, peering through the smoke that was trying to ruin the view. Roughly a hundred feet beneath them, the fire Sam had started was still raging, engulfing the entire hunting grounds, and turning his battleground to ash.

Without looking back at Glass, Sam gave his answer.

'All those people. Those men. Those women. Those *kids*.' Sam spat with venom. 'All the ones who faced whatever horror your customers paid for.'

'Yes, my customers.' Glass sneered. 'I never did anything. I just…'

Sam turned and fixed him with a look colder than the chill on the wind, which was still fighting against the heat of the inferno.

'You just made it possible.' Sam stepped forward and hauled Glass to his feet, the two of them standing a few feet from the perilous drop to flames below. He pulled him in close, peering into Glass' swollen eyes with a hatred he hadn't felt since he looked down at Miles Hillock all those years ago. 'You had Ranjit murdered. You killed Renée Corbin. You should face the consequences of your crimes.'

A relieved sigh escaped Glass' bloodied mouth.

'I will and I promise, I will help you bring it all down. Just hand me over to the police. We can put things right.'

Sam frowned. A man of Glass' wealth would never so much as receive a rap on his knuckles, let alone the full penalty of the law.

'I am putting things right.'

Sam mustered all of the energy left in his battered body, and he lifted Glass off the ground and in one mighty heave, hurled the billionaire off the side of the helipad. Glass' horrified shriek soon disappeared into the smoke, as he plummeted down from the roof of his ironically named

Sanctuary, and down into the fiery pits of the hunting ground below.

Sam dropped to his knees, allowing himself a few moments of grief, as the cold drizzle lashed at the exposed wounds on his arms. As he wiped away tears, not just for his fallen friends but for the holes they would leave in their passing, Sam took a deep breath and pushed himself to his feet.

Sebastian Glass was dead.

Veilmont was crumbling to ashes below his feet.

But it wasn't over.

Not yet.

Sam turned and headed back towards the door, heading for anywhere that would get him away from the crime scene. As he passed through the building, he made one final stop to say a silent goodbye to Corbin, before he headed outside to the car park.

Minutes later, he was heading back down the winding track, cutting through the woodlands in the luxury car that had been left with the keys in the cup holder. As Sam headed back towards civilization and the Swedish capital, the fire that was engulfing the Sanctuary roared high into the night sky and wouldn't stop until the entire structure had fallen to ash.

CHAPTER THIRTY

Nearly two full weeks had passed since Director Vivier had handed Agent Corbin over to Sebastian Glass, and somehow, despite the confirmation of her death in the blaze that had devastated some of the Swedish woodland, the guilt was ever so slightly subsiding. There had been no compensation for his role, as Glass' had also been confirmed as one of the dead bodies at the horrendous disaster. Whilst Corbin's charred remains had been identified by her near perfect teeth, Glass was by process of elimination by matching the loose teeth found in the ashes with the only chard remains that were missing them.

Someone had removed them.

Vivier had a pretty good idea who it was.

Using his position as director, Vivier had threatened a few junior tech administrators at the DGSE with an uncomfortable career path unless they hacked into Corbin's phone records and recovered the recordings from the cloud storage. Every company, no matter how much they lied to the public, logged everything, and it was available to those with the money or the power to access it.

He found the last few phone calls of Corbin's life,

confirming to him that it was indeed Sam Pope who was the man hammering his fist against Veilmont's front door.

The same man who had laid siege to Ducard's compound a year ago.

The news brought a sense of relief to Vivier, who was already greasing the wheels to ensure that when they began turning, it was Sam Pope who was fitting the bill.

He was the one who abducted Cheyrou and opened fire on brave DGSE agents in the centre of Paris.

He was the one who attacked police officers in the Paris Metro.

The man who left several dead bodies in a hostel, including the innocent proprietor.

The horror show at the Haven just north of the city.

The fire in Stockholm that claimed the lives of some of Europe's most prominent businessmen and women.

That claimed the life of Agent Renée Corbin.

It would be a tricky narrative to weave, but Vivier had low friends in high places, and those who could swing the media in his favour were in just as much trouble as he was. The head of the Paris Press had been a frequent visitor to the Haven, and Vivier knew that the man didn't want anything to come out.

Nobody did.

There were hundreds of men like Vivier, all with families and careers hanging by the thread that Sam Pope was now threatening to cut. The only way out was to bury Sam underneath the violence he had left in his wake, and hope he ended up too far down to be heard. That relief filtered through his body as he looked out over the *Père Lachaise Cemetery*, where rows of seats were filled by black-clad mourners, all of whom were grieving the loss of Agent Renée Corbin. In the front row, Jeanette Agard sat, with her boys Louis and Marc, all three of them sobbing as they watched Corbin's coffin begin its descent into the earth.

Vivier had given a heartfelt speech about her, swallowing his own guilt as he recounted her bravery and dedication to her country.

How she had won a bravery award for the successful apprehension of Pierre Ducard, a noble act that had caused her notable stress in the aftermath. Vivier found that lying was as natural to him as breathing and began to plant the seeds that Corbin was at the Sanctuary for her own nefarious needs.

That the stress of bringing down a popular political figure had seen her turn to drink, which had seen her follow a dark path that had eventually led to a burning building in the Swedish highlands. Vivier laid on his sorrow thick, even dabbing away tears that were more to do with his own role in Corbin's death than the fact that she was gone.

It had been a year since he had stood a few rows down, giving the same address about Agent Agard, and now, another agent was being put in the ground. Those in the surrounding seats would remember her, and a flag and plaque would be sent to her parents.

Renée Corbin's name would be etched onto the wall of fallen agents in the CAT building, all of whom had died in the line of duty.

But only Vivier would know the truth, and as he joined the morbid party for a drink to celebrate the life of Agent Corbin, he knew one too many, and that truth might slip out. It was a truth he would keep until his dying day, and as he sat and listened to the heartbreak that was being batted around the room, he could feel the guilt swelling in his chest.

Filling that with smoke seemed like a decent solution, and so Vivier excused himself, headed out through the side door of the local bar where the wake was being held, and stepped out into the sanctuary of the empty alleyway.

Vivier lit a cigarette with a shaking hand, took a long, exaggerated pull, and then let the smoke filter out of his mouth and into the bitter chill of the wind.

Footsteps.

Vivier turned, and rolled his eyes, as a hooded man with a hunched back stumbled into the wall, clearly inebriated.

'*Va te faire foutre.*' Vivier barked as the man stumbled nearer, clearly out of his mind on some concoction of drugs and alcohol. It was a damning indictment of the city, that in the middle of the afternoon, one of its residents could be in such a diabolical state. As the man took a step too close, Vivier drew back his arm to show his identification.

The man drilled a vicious knee right into Vivier's crotch, crushing his testicles and sending him collapsing to the ground, gasping in agony as he clutched his battered privates. As he began to call for help, he felt a hand grab his ankle, and in an impressive show of strength, dragged Vivier's portly frame further down the alleyway and out of the sight of the public.

Vivier screamed, received a hard boot in the stomach for his troubles, and then looked up at his attacker as the man removed his hood.

Vivier's eyes widened in horror.

Sam Pope.

With his head almost shaved to the scalp, and his strong jaw now covered in thick, grey-tinged stubble, Sam looked different to the well-dressed man who had handily led Cheyrou through the city. But Vivier knew it was the man who had taken the fight to Sebastian Glass and had burnt down the most powerful organisation in the world.

Which meant he was the only man alive who knew what Vivier had done.

Vivier winced as he tried to sit and tried to add bass into his shaking voice.

'Don't do anything you will regret, Sam.'

'Ah, good, you do speak English.' Sam nodded, squatting down beside him. 'However, I'm not the one with the guilty conscience here, am I?'

'You don't understand. Agent Corbin was getting too close, and I needed...'

Metal struck Vivier above the eyebrow, slicing it open and causing him to roll backwards and squeal, his hand pressed to the open gash that was now dripping blood. Sam held the Glock in his hand, keeping it in clear view of Vivier's eyeline.

'Renée Corbin didn't deserve to die. She certainly didn't deserve to have the man she trusted hand her over to be killed.'

'And you?' Vivier snapped back, his face now smeared with blood. 'You were the one who pulled her into this. It is *your* fault she is dead. Not mine.'

Sam nodded and then struck Vivier with the grip of the pistol once again, this time in the mouth, busting his lip open and loosening a few teeth. Vivier groaned with pain and rolled back again, and Sam calmly fetched something from inside his hooded jacket.

It was a sheet of paper.

He dropped it on Vivier's chest.

'That there is a list of every payment you made to Sebastian Glass. Every communication you had with Veilmont and every transcript of every phone call.' Sam stood, shaking his head. 'There's a whole booklet of them, and that page there, that proves you agreed to deliver Agent Corbin over to Glass to be murdered.

Vivier's eyes scanned the document, and the colour drained from his face as the reality kicked in. He looked up at Sam with hatred in his eyes.

'Where did you get this?'

'Glass' former assistant. Charles Glover.' Sam explained curtly. 'Turns out, working for Sebastian Glass wasn't all it was cracked up to be and he saw me as a way out. Knowing I'd come for him after I killed his boss, Glover made a deal. Every single record that could bring down *everyone* who ever benefited from or used the Veilmont service, in exchange for his name being left off the list and half of Glass' fortune being donated to numerous charities around the world. The other half, Glover has used to disappear.'

Vivier scrunched the paper as his arms went rigid with anger.

'The little shit.'

'Some of that information has been sent to every major news outlet in the world. I've told them in twenty-four hours' time; I will send them the proof.' Sam squatted back down to face Vivier eye to eye. 'Meaning you have twenty-four hours to come clean, make a deal, and serve your time for what you did to my friend.'

Vivier looked at the scrunched paper in his hand and swallowed the lump in his throat. Tears flooded his eyes, as the only decision he now had to make, was whether he owned up to his crimes, or allowed the press to display them for the world to see.

The light at the end of the tunnel had been shut off, and he turned to Sam with a pathetic look of hope.

'Just kill me.' He begged.

Sam lifted the gun, and Vivier closed his eyes.

'I'm not going to kill you, Director Vivier,' Sam said. 'But I will give you a helping hand.'

Sam turned, pressed the gun down on the back of Vivier's hand, pinning it to the floor and he pulled the trigger. The bullet burrowed through the bone and cartilage, lodging in place as it hit the concrete below and Vivier howled in pain as he rolled over and clutched his hand. The red-hot bullet was scorching the inside of his hand, searing the nerve tendons, and causing him to weep with agony.

Sam stood, looked down at the pathetic man who had sent his friend to die, and knew he had avenged her. Vivier would spend the rest of his life in prison, and over the coming weeks and months, every major law enforcement agency would be investigating the names on the list that would be made public.

Justice had been done.

Veilmont and Sebastian Glass had been burnt to the ground.

Everyone who had been involved would soon face the full penalty of the law.

The world would be a better place for it.

But it had come at a cost.

Ranjit Siddique.

Renée Corbin.

Two more people who had lost their lives in the continuous fight that Sam raged against the systems that had promised to keep them safe. Against the organised crime syndicates and the shady organisations that operated either out of the law's reach, or hand in hand with those who should have done better.

Discovering the horrors of Veilmont, Sam knew he was needed more than ever, and the only way he would be able forgive himself for those deaths, would be to make them mean something.

To ensure they didn't die in vain.

Veilmont was gone, but the world was still a grim and grimy place, where the oppressive boot of the powerful crunched down on those without the means to stop it from happening.

Somebody *had* to fight back.

Sam turned and headed down the alleyway, tucking the Glock into his jeans and pulling his hood up over his freshly shorn head. Vivier's pitiful groans of pain echoed behind him, but Sam reached the end of the alleyway, turned onto the high street, and lost himself in a world that would forever need him.

That could always count on him to do the right thing.

Fight back.

Even if it was never enough.

EPILOGUE

THREE MONTHS LATER...

The heat from the sun relentlessly pounded down upon the Brazilian favelas, scorching the corrugated metal roofs of the shacks and raising the temperatures inside. Poverty flowed through the slums like the Amazon River, and those with anything other than their wits and the clothes on their back were considered lucky.

This was not a place of wealth nor status, and the fact that he had needed to come to such a depressing part of his city has already gnawed away at Renaldo Almeida's infamous temper. He had been born and bred in a place not too dissimilar, although the favela in which his single mother had raised him and his older sister had been on the outskirts of Sao Paulo. Now here he was, walking up the steps that rose between two run-down shacks that some unfortunate people had called home, in a place that felt airlifted nearly three hundred miles from his childhood.

In Rio De Janeiro, Almeida was a somebody. As a leading light for the city's National Congress, Almeida was seen as a viable candidate to succeed the current mayor in the upcoming election. Charming and handsome, with enough grit to appeal to the common man, Almeida was seen as a new breed of politician, who saw through the usual dick-measuring of political parties and focused in on the genuine issues at hand.

The informal power structure that ran places such as these favelas, where the drug cartels and the militia on their payroll ruled the streets with fear and bullets, and the law was as welcome as a whore in church. The 'parallel power' between the two groups had reached a level of understanding that made them damn near unstoppable, and numerous high-ranking officers of several law enforcement agencies had been exposed as being on their payroll.

Why beat them when you can join them.

But Almeida was hellbent on beating them and bringing a sense of justice to the makeshift streets of the favelas that continued to grow despite being forgotten about.

He was loud.

He was bullish.

And Almeida had made little to no secret that he was planning on changing things.

It made him a target, and the three highly trained, heavily armed bodyguards who cleared his pathway through the slums were a necessary precaution for the mission ahead.

But as he reached the top of the staircase, Almeida looked out across the vast, rolling metal roofs that comprised the enormous favela and felt his heart break.

Not just for the people who called it home.

But for the woman lost somewhere within its walls who didn't belong there.

Almeida's political goals had made him a target.

It had also made targets out of the ones he loved.

Eliana Almeida was part of his strategy team, and ever since they were kids, had always been a doting older sister. They'd survived the harsh realities of the favela together and always made sure the other was looked after. They'd cared for and then buried their mother in Sao Paolo and then made the trip to Rio when Almeida had turned twenty. Four years his senior, Eliana had found them a place to live and worked three different jobs as he studied relentlessly for his chosen political career.

She'd sacrificed a lot for him, Almeida knew that, including starting a family of her own. Which was why now, in her early forties, he was thrilled she had found love and although she hadn't married, she was expecting a daughter in three months' time.

If she survived.

Because it had been twenty-four hours since she had been kidnapped. The fact that it had happened a week before Almeida was due to announce his candidacy for the upcoming election was no coincidence.

Almeida had refused to comment in the press about the apparent abduction, and he was emptying his savings to afford the private security and investigators that were knocking on doors in the favela to find her.

But George Trafford had surprised him.

As the father to Almedia's unborn niece, George was a nice if not slightly irritating man. A decade older than his sister, George had arrived in Brazil from the United Kingdom over five years ago, with little desire to share his reasons or his past with anyone, but happy to share his apparent fortune with those he cared for.

Eliana and George had fallen in love pretty quickly, and although Almeida's career meant he didn't spend a lot of time with them anymore, he knew George loved her deeply.

Was excited to become a father, even if a little later in life.

When they were abducted, Almeida had promised George he'd have them returned.

It was then that George had surprised him, snapping into a seemingly previous life as he booted up his computer and began to syphon as much information as he could. Quicker than any agency, George had managed to pull all the information of the abduction, including identities of the two kidnappers, who they worked for, and their links to the cartels that would now be holding Eliana until Almeida backed down.

It was impressive.

It was also surprising.

They'd been able to isolate one member of the gang, who after some persuasion courtesy of a pair of pliers and a bloodthirsty member of Almeida's security detail, had given them the lie of the land. Half of the favela was under the rule of the 'Redeemers', a militia operation that believed the statue that overlooked the favela from atop the Corcovado Mountain was guiding their movements.

A full-scale sweep of the streets would be an act of war, one that would not only lose Almeida the election, but would certainly see him lose his sister and unborn niece, too.

George told him he had another idea. And as the two of them stood on the balcony of the shack that George had revealed he'd acquired as a hideout, it raised more questions with Almeida that he would one day need answered. His idea raised even more.

'We need to send in one person,' George said with the authority of a soldier. 'One person can get a lot further than a whole team without being detected and getting them out would be a lot easier too. Fewer casualties. Less fuss. Hopefully less blowback.'

'And when he gets killed, we have zero chance of finding my sister.' Almeida snapped in broken English. 'Besides, there is no one who will take that fight.'

George took a deep breath. He knew what he was about to do carried a lot of potential consequences.

But to rescue the love of your life and your unborn child, those consequences were worth the risk.

'I know someone,' George said with a firm nod. 'But I need to go to England. Today.'

Almeida's head snapped to George in confusion, and his brow furrowed. The favela glistened beneath them in the vast glow of the sun, the heat bathing the rooftops in a strong blur.

'Who are you?' Almeida asked, his eyes narrowed as he looked at the man he'd known for the past five years as if he was a stranger.

George had tried to be a different man.

A better man.

But he needed to go back to who he was, to save what he now had.

And that meant, when he found Sam Pope and begged him to walk into hell for his family, Sam wouldn't embrace him after all these years and call him George.

He'd call him by his actual name.

Paul Etheridge.

Minutes later, Paul was heading to the airport, knowing his entire world was on a stopwatch.

And the time was ticking down.

GET EXCLUSIVE ROBERT ENRIGHT MATERIAL

Hey there,

I really hope you enjoyed the book and hopefully, you will want to continue following Sam Pope's war on crime. If so, then why not sign up to my reader group? I send out regular updates, polls and special offers as well as some cool free stuff. Sound good?

Well, if you do sign up to the reader group I'll send you FREE copies of THE RIGHT REASON and RAINFALL, two thrilling Sam Pope prequel novellas. (RRP: 1.99)

You can get your FREE books by signing up at www.robertenright.co.uk

SAM POPE NOVELS

For more information about the Sam Pope series and other books by Robert Enright, please visit:

www.robertenright.co.uk

ABOUT THE AUTHOR

Robert lives in Buckinghamshire with his family, writing books and working on his Magnum Opus.

For more information:
www.robertenright.co.uk
robert@robertenright.co.uk

You can also connect with Robert on Social Media:

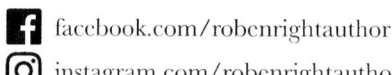 faccbook.com/robenrightauthor
instagram.com/robenrightauthor

Printed in Dunstable, United Kingdom